ALSO BY CRAIG A. ROBERTSON

RISE OF ANCIENT GODS SERIES

RETURN OF THE ANCIENT GODS, **BOOK 1**
RAGE OF THE ANCIENT GODS, **BOOK 2**
TORMENT OF THE ANCIENT GODS, **BOOK 3**
WRATH OF THE ANCIENT GODS, Book 4 (Due in early 2019)

STAND-ALONE NOVELS:

THE CORPORATE VIRUS (2016)
TIME DIVING (2013)
THE INNERgLOW EFFECT (2010)
WRITE NOW! The Prisoner of NaNoWriMo (2009)
ANON TIME (2009)

THE FOREVER ALLIANCE

BOOK FIVE OF THE *FOREVER SERIES*

by Craig Robertson

There Is Hope, But Only If You Forge It.

Imagine-It Publishing
El Dorado Hills, CA

ISBN: 978-0-9973073-7-5 (Paperback)
978-0-9973073-8-2 (E-Book)

Cover art work and design by Starla Huchton
Available at http://www.designedbystarla.com

Editing and Formatting by Polgarus Studio
Available at http://www.polgarusstudio.com

Additional editorial assistance by Michael Blanche

First Edition 2017
Second Edition 2018
Third Edition 2019

Imagine-It Publishing

This book is dedicated to Spain.

Mi cuerpo nació en los EEUU,
pero mi alma brotó en Espana.
No puedo agradecer te bastante,
paiz de mi corazón.

Note: Glossary of Terms is Located at the End of the Book.

PROLOGUE

"It has been so long since I've tasted the soul of a mortal. I almost forget the bliss it brings. I must know this again. *We* must know this once again."

"Eas-el, there was a time for that and it has passed. We now feed on the infinite light. It is our way. It is a better way." Grees-el understood his brother's words, but he could not share in them.

"The infinite light nourishes our being, but not our passion. When did we lose the will to enjoy ourselves? More importantly, why did we lose the drive to know bliss to excess?"

"The path to bliss as you envision it inevitably leads to struggle, to fighting, to annihilation. We cannot afford more loss. We must be fulfilled within ourselves and resist the temptation to destroy. You know these things, brother. Why do you speak of that which is forbidden?"

"*Forbidden*? Who can forbid the Last Nightmare? Not only does the power to do such an act not exist, it is inconceivable. If we want a thing, we take it. If we seize a thing, it becomes ours to do with as we please. You know *that*, brother."

"In the time of the First Universe, we were many and we were voracious. By the time the Fourth Universe dissolved into chaos, we were few, but we remained insatiable. We learned *nothing*. Now, after the Twelfth Universe, we live well—the paltry few who remain. Would you see the Last Nightmare disappear for all eternity?"

"If it pleased me, yes."

"The Neverwhere will tear itself apart at an ever-increasing rate if your lust continues. If you act to enter a new universe, the destruction here will accelerate. Where would you have us go after obliterating the Thirteenth Universe, if *this* place is not here to return to?"

"There are infinitely many universes for us to burden with our existence. Why do you worry as if you are an old woman?"

"An old *woman*." Grees-el repeated the words in his being, feeling them, tasting them. "I have not thought of old women in a very long time. Surely they are all gone by now."

"No, brother, one remains. She is a Last Nightmare named Grees-el of the Demarcation Clan."

"Humor? I would not have thought it possible. Two ancient concepts in one day. You are a beast of nostalgia, Eas-el."

"No. I am an eternal beast who hungers for more. I would welcome oblivion over the passive death the Infinite Light would afford me."

"You cannot act alone. We must stand together, as we always have. It *is* the only way."

"Perhaps we must remain as one. I can, however, pull the Last Nightmare off their funeral slabs and drag them into action. This you know I can do."

"No, brother, this I know you *will* do. As surely as I see the future, I see the end of the Last Nightmare."

"Then let us make it one damnation of a good party."

ONE

We were settling in nicely on Azsuram. Kayla had given birth to our son. Jon the fifty second, or something. Okay, she insisted our first son be named junior. By then, there had been Jonathan Ryan IIs, IIIs, and IVs, and some number fives were threatening to be born soon. I groused about what number we should even choose. I wanted no part in the legacy thing, but happy wife, happy life and all, so I went along with her wishes. I suggested Jon the Tenth, so we'd be the first to get there. We could then stick a flag in the kid or something. That suggestion didn't make her smile.

After a significant number of angry looks, we settled on Jon Ryan III. She let me keep JJ as second in the lineage of my mind. So Jon III it was. Anyway, after my second battle with the Berrillians, I was anxious to go home and decompress. Warring against hopeless odds again and again was draining my batteries, probably literally. The colony of Azsuram, a small nation by then, was doing spectacularly. They didn't need my help anymore, which was fine by me. I was more than okay with being a figurehead. I'd go to the occasional meeting or ribbon cutting, say profound words, and fish a lot.

And that's what we did for a few years. Then, I noticed a change in my dear sweet wife. Whereas before she was a vision of beauty and a powerhouse of a person, she became a bit less dynamic. Not sure if that's the right word, but something in her pretty little head was off. Of course, when I'd hint at the fact, or even obliquely refer to it, she'd deny everything vehemently. She insisted that life was slightly north of perfect. Matters couldn't be better, given the laws of physics. I kept flashing back on Shakespeare's line in *Hamlet.* "The lady doth protest too much, methinks. "

It took me a month of focused attacks on the castle walls of her denial, but she finally fessed up to her mood malady. She felt out of place. What's more, Kayla wasn't super-excited about raising our human children in a Kaljaxian society. She didn't dislike them or anything. She just wanted a more normal upbringing for our kids. She really landed a sucker punch when she mentioned she wanted to see our daughter in a prom dress and our son steal my beer when he got to high school. Ouch. I stole my dad's beer in high school. It was a rite of passage, as far as I was concerned. Crap, here I was denying my infant son the chance to commit petty larceny and get drunk with his football teammates. I was a bad father. Heck, I was a bad *human*.

It did strike me as odd that she'd had such similar experiences growing up, wherever she and her brother Karnean *had* grown up. Whenever I asked about that, she turned my words back on me and always said that I was missing the point. She'd read about American traditions and wanted to make those her children's. She'd also endured—her word not mine—my telling and retelling of endless tales from my misspent youth. She'd come to want those same things for our kids. I think that was a compliment, but I wasn't sure.

I pressed her. Since Middle America was gone—on account of being sucked up by Jupiter—where did she want to move? Her home world? The worldship fleet? Middle Earth, right where it bordered the Land of Oz? The last comment got me three nights of sleep in my own room, but it was worth it. Hey, when the muse delivered, I had to pass it along, now, didn't I?

She wasn't sure, as it turned out. She just knew our forever home wasn't Azsuram. I think that also had to do with Azsuram being *my* world; mine and Sapale's. She found it hard to compete with a dead legend. She didn't have to, but I didn't think she could help it. She left it to me to decide what would be best. That made it a simple assignment. All I had to do was guess what she was thinking and, in turn, feel that way myself. Same revolver to my head, just different bullets.

I favored relocating to the worldfleet, which suggested to me that that was the *most* incorrect answer. Plus, moving to the worldfleet wasn't just *a* decision, it was a *Jon* decision. Those were the least SNAG decisions possible and were always suspect. Oh, sorry. Sensitive New Age Guy. Some would erroneously accuse me of not being the sensitive empathetic type. Can you imagine?

If I couldn't choose the worldfleet, my second choice would be Azsuram, with frequent visits to the worldfleet. Wrong answer. Duh. She was already unhappy here. Worse yet, I'd placed *my* desires on my list. I couldn't very well choose where she grew up, since I'd never been there and she rarely spoke of it. Ah-ha. That had to be the best, least Jon-lethal answer. So, I told Kayla I wanted to raise our family on Chorum, the place she most identified as her family home world. Outstanding response. Not only did she not kill me, but she actually stroked my cheek and told me I was the sweetest man she'd even met. Score one for Team Dude.

Even though she knew her home world was an option, she had sort of figured I'd choose an American worldship. As a result, she'd slowly come around to that way of thinking. But I was still as sweet as concentrated honey for wanting to take her home.

So, we were moving to floating America. I was down with that. I contacted President Gore and let her know our desire. She was more than happy to help. She arranged for a much larger than normal residence near the capital. She assigned my great-grandson Heath to be my official full-time aide. Since Amanda and he had left office, he worked as a lobbyist. The kid was ecstatic to have a real, honest job again. It sounded to me like he'd have the easiest job in the US government, which meant I could torture him about what a slacker he was with a clear conscious. My life just kept getting better.

Leaving the place I'd made my home was just as hard as I thought it would be. My extended family numbered in the hundreds, and to be honest, leaving JJ was the hardest of all. We were as close as a father and son could be. He was head of the Council of Elders, a grandfather himself, and as good a man as I'd ever met. I could visit anytime I wanted, but we both knew my leaving was a big step, and that a significant separation loomed in our future.

"Are you sure you have to go?" he asked for the tenth time.

"Yeah. You have a brood's-mate. You know as well as I do that when they speak, we listen. When they suggest we jump, we ask how high might be sufficient."

"Roger that," he said with a frown. "But I'm going to miss you like I'd miss oxygen. Like I'd miss beer."

"Yo," I responded, "oxygen, okay, but let's not joke about beer."

We laughed. I wished for the millionth time I had some form of communication that didn't involve me climbing in my vortex and folding halfway across existence, just to keep in touch. I'd asked Kymee about such a radio before, but he always shrugged and changed the subject. Either their technology didn't have such a device, or he didn't want to give it to me. It was a shame either way. It would have been nice to text JJ, or holo the grandkids on a whim.

Toño was the only loose end left. He'd been on Azsuram as long as I had, longer if you counted the time I spent searching for the alternate timeline version of myself. I let him know he was free to stay or come with us, whichever he preferred. I also gave him the option of emigrating later, since I'd be returning to Azsuram fairly often. He took a few weeks to decide, but in the end he chose to come with us. He felt perfectly at home on Azsuram, but also knew he was no longer mission critical for the colony, either. Several scientists and physicians from Kaljax had taken over that role. I suspected Toño wanted to live among his people again, for the first time in nearly a century.

Gallenda was the cutest toddler and Jon III still a wrinkly prune when I loaded up the cube and moved us to *Exeter*. I took *Shearwater*, including the AIs Al and Lily. I left JJ my original ship, *Ark 1*. It wasn't like he could use it to visit me, but it at least afforded him the option of space travel. Plus, it was his mother's and my home for a long time, so it would remind him of us. He also appreciated being the only guy on Azsuram with his own personal bitching ride. I had my boy's back.

Heath met us as soon as we materialized on my private landing pad. He had a team of moving men to help unload our stuff. It was so weird. I hadn't "moved" in two centuries. I'd traveled, relocated, and been shanghaied. But I hadn't moved a household since I was a fighter pilot dragging my ex around the now-defunct globe. There they stood, burly guys in bib overalls. Nothing had changed. If I didn't know I was inside an asteroid speeding along at sixty thousand kilometers per hour, I'd have sworn I was in Anytown, USA.

Our place was very nice, better than Alexis Gore had led me to believe. It was a two-story colonial that had a lawn and veranda. Several large oak trees provided shade from the ubiquitous artificial light sources. The inside was just as nice, well-appointed with modern furniture, hardwood floors, and a deluxe kitchen. I had to wonder what high-ranking government official now hated my guts for kicking him and his family out of such a prized piece of real estate.

Kayla was totally impressed. As someone who'd spent most of her life in space, such quarters must have seemed unbelievably extravagant. I did notice she didn't say anything about what would we do with all the space. No, her eyes were like a rich kid's on Christmas morning. She made me promise to bring Karnean to visit as soon as we were settled in. She wanted to impress her big brother.

After we'd set up the house, I had to decide what I'd do with myself. Toño hooked up with Carlos immediately, and the two android scientists were in hog heaven working together. I had no idea what they were laboring on, but they applied themselves to it like newlyweds to their honeymoon. I met with all my old friends—Amanda, Bin Li, and many others. They all either offered me a job or said they'd arrange whatever I wanted. That was nice, but it didn't help me decide exactly what I wanted to do.

Politics was out. I never liked it in the first place. All my experiences to date only convinced me it wasn't the life for me. I was still a general in what succeeded the USAF, but the military no longer held any fascination for me. If there was fighting to be done, I'd be in the vanguard. Being in uniform during peace only promised to weigh me down with administrative duties and silly ceremonies. Those were as bad a politics. I could do tours or give lectures, but that sounded like a prison sentence, not a career. Academia? Maybe. I had a Ph.D. in physics. I also knew more about interspecies relationships than any other human. It was a possibility, but it had yet to light my fire, so to speak.

But there was no hurry. I could handle as much downtime as the universe was likely to give me. I'd worked, fought, and struggled almost nonstop for the last two centuries. For the near term, I was content to be a dad and a husband. I actually liked doing minor home repairs. And mowing the lawn?

Dude, I loved it. It was such a treat to be so darn normal. A cold beer after yard work on a warm Saturday afternoon was brand new to me.

A dirty secret revealed was that I looked forward to attending live sporting events, especially my beloved football. Sure, I could watch a million games, broadcast live or recorded. But there was nothing like sitting in the bleachers with a beer in one hand and my arm around Kayla, watching huge sweaty men crash into one another. That would never get old. Lest one conclude my life was too centered on beer, let me say this. Get over yourself.

Alexis called me often and invited me to important meetings. She truly valued my input. Eventually, she offered me a cabinet-level position, but I turned her down. Too political. She ended up appointing me her Alien Affairs Advisor. That was a job I could do. I answered only to her, and I worked when I wanted to. She turned out to be a good boss. She was thoughtful, kind, and she was an excellent leader. Like Harry Truman or Teddy Roosevelt, she knew what it was to be a leader and knew how important good leadership was to the general population. Times were hard, and the external threats were all too real. The people needed someone to look up to, one who they felt deserved their trust.

So, a couple hundred years into my goofy life, I became conventional. I had a wife, a steady job with an office, kids to bounce on my knees, and a lawn to mow. I felt like the dad in all those mid-twentieth-century sitcoms I watched on long space flights. I was this close to buying a cardigan sweater. Move over, Mr. Rogers. Mr. Ryan was sliding onto your bench.

TWO

"I'd like to call this council meeting to order," said JJ as he lightly tapped the gavel on the sound block. "I'd hoped my father would return in time to join us, but apparently he won't be here. I'd like the record to formally note that since our last meeting, Toño DeJesus and my father have left Azsuram. They now live on *Exeter,* in the worldship fleet."

"The *human* worldship fleet," added Dolirca acerbically.

JJ turned to look at her. "Does that actually matter, sis? You say *human* like it's some form of disease."

"First off, please do not refer to me as *sis* in the formal setting of a Council of Elders meeting. My name is *Dolirca*, in case you forgot. Second, I say *human* worldship fleet because it is just that. It has absolutely nothing to do with the proud sons and daughters of Kaljax. Third, I say their species name like it is a disease because it will be, soon. They are at this very moment speeding toward our homeland with the intent of forcing themselves on our sovereign nation. If that's not a disease, then I'd like for you to tell me what it is."

"Yeah, *sis*, but how do you really feel about life? I'm sure there might be one person present who'd conceivably like to hear it."

Scattered chuckles registered in the large crowd.

"Mock me at your peril, brother. Many of my concerns are shared by my supporters in this room."

"Ya think I should be scared, or maybe I should just skip straight to groveling for your blessed mercy? Hmm?"

"Play the fool, like the human android who imprisoned our mother as his sex slave. I personally think the matter of the humans is far too important to joke about."

"Dolirca, *you're* the joke, not the humans. They're our future co-inhabitants of Azsuram, and we will welcome them upon their arrival. You know that not a single person alive today will be around when they actually do arrive, don't you? No one's *grandkids* will be alive when they hit town. As to the matter of our mother and father, I will have that turd of hate you just coughed up stricken from the record. No one deserves to hear such a vulgar lie. Let the record reflect that if you say such a thing again, I will put you over my knee and spank you."

"You are the council chair, for the time being, and can corrupt the record however you like. We all know you're a pet to your human handlers. But the day will come—"

"When you shut up and let us proceed with this routine meeting?" JJ finished the sentence for her.

Dolirca stood. Her Toe guards did likewise. "I don't have to sit here and be insulted." She stormed out, her Toe following close behind her.

"Thank Tralmore and the Holy Veils. And no, *sis*, you can leave *and* be insulted by us. It's more fun that way."

It took awhile for the laughter to die down. Only when the room was quiet did a handful of citizens make a show of packing up and leaving.

Once they had left, JJ spoke with a straight face. "Let the secretary record that the Dolirca Coalition is heard from and has silently and thankfully left the building."

Walking home from the meeting, Challaria put her arm around her brood-mate's waist and asked, "JJ, do you think it's smart to make fun of your sister like that? I mean, yes, she's nuts. But she does have the right to speak."

"My pop used to call it the difference between liberty versus license. Free speech versus false speech. Sure, she can speak. But the minute she crosses the line she so loves to cross, the stupidity of her remarks must be pointed out."

"I think she's gathering more followers. They could become a problem. Maybe you should try and appease them. rather than alienate them."

"I'm the leader now that mom is dead and dad is gone. I must protect my people. It isn't hard to panic a herd into heinous acts with unchecked hate and bald-faced lies. These lunatics must be challenged. It's not like Dolirca's going to change or hate me any less, no matter what I do."

"She certainly does have strong feelings about her uncle, doesn't she?"

"I half expect to wake up some morning with one of her Toe chewing on my face."

"Don't even say that. She may be crazy, and those bears may be way too loyal, but let's not start the rumor that either of them might be dangerous." She smiled nervously at JJ.

"I'm not sure it's all that farfetched. I wish it was. Unfortunately, I suspect my little niece is capable of some major badness."

"You're just being dramatic. She's not a threat to anything except the concept of public decency."

He kissed her forehead. "Let's hope you're right."

THREE

The most pressing issue was when the Berrillians would attack again. No one doubted that certainty. It was only a question of when. What would be their counterstrategy to the unknown force of ours that caused them to lose so decisively in the last attack? That led to a lot of discussions between the UN, the military types, and yours truly. I still hadn't told anyone about the quantum decoupler, though many suspected I was withholding information on a secret weapon. The cool thing about being the only one with a cube was that nobody was anxious to piss me off by pressing me to be more forthright.

"Does your vortex detect any warp signatures?" asked Fleet Admiral Katashi Matsumoto. Though he was getting a bit long in the tooth, he was still an imposing man. He reminded me of a Japanese actor from long ago, Toshiro Mifune. Dude had a real badass look going.

"No, last I checked, there were none. I make it a point to ask Manly every few days."

"We detect none, either," Toño said. "Jon, at what range do you think the vortex manipulator can detect those signatures?"

"I'm not too sure. He says that warp space is harder to interpret than normal space. I think I pinned him down to having a reliable range of three or four light years. Past that, it would be blind luck to pick up a signal, and he wouldn't be able to pinpoint their location."

"And in our estimate, what is the maximal cruising speed that the Berrillian fleet can maintain?" asked Katashi.

"That is also hard to estimate. I personally feel their practical limit is three or three and a half times the speed of light," responded Toño.

"So I can count on a minimum of a year's warning when they next attack?" asked the admiral.

"It's hard to be certain, but that's my best guess," replied Toño.

"I concur," added Carlos. "If all our ducks line up properly, a two-year alert is probably as much as we can hope for."

"Jon, we've discussed this before. What are the chances that your ship can make random flights into deep space to try to detect warp signatures at a greater distance?" asked Katashi.

We had discussed that option before. It was stupid. We had no idea what direction the Berrillians would be coming from. I could make all the probing attempts I wanted, but randomly choosing a path anywhere near where they'd be was inconceivable. There was too much real estate out there.

"If I spent all my time doing that, I believe I'd waste all my time." That was the most tactful way I could respond. Yeah, I had limits, didn't I?

"But if you made a few reconnaissance missions every now and then, you might get lucky. You'd buy us valuable intelligence if you located them when they were farther away."

"I have to side with Jon on this matter, Admiral," responded Toño. "It would be unfair to ask one man to burden himself so greatly for such an unlikely chance of a useful outcome."

"I would feel better if you did, General Ryan," replied Katashi. "But I am willing to make allowances for a person's time and devotion to their *personal* interests."

In other words, if you want to be a selfish baby and put your needs in front of the defenseless masses you swore to protect, I can't stop you. Would if I could, but can't. As always, he and I didn't see eye to eye.

After the meeting broke up I sought out Toño. Carlos and he were scurrying away so fast I barely caught them.

"You know, if I didn't know better I'd swear you two were newlyweds running off together all the time. What gives? Is there a nasty rumor I'd love to start just below the surface?"

"That's horrible," replied Carlos. "I'm a married man with a family."

"You wouldn't be the first with a big secret. Come on, you can tell Dr. Jon. I would *never* betray your dirty secret. Well, not until I found a computer terminal."

"We're working on a project together that is both stimulating and nearing an important breakthrough," said Toño sternly.

"That'll make a really lame rumor. I'll have to embellish it, somehow. Hey, I heard you bought a chicken suit online." I bobbed my eyebrows. "That might be the key element I need to spice the story up."

"If it will shut you up and let us get back to work, I'll tell you what we're doing," said Toño. "But please keep it to yourself. I don't want others to pressure us for results, if you know what I mean?"

"I won't breathe a word of it to the big mean admiral," I replied, drawing an X over my lips with my finger.

"You're very challenging not to dislike," said Carlos. He knew me pretty well, didn't he?

"We have finally made some headway in understanding the Berrillian technology we obtained on Azsuram."

"Wow," I remarked. "That is big."

"It will be when we can fully reproduce it. We're close, Jon. Very close," said Toño. His excitement was palpable.

"What element of their tech are we talking about, here?"

"All of it, really," responded Carlos. "It's mostly a matter of understanding their computer language and breaking their code. Once we achieve that, the tech itself will be easy to decipher."

"So, you're only trying to hack their computers?"

Toño got that irritated look on his face he reserved exclusively for me. "To understand how an alien brain conceives a computer language is very tough. Past that, we have to deal with the encryptions and barriers they would naturally have in place. It took me six months to determine that they did *not* use a binary code, as we do. For some reason they chose to program in a quaternion system."

"That employs four symbols, not our two," added Carlos.

"I know what *quaternion* means," I lied. Not sure why I lied, but it felt like I needed to.

"In any case, that part is behind us. Since I returned, Carlos has provided keen insights that have allowed us to understand their programing and unlock the code. Now we're reading the information. Some was corrupted in the crash, but I think we're going to be able to duplicate their gravity wave device."

I whistled. "Nice."

"Aren't you going to ask? I know it's killing you," remarked Toño.

"Oh, yeah, what's your favorite color, Doc?"

He balled up his fists and shut his eyes.

"And, any idea when you'll have a working model of the gravity machine?"

"No. Don't ask again. We'll tell you as soon as there's something to tell."

"Works for me. What about the color? Your birthday's coming up and I want to get you two matching tutus to wear around the lab."

"Go. Please, go *now*," responded Toño. Dude was having trouble not smiling. I almost had him. Try, try again was on my side. Oh yes, it was.

FOUR

"My lady, I fully understand your anger, but surely what you suggest is treason." Zantral had trouble saying those words, but she felt it was her duty to be honest with her mistress.

Dolirca stiffened. One edged closer to Zantral, while Two drew toward her master. Dolirca forced herself to relax. "Thank you for your candor, my friend. As much as your words wound me, I must thank you for them."

"I wouldn't say such an affront if I wasn't so committed to your ascension." Zantral bowed deeply. Both Toe then relaxed back to their neutral stances.

"I can assure you, my thoughts and words are not treasonous. They *can't* be. I speak for all Azsuram, all Kaljaxians, for that matter. My uncle and his puppets cannot be allowed to muddy my mother's prescient vision for this new land. I will collapse the false structure they have beguiled the people into making and lead them to the true fulfillment of the promise that is Azsuram."

"Of course you will. But speaking too boldly or before your political base is more secure could put your designs in jeopardy."

"Zantral, my child," she said, stroking Zantral's cheek with the back of her hand, "could I put in peril the rising of the sun tomorrow or the coming of winter? No. The blessed will come to pass. I will shepherd in a new, nurturing era on Azsuram. I will build a monument befitting my mother and tear down all vestiges of that agent of Brathos, Jon Ryan. What Davdiad bids cannot be corrupted."

Dolirca turned to a Toe. "One, will you remind Zantral what happens if one doubts the will of Davdiad."

"*No*, my lady."

One seized Zantral's arm and bit into it deeply. She started tearing at the flesh.

"Enough, my pet," shouted Dolirca.

One released the arm and stood, as if she had not just committed a horrific act.

"There, there, sweet Zantral," purred Dolirca as she held the mangled arm up. "Let's get you to the doctor. This injury caused by your fall from a tree must be tended to promptly, or you might bleed to death. I couldn't live with myself if you were gone." She began wrapping Zantral's arm in a towel.

"You say you fell from a tree?" asked an incredulous Tomton-Bray. He was the physician on duty that afternoon. He was among the latest batch of Kaljaxians to relocate to Azsuram.

"Yes," Dolirca answered for her mute friend.

"This looks more like an animal bite than blunt trauma."

"It was a very *tall* tree," replied Dolirca.

"Zantral, did the fall effect your speech? When I ask *you* a question, *she* responds. I'm wondering why that is."

"I'm f … fine, sir," Zantral managed.

"She's traumatized, you fool. I'm her friend and I speak for her because she's shaken. Please worry more about your job and less about challenging a member of the ruling family of Azsuram."

He stared at Dolirca long and hard. "I was not aware there *was* a ruling family on Azsuram. I hear we're all equals in the eyes of the council."

"Please summon another physician. You are clearly more interested in polemics and politics than the healing arts."

"I'm the only one on duty. Unless your friend here would like to wait ten hours for my relief to show up, I suggest you hold that whip like tongue of yours, your royal holiness."

"That is unacceptable. I demand to see your supervisor immediately."

"You're looking at him, sweet cake. It's just the receptionist, my aide, and me. You're welcome to complain to both of them, though, if it suits your divine whim."

"Your insolence and unprofessionalism will be brought up at the next council meeting. I promise you that."

"And I promise I could not care less. Now, take your two mobile carpets, leave the room, and let me do my job. Otherwise, take care of your friend here by yourself in the Palace of Azsuram. In case you're uncertain, it's located somewhere in your insane head. Make a right turn past your massive ego. Mind you don't bump your head on your low intelligence level. I don't need another patient."

The Toe, who accompanied Dolirca everywhere, growled menacingly, and Two inched toward Tomton-Bray.

"Ah, now I'm beginning to see what tree Zantral fell from. A walking, furry one," said Tomton-Bray with a wicked smile. He also reached into his waistband and produced a rail pistol. "Never know when an ungrateful patient might get physical. A word to the wise. I don't *do* veterinary work. If I shoot them, they stay dead."

"You will pay for this," replied Dolirca. "I shall see that smile struck off your face."

"No, *you* will pay on your way out the door. When you come to the realization that you need major psychiatric help, please seek treatment elsewhere. I'm not nearly smart enough to cure you."

Dolirca gave the doctor a look that fell short of killing, but not by much. She stormed out of the office.

"I'll get my assistant to witness your consent to treatment, then I'll patch up your bite wounds."

Zantral lowered her head and nodded.

FIVE

Anganctus strode on his hind legs along a catwalk. His view of the space dockyard was expansive. He towered over the group of pentapeds who groveled in tow. They were Leck technicians, working for the Faxél. Most reluctant workers, to say the least. Leck was one of the many worlds conquered by the Faxél for the express purpose of enslaving the able-bodied population to build the Berrillian war machine. The rest of the population, the majority in most cases, were consumed. All served the Faxél, as best they could.

"Your production is of adequate quality, but much too little quantity. If you cannot build ships-of-the-line faster, you will be sent to the packing house and replaced with a more motivated servant. Is that clear, Monrove?"

The lead scientist for that shipyard bowed nervously. "Yes, lord. If we fail you, we deserve to die."

"No, Monrove. You already deserve to die. What is in question is whether it will be of old age in the ground, or as a result of roasting in an oven."

"Of course, highest. It *is* as you so kindly say."

"So, what are the specific plans you have to increase production? You have three shifts working around the clock. All bays are occupied with ships under construction."

"I will see to it that more dockyards are built."

"That is much too slow. It takes years to fabricate an entire dockyard. Tell me, Monrove, have I eaten all your children yet?"

"N … no, sir. I have two remaining. I beg mercy—"

"The Faxél don't possess mercy. There is not even a word for it in our language. Please know I do not tolerate simpering beggars. You will meet my demands, or you will wish you had."

"I can convert more existing factories to ship production. Refitting will require little time at all."

"You cannot delay the manufacture of other war materials. I will not allow that."

"No, of course not, lord of lords. I will see to it all non-martial production is ended. We will produce only goods for the Berrillian Empire and the power needed to build those supplies."

"Make it so, and I will see if you live." He laughed loudly. "I guess housing construction can be ended without an impact. I've packaged enough of your otherwise useless race to make plenty of room for those who remain." He laughed again.

The Leck genuflected in near panic.

"Show me my new flagship," growled Anganctus.

"It is my honor. This way, most regal."

They descended a few sets of stairs and crossed the dock leading to the rear hatch of a truly tremendous warship. The *Color of Blood* was typical of Faxél design, but much larger. Its gravity wave generators were correspondingly bigger. She would be like the battleships of old Earth, massive and powerful.

As the group stepped aboard, the first thing the Leck noted was the horrific smell. The large cats working in close quarters inside produced an odor that was desirable to the cats, but to no other species. Ammonia, pheromones, and decaying meat assaulted the Leck's nostrils. Anganctus breathed it in deeply, like a fresh sea breeze. One of the Leck technicians collapsed in a fit of gagging.

"Take him to the galley," said Anganctus without delay. "My crew will have fresh meat."

The now smaller group proceeded down a corridor.

"Take me to the bridge," said Anganctus.

Monrove stepped to the front and led the way. When they arrived, it was a hive of activity. Mostly Faxél personnel were installing the sensitive inner workings, such as computers and communication equipment. When they noted Anganctus's entry, they all stood and saluted.

"Thank you, my friends. Please, don't stop work on my behalf. The sooner this ship is complete, the sooner she will see the color of blood."

A loud cheer, in the form of a growl, rose from the crowd.

"The ship will be ready for its maiden voyage very shortly, lord," said Monrove addressing the floor.

"I hope, for your remaining children's sake, that is the case."

In a sense, everyone on Leck knew such were idle threats. Whenever the Faxél were done decimating a world, they canned or froze all consumables before leaving. The faster the Leck worked, the sooner they would perish as a society. But a death in the future topped one in the present, so on they labored.

Back in his quarters later that day, Anganctus spoke with his top advisors.

"Has the last of my fleet set sail for the human space?"

"Yes, lord," said his chief of staff Quentib. "The final flotilla has set a course for the last known position of their worldship fleet. They are at maximal drive and will hopefully arrive within two years."

"I do not wish to delay my divine retribution for two years. Tell the captains to make better speed or I will fire on them when they arrive home."

"Sir, it will be so. However, the inherent instability of the warp—"

"I care nothing for physics, or similar trivialities. The crew will find a way, or perish in their attempt. Is that clear, Quentib?"

"Yes. Perfectly. I will send the order myself."

"Good. At least I have one reliable servant." He scanned the others present with an evil look.

"Have you finalized your battle plan?" he asked of his fleet admiral.

"Yes. Given what we knew as of our last encounter, I expect we will need to implement changes once we have the prey in sight. But as of this moment, we are as ready as we can be."

"Excellent."

"I followed your vision to the letter, lord. We will attack like lightning, and we will be spread out as thinly as the molecules in space. We *cannot* fail."

Anganctus leaned toward the admiral hatefully. "Do you mock me? Do you say failure is not possible, or do you say failure cannot be tolerated?"

"Lord, the very thought. I could not mock you if I wanted to. I clearly meant to say failure was impossible, given your all-encompassing vision. If I have insulted you, please allow me to fall on my sword."

"No. That will not be necessary."

"Thank you, gracious one."

"You may fall on *my* sword. It longs for the taste of blood. Yours, though thinned by your treachery, will quench the blade for the time being."

SIX

Kayla and I were settling in nicely. Since both of us had spent so much time in space together nearly alone, we were uncertain if we'd like the teeming populace of a worldship. The first impression I got, having lived on Earth for forty years, was that *Exeter* was very much like living in a big city such as LA or Houston. I didn't get the feeling of being on a spacecraft at all. Of course, that was part of the design, trying to fool the senses into not getting island fever. Mass hysteria was a real possibility, if a large segment of the population started focusing on their extreme isolation.

With a much larger than average home and an endless number of people who wanted to meet the legend—me—we had a lot of company. Kayla flourished at that. Who knew she was a hostess with the mostest? Serving as first officer on a pirate ship didn't exactly give a gal the background needed to entertain gracefully. But she made guests feel welcome, stimulated the shy to speak, and the drunken to quiet down. She wasn't a half-bad cook, either.

Before I knew it, and certainly before I could handle it, Kayla was pregnant with our third child. Little Gallenda was about to start school. Despite looking like I was still thirty-eight, I felt *very* old. I'd been through all this with Sapale and my stepchildren, but the intimacy of this version was disquieting. I might have to give in to becoming a grown up pretty soon. That was a jarring thought, because if I did, I'd then have to start *acting* like an adult. Yuck.

Somewhere in my period of domestic bliss, Toño asked me to come to his lab. He and Carlos had something they wanted to share.

"Good afternoon, professors," I called out as I entered. "You have a new toaster you wanted to show me?"

Toño smiled like a kid put in charge of a candy shop. "Think bigger," he said barely able to contain himself.

"Wow, not a newer, bigger toaster *oven*? I can't tell you how much I need one of those."

He frowned. "You have a way of deflating the most joyous of times," said Toño with a pout.

"Aw, I'm sorry. What miracle did you come up with?" I figured it was something to do with the gravity wave generators.

"Not a miracle," replied Carlos, "but not all that far from one. Look at this," he gestured to a control panel.

"Ah. You invented the computer?"

"No," snapped an irritated Carlos. "But we did get this one up and running."

"Here," said Toño.

He flipped a switch and hit a few buttons. A sound I couldn't place came out of the speakers. It wasn't radio noise, because it had a periodicity to it. Otherwise, it sounded maybe like boring music.

"I give up. What am I listening to?"

"Here," Toño said hitting another button. "Let me cut in this filter."

Instantly the wavy, electronic signal became a set of discrete sounds. The result was like one of those voice scramblers kids loved to play with.

"And now this," he said tapping a final icon.

"…routine maintenance reports will be issued on the prowl. Delinquent reports will be noted in the issuer's file and may be cause for disciplinary action if the offense endangers any part of the total operation, its goals, or its intent. Remediation of infractions—"

"Wow, that is *dull*," I said shaking my head. "Those have to be the most boring people in existence. *Rocks* would find those guys ponderous."

"No. Guess again. I'll give you a hint. You don't like them at all," responded Toño with a wicked grin.

"That's a non-short list."

"One guess please, if only to see you fail."

"You want to *see* me fail? That's harsh, Doc."

"You're right. I should say, fail *again*. Go on, guess."

"The Listhelons?"

"No, but not a bad guess. The voice your hearing is a Berrillian AI." Toño said that so triumphantly, I felt bad not getting the exact importance of his point.

"You have a recording of a Berrillian AI. *That's* supposed to impress me?"

"It is not a recording, Jon. It's a live broadcast." Carlos was about to explode, too. "It comes to us from *warp* space."

"Not really getting … *whoa*. Are you saying we can listen to them live in warp space?"

"Real space, too," squealed Toño. "We figured out their communications pathways and broke their codes."

"But how? It shouldn't be possible, right? They're millions of parsecs away, in a warp bubble."

"A truly magnificent piece of engineering on their part. To make travel in warp space possible for a fleet, they devised a way to communicate. Without it, they'd be slowed considerably. The technology creates a tiny warp bubble here." Toño pointed to a large metal-jacketed box. "For whatever twist of physics, bubble-to-bubble signaling is possible, and can be sent in real time."

"So we know what they're doing as soon as they do?"

"Yes. It's a game changer." Toño clasped his hands together in excitement.

"More than a game changer," I marveled. "It renders them a nuance, not a threat. This is *huge*, you two beautiful geniuses."

"Well, that's for you military types to determine. We only make the tool available," responded Carlos with false modesty.

"I'm calling the Swedish command worldship. Hand me that phone."

"Wh … why would you call them?"

"You two are getting a Nobel Prize before the sun sets on your cute little faces."

"They don't award them anymore," replied a very serious Carlos. "Not since we left Earth."

"I know. That's why it'll take me a couple calls."

The next morning, we had a meeting with Alexis and all her military muckety-mucks. Toño announced the breakthrough to an absolutely stunned room of people. When he was finished presenting, the two of them got a standing ovation, as well as bear hugs from Alexis. After the hoopla died down, Alexis asked if they were any closer to duplicating the gravity wave generators. They said they'd made progress, but didn't expect success for at least several months. It was funny. The two scientists were so crestfallen to report that delay. Here they whelp a miracle but are then chagrined they couldn't make it a double. White coats.

Alexis, of course, saved the day, bless her soul. "I wish I could knight you both. Hell, no, I'd make you dukes or something. Humanity owes you two so much, that words of thanks alone simply cannot express our debt. Suffice it to say, your contributions will never be forgotten."

That perked them up. Both looked like a couple of embarrassed boys in front of the whole school. Darn cute. It was one of those moments I never expected but was privileged to be a part of. Life felt good just then. I began to fantasize that we'd turned a corner and that humankind's travels in space were going to fall into a comfortable normalcy.

In retrospect, my big mistake was not staying on guard. The alternate timeline version of me had said the baton was mine alone. But experiencing normal life for the first time was a narcotic to me. I lost the desire to worry about, manage, and police the galaxy. I also put Azsuram so far back in my head, I didn't think of paying them a visit as often as I should have, as often as I owed it to Sapale. I *was* only human. I made a set of misjudgments. Maybe that cost us big in the long run. Maybe it wouldn't have changed a damn thing. The best outcome at that juncture would honestly be if the alternate timeline Jon would have shown up and kicked my ass.

SEVEN

"No, Dolirca, you can't. What you are is out of order. The Council of Elders has rules. This is not a bar. You wait your turn, or I'll have you thrown out." JJ was furious with his niece. He was a man who rarely got mad, so all in attendance understood the gravity of his explosion.

"But this is important. I insist I be allowed to speak first." Dolirca struggled to remain calm. She wanted to appear the more composed of the two.

"I'm betting it's only important in *your* mind, not from a *rational* person's perspective."

"I must point out it is forbidden to cast insults in a council meeting. *You're* out of order. I will have *you* thrown out," Dolirca spat back, defiantly.

The session was degenerating badly. As head of the council, JJ needed to retake control. Plus, he was not about to let his crazy niece have her spoiled way.

Summoning all his inner strength he spoke evenly. "Will the sergeant-at-arms please remove Dolirca from the room. Please see to it that she does not interfere with the proceedings in any other manner. The subject of her punishment will be discussed at an appropriate point in this meeting."

JJ flopped into his chair. What a mess. Plus, Dolirca's brood-mate was the current sergeant at arms. What a muddle. Burlinhar was spineless on his best day. He might be incapable of forcing his brood's-mate from where she sat.

"If the SAA needs more help, the room's full of anxious volunteers," JJ sniped as an addition.

"No," Dolirca shouted, "he does *not* require aid. I shall gladly leave this mockery of a deliberative body." She stormed out of the room, her Toe by her side.

Burlinhar followed closely behind, visibly crushed. He caught up with Dolirca halfway home. When he firmly grabbed her arm to stop her, both Toe growled viciously.

"Dory, wait," he said as he pulled to slow her flight. "Come on, let's talk. That will help."

She ripped her arm free and began to run.

He matched her pace and reached for her again. One batted his arm away and stopped to block him. When he tried to step around the Toe, she lifted him in her furry arms.

He stared wide-eyed at One, not knowing if he was about to be torn to shreds. One was clearly uncertain, also.

"Dory," he shouted, "help. Make her put me down."

She slowed quickly to a stop and reluctantly turned around. "One, release him and come here."

One did so and trotted over quickly.

"Do us both a favor and never come home," she said in a passionless tone. "Never speak to me. Don't even look at me. Next time I will not call my guards off." She turned and began walking away.

"Dory, wait. You can't mean that. We're one, you and me. What about our children? I have to see my kids."

She stopped and stood stiffly with her back to him. Her first thought was to have the Toe kill him. But that would raise questions in others's minds, and there could be repercussions. If Burlinhar was found in tiny pieces, it would be easy to forensically prove her guards were responsible. A call might be made to destroy the only things she truly loved. Burlinhar would not cost her so dearly.

"Take him to the Cliff of Atlas and throw him off. But be gentle. I want it to look like a simple suicide." Dolirca wagged a scolding finger at the Toe. "Do you hear me? Not one mark on him the rocks and the water don't cause."

That would do nicely. Everyone was at the council meeting. No witnesses.

She'd claim they argued after the meeting. Her dearest Burlinhar fled into the night. She worried about him so, because he blamed himself for her expulsion. She'd even cry when they told her they'd found his worthless corpse.

Two days later, Dolirca's mother Fashallana and a group of her siblings came to her door. JJ was conspicuously not among them. Their faces were grave. They told her that Dolirca's worst fears were confirmed. Her brood-mate's badly mangled remains were found washed ashore below the cliffs. Her sisters carried her to the couch when Dolirca's legs collapsed. Her tears were unconsolable, her grief manifest. Before leaving, Fashallana mentioned that the sheriff would be by the following day to take her official statement. Burlinhar's autopsy was already in progress, so the burial could be performed in accordance with the time constraints tradition dictated.

After closing the door on the last of her cursed kin, Dolirca leaned back onto the portal. A statement? How offensive. Her fool brood-mate jumped off a cliff. Why were statements and autopsies needed? They suspected her. That was the reason; she was being accused. They all clearly hated her. They were all jealous. They knew she was the rightful heiress to Sapale's golden crown, and they hated her because of that.

But they would never stop her. No. They were inferiors, each and every one of them. Slime on the underside of a rock. She would rule supreme, and they would bow down to her. And she would rule them with wisdom, grace, and love, because Dolirca *was* love. She was mother to all her kind. That was why she loved the unlovable and would cherish the undeserving lot of them. Soon, the preposterous statue to her grandmother would be hammered to dust by an adoring crowd, and a proper monument would be raised to Azsuram's first and only queen.

EIGHT

Eas-el stood in a universe he'd never known. He closed his eyes and saw everything that was. Infinities were such a wonder of endless possibilities. He felt as if blood surged in his body, stirring in the heart he didn't have, warming his barren interior. It was good to be alive again, not suspended in quasi-death, trapped in some ill-defined nexus. He sensed life abounding in this universe. It was everywhere and it was joyous. He knew it was his to crush, his light to extinguish. It would be good to destroy again, to create fear, to end happiness, and to cancel out meaning. As his brothers and sisters dragged themselves reluctantly into existence near him, Eas-el smelled their longing, their acceptance of the need to squeeze all that was from this universe. What else could the Last Nightmare do? The oblivion they spread was their way.

"Eas-el, you were always the smallest and the weakest of us, yet you force us to come here. I share your lust for shattering this vibrant universe. We all do. But the peril we are causes inhabitants to resist us every time. We will lose brothers and sisters in the apocalypse that we will spawn. It has always been so. I hold you responsible for each of them." So spoke Des-al, the most powerful of the Last Nightmares that remained.

"I chose to reformat myself here. You could have remained in your eggs and cried so much that you drowned in the tears."

"You know we move as one or we move not at all. It is far too late to reverse the havoc you have unleashed. Know that I called your treason what it was. If you outlast this universe, you must carry that weight."

"Speak more clearly. All I hear from your mind is a cackling sound, that of a giant chicken." Eas-el spoke of chickens because he knew everything there was to know about this universe already. Chickens once existed on a ravaged planet named Earth.

His brothers knew of chickens and laughed at Des-al. In his rage, Des-al grabbed the supermassive black hole in a nearby galaxy and hurled it at Eas-el. It erupted into nothingness around Eas-el. But his laughing could be heard through the torment space-time experienced. Finally, Des-al joined in the laughter. The destruction had begun. It could not be stopped. All was good, because the Last Nightmare *were* again.

"As the first to condense here, yours is the first path," Tro-il said to Eas-el. "How will your reign begin?"

"I will seek out the most miserable, the weakest, the most pitiful creature there is in this universe and crown him king, ruler of all that is. I will make the one most completely bereft of power into the mightiest force conceivable to the sentients of this space-time. That is how I will begin."

"You have always been unsteady, weak Eas-el," responded Des-al. "Why would you interfere in such a limp manner? We crush, kill, and destroy. We do not make puppets and have them perform for our liking."

"It is mine to do. That is how I will do it. I will build up the most pathetic being and allow him to know hope, power, and control. I will then lead him to the absolute pit of despair, and I will eat his soul. He will know the completeness of his failure, and then he will die." Eas-el roared so loud the stars shook in the heavens. "It will be as I think it."

Then Eas-el focused his mind on the universe. He sought the one he would destroy the most.

NINE

I had to pinch myself. It just kept getting better and better. My personal life was soaring way past its all-time high. Toño and Carlos had all but neutralized the Berrillian threat. There was no sign of the Listhelons, and Stuart Marshall was still dead. My vortex was the ultimate weapon in the universe. I'd long since stopped asking stupid stuff like "What could possibly go wrong?" The answer was always something worse than I suspected, and it perennially lodged itself quite high up my butt. Still, I had to wonder if things would ever be as bad as they had been. Were all our bases finally actually covered? I know, silly me.

One day Kayla asked me to take her and the kids to visit uncle Karnean. I still wasn't a big fan, but he was family. We rendezvoused with his new ship during some mission of dubious legality. It was a nice visit. As lukewarm as he was toward me, he was great with his niece and nephews. The trip reminded me that I hadn't been to Azsuram in way too long. I missed that family. I also had an obligation to make sure the colony continued moving forward.

We returned to *Exeter* after a week with Uncle Kar-kar, as Gallenda had dubbed him. I checked in with Alexis and Toño to make sure there were no new crises on the horizon. As there were none, I made the trip to Azsuram. I was especially psyched because Toño had made me a Berrillian warp-communication unit to leave on Azsuram. After this visit, I would be able to call them and, more importantly, they could call me if there was trouble.

My designated landing pad was next to my old house. JJ lived there now, with his rapidly growing family. I'd been gone so long, I did that awkward thing where you stand in front of the door, not knowing whether to knock first or just enter. I chickened out and hit the call button.

JJ opened the door, jumped with joy, and vaulted into my arms. Honestly, a man his age acting in such a juvenile manner. I was shocked and dismayed. We hugged for the better part of two minutes.

"Dad, you pissed me off," was his first remark to me.

"I can live with that. Just curious, what'd I do to warrant it?"

"You rang the bell." He gently slapped the side of my head. "*Hello*. Your house. You just key that pad and waltz on in. Do I make myself clear?"

I saluted him. "Yes, sir. It'll never happen again."

"In that case, you may enter my domain." He stepped aside and ushered me in.

His kids ran over and hugged my legs. God, they reminded me of their father. Of course, that reminded me painfully of their grandmother. I would never stop missing her.

Challaria heard the commotion and came to investigate. When she saw the source of the noise, she piled on. Hugs all around. It was sublime. She insisted I looked too thin, though we all knew that was impossible. She dragged me to the kitchen table. Two of the kids pushed my butt from behind because they figured that Mom needed help.

"Sit," she said with remarkable authority. "I'll get you something to eat. And JJ," she karate chopped the air in his direction, "no beer until sunset. You got that?"

"She's just negotiating, Pops. I'll sneak us some of my latest concoction, as soon as her back is turned," responded JJ.

That's my boy.

Shortly, Challaria plopped a huge bowl of calrf down right under my nose. That's the worst place for a big bowl of calrf to be. And it was the eucalyptus-aromatic one even most Kaljaxians didn't like. It was their culture's version of hákarl, fermented shark. You ate it, because it proved you were just that tough. Me, I'd happily choose starvation over either abomination.

My little granddaughter Bottsal handed me a spoon and said, "Eat, Tato.

It's good for you." Tato was a child's Hirn diminutive for grandfather.

I was torn. She looked so sincere, so intent on pleasing me. But I wasn't sure there was enough love in the universe for me to put that vile, lumpy paste in my mouth.

She turned to her father. "I tried, Daddy. He won't eat it like you wanted him to. I'm sorry. You're not mad at me, are you?"

Challaria snickered, and JJ laughed as he swept Bottsal into his arms. "Never, sweetness. Your Tato just isn't hungry right now. He'll eat it later. He promises, don't you, Tato?"

"I smell a rat," I replied.

"No, that's just the sunne calrf," responded Challaria through her cackles.

"I mean, I sense a setup here. A dark conspiracy to guilt me into consuming this poiso … I mean porridge." I didn't want to confuse innocent little Bottsal.

After that, we settled into a wonderful day of family. I played with my grandkids, showed them holos of my other family, and shot the breeze with JJ. I really missed that. He was almost as brilliant a liar and bullshitter as I was. He was good company. Finally, our conversation came around to politics and how the colony was doing. That brought an unfamiliar sour mood to JJ's face.

"What?" I asked. "That's the sad JJ look. What gives?"

"Objectively, things are great, better than Mom ever dreamed. Factory production is finally ramping up, the crops are growing faster than the weeds, and there's a lot more game to be had than we suspected. The education system is clearly better than anything on Kaljax, including our university. Thanks to you, the top people are all here. Hey, the medical school graduated its first class a few months back. You should have seen them, all dressed in those silly gowns."

"Yes," I said somberly, "I should have seen them. I've been lax in my duties to Azsuram."

"Don't be so dramatic. Those are *our* duties now. You're a figurehead, Pops. Get over yourself."

I could always count on a nice broadside from my wiseass boy.

"That only leaves the part where you tell me where something has gone to hell in a hand basket."

"That would be Dolirca."

I did *not* see that coming. Little Dory a problem? Not in a big way at least. Sure, one of us had to redirect her once in a while, but she never seemed bad. JJ filled me in, up to and including the still unconfirmed suicide of Burlinhar. I was well beyond dumbfounded.

"You think she killed her own brood-mate? JJ, that's a powerful accusation, especially without witnesses or evidence."

"No, she couldn't have. She's thin as a fencepost, much worse than the last time you saw her. No, I know she had her Toe do it. I'm positive."

"How can you be so certain about something so awful? And her Toe? Come on. I spent years with their mother. She was as kind and gentle a creature as there ever was."

"Dad, Burlinhar was a sniveling coward. There's no way he jumps off those scary cliffs into that rough sea. Zero chance. A railgun to his head, maybe. But otherwise no way. And those Toe aren't like the one you knew." He focused on the floor. "She's trained them to be vicious, mean, and absolutely obedient. They scare the hell out of me. I do believe, by the way, that's her desire."

He told me about the incident with Dolirca and Dr. Tomton-Bray. The doctor had confided in JJ that Zantral's wounds could never happen from a fall. That was the topic Dolirca wanted to bring up at the meeting that led to her expulsion. She wanted the doctor sent back to Kaljax.

"No way," I responded. "You're making this up. There are totally no provisions for such a deportation. Since I helped write the laws, I'd know. That's crazy."

"Therein lies the problem, Dad. Dolirca's insane. I mean that medically as head of the council, not as her uncle. And there's no protocol for what to do with a crazy person either."

"Before we get any deeper here, let me talk with her. I'm sure I can figure out some solution."

"I doubt it, Pops. You really don't know her now. She's a xenophobe."

"Now I'm speechless. No way I can believe *that*."

"She is. Trust me."

"No, I can't believe you used the word *xenophobe*. No way. Drop and cover, the sky is about to fall."

"Dad, this is serious. Please be serious for just a second."

I made a huge show of flailing in my chair.

"I can't believe I raised you so poorly. Demanding seriousness. That's so wrong."

"Sorry. I'm head of the council, and she's my niece. Dad, this is the most serious threat I've ever faced. For you, the savior of the galaxy, this may seem trivial, but it's ripping my heart out."

I sat up straight. "Sorry. You're right. Is she at her house now?"

"Yes. I'm coming with you."

"No. I need to do this alone. I don't want her focusing on you."

"She's got those Toe."

I held up my laser finger. "I'm not the one you need to worry about, son."

My mind was numb as I walked to Dolirca's small house near the edge of town. JJ was correct. When my granddaughter opened the door, her face turned to stone. She was not happy to see me.

I stood in the doorway an uncomfortably long time. Finally, I asked if she was going to invite me in.

"No. You can deliver whatever brief message you have from where you stand."

That brought Fashallana to the door like she'd been shot from a cannon. She must have been on the couch. "Dolirca, what in Davdiad's mercy are you saying? Dad, please come in." She took my arm and pulled me past her daughter.

"Hi, Fash," I said with a genuine smile.

"It's great to see you. I've missed you. JJ's really missed you" said Fashallana with a very worried look on her face. She positioned me on the couch. "Can I get you something?" She looked disapprovingly at her daughter. "Can *we* get you anything?"

"No, sweetheart, I'm fine. I'm just here to see what's up with my favorite granddaughter."

"Well, I'll leave you two alone. Dory, dear, will you be okay?" asked Fashallana.

"Of course, silly. Why wouldn't I be? This human replica won't linger long. I have to get the children from school."

Fashallana exploded in fury. "I will *not* allow you to speak about my father in that manner. This man is a hero to me and to everyone else living on Azsuram. He's saved our lives so many times I've stopped counting. If you are *anything* but a perfect host to him, I will make you sorry you weren't."

"He's not your father. Your mother couldn't remember which of the *many* possible sperm donors yours was."

Fashallana slapped her hard across the face. Both Toe roared and advanced on Fashallana. I extended my probes and held them both aloft. Their fierce struggles were for naught.

"Release my guards," demanded Dolirca. "I'm not safe in the presence of my enemies."

"Fash, why don't you go home? I'll stop by after Dory and I have a nice, long chat."

"You'll be okay?" she asked me.

I pointed to the suspended Toe. "I'm not too worried."

She left, but she was sure a bundle of nerves.

"Dory, sit," I said in my command voice.

"I do not take orders from human robots."

"Good. Neither do I. Sit down young woman, or I'll come over and physically toss your butt into a chair."

Reluctantly she sat. She knew I wasn't kidding.

"Put them down at once. You're scaring the poor darlings."

"They're scaring me, too. First, there's something I need to do."

In my mind I asked of One: *did you throw Burlinhar off a cliff?* I then asked the same of Two. Being as simpleminded as their mother, neither tried to resist.

They both confirmed that they had.

Why?

Because Dory told them to.

Son of a bitch. *Go to sleep.* The Toe rolled into balls, and I sat them down.

"If you've harmed—"

"Shut up. They're asleep. They'll have to be put down for what you made them do. Dory, I've never been more ashamed of a person in my life. How could you?"

Her face tightened. "How could I what? I have—"

"Stop lying. You told them to pitch your brood-mate off a cliff. That makes you a murderer and them dangerous pets. I cannot believe I'm even *having* this conversation. I told you what we do to unsafe pets. Do you know what we do to women who murder their spouses?"

"You can't prove a thing, so don't try to bluff me into confessing, robot."

I scoured my face with my palms. "Dory, your grandmother and I helped write the laws of this planet. You're either going to be deemed mentally incompetent and locked up for good, or you'll be executed. I didn't want that part of the law, but it turns out Kaljaxians are pretty vengeful when it comes to cold-blooded murders."

"I cannot be convicted on the opinion of a machine." She turned her face away from me.

"Ah, yes you can. I can download what your Toe told me. A jury of your peers will watch the holo and convict you faster than you can say *lynch mob*. Honey, what's going to happen to your kids? Did you think about them?"

"The welfare of my children is no concern of yours, toy human."

"You know what? You can keep saying that until your tongue falls out, and it won't bother me in the least. You're mentally ill, Dory. You're also remarkably stupid. Combine that with smug and heartless, and I'm not taking your abuse too much to heart."

I pulled out my handheld.

"JJ. Hi. Look, I found out you were right. Yes, she told them to. They're asleep on the floor. Fine, yes. Definitely, and have them bring cages. Thanks. Tell her I really appreciate her picking up the kids. At her house is fine. I'll meet her there after you come get Dory. For sure, bring a few. The more witnesses, the better. I know. They probably won't interfere, but why risk it? Okay, see you soon."

She glowered at me, seething rage boiling up in her face.

"You look as ugly on the outside as you are on the inside."

"I will see you're turned off for this, computing machine."

"Now I'm worried. Wait, no I'm not. You're a cruel little girl who'll be locked up for the rest of her life. I feel so much safer all of a sudden."

We sat in silence, waiting for JJ and the zoo officials to arrive. Quicker than I expected, JJ was there with several police officers. They took Dory away. She never looked at me or her uncle the entire time. The zoo workers rolled the sleeping Toe into cages and left with them. Time would tell if they'd be put down or simply become display specimens. Either way, they weren't going to be hurting anyone else.

"Shit, JJ, all this is so wrong," I said in a whisper. "How did it ever get this bad?"

"No idea. Really. She's always been a little prissy, but this psycho thing came out of nowhere on a greased lightning bolt."

"The law is clear as to what comes next."

"Yes. The council will order psychiatric evaluations. They'll prove she's nuts. Then we'll probably ask you to take her back to Kaljax for better long-term care. But, hey, let's worry about that when the time comes."

"Amen. No need to rush the unpleasant. Poor girl."

"Poor Burlinhar. Poor innocent little kids. Both their parents gone. Dory brought this on herself. They didn't. She'll get no tears from me."

"It's a tragedy every way you look at it. I'm sick inside."

He put his arm around my neck. "Let's go find that brew. I think we both need it more than we want it."

TEN

"I think the One That Is All went pretty easy on you," Yibitriander said as harshly as he could to the man who was his father, a man he still loved dearly.

"I don't care either way. I did what I knew had to be done. It was as plain as the three legs you stand on that the Berrillians needed to be stopped," replied Kymee.

"Please don't say you don't care what the collective thinks. If they should hear you—"

"*If?* I assume they heard me when I shouted those very words in their conjoined heads."

"I speak only as your oldest friend. I wish to see no harm come to you."

"And none will. You must believe me on this point. If the One That Is All was that morally bankrupt, I'd be long gone. I'd jump in a vortex and never look back."

"No one has ever left. You can't leave. They wouldn't allow it. *I* wouldn't allow it."

"Farthdoran left."

"No. He *died*."

"And the difference is? We not only allowed him to die, but we also did the dirty deed." Kymee waved his hands in frustration. "Clear consciences all around, too."

"Please calm down and let this go. You acted independently, One That Is All censured you, which means nothing. It's done."

"It's as far from over as One That Is All is from being a fish."

Yibitriander closed his eyes and rubbed the lids. "I believe you're mixing a metaphor. Can we ease back on the anger here, please?"

"You are free to do whatever you like. No, wait, I take that back. You're as bound to obey as I am. We are, in fact, *not* free to do as we may. I can't let this go. When there's a next time, what'll they do? What'll I do?"

"Let's not even discuss a repeat performance. That way we won't have to stress over the consequences."

"Do I look like I'm stressing? I'm not. I'm morally outraged. I'm deeply hurt. What's more, I'm pissed. Don't you see? They censured me for giving the humans the technology needed to not die as a species. In translation, it means One That Is All is completely indifferent whether or not evil triumphs and good people are murdered."

"We are here ... we have isolated ourselves on Oowaoa forever, so as not to get involved." Yibitriander stammered when he was this upset.

"No. We returned home because we were a blight on the universe. We came here to better ourselves. That's diametrically opposed to simple isolationism."

"Yes. We are poison. So, we confined the poison and *all* its effects here."

"I was there when we made the decision. You were, too. We were forced to face the fact that we had become monsters. We decided it was morally imperative that we improve ourselves. We retreated home, because it was the best way to stop our transcendent evil."

"If I agree with you, will you stop lecturing me?"

"Yes. Unless of course you need further lecturing, in which case I'll help you as much as I can."

"I'm too old for this." Yibitriander covered his face with all three palms. "I think I'll call it a day, go live in a cave, and cover the opening with rocks and brush."

"You're the dramatic one, aren't you? What's next? Theatrical productions? Public performances for spare change?" Kymee smiled mischievously.

"I wish to make two serious points clear. One, there was support for your action among some of One That Is All. It didn't rise to the level of dissent, but it was there. If you didn't notice it, you should know it was present."

"And two," interrupted Kymee, "don't ever do it again. That's what you were going to say."

"And your response was going to be that you'd never do it again unless there was just cause."

"There you have it. We perfectly understand each other. Blood *is* thicker than complacent intellects."

"Please mind the metaphors. They're a privilege, not a right. If you can't use them properly, do not employ them at all."

Kymee stuck his tongue out at his son.

"Oh, *that's* a mature response. Now I feel so much better about your future safety."

ELEVEN

Dolirca sat in her jail cell, alone and brokenhearted. The side of her head rested on her elbow and she stared out the window. She did not, however, even notice the lovely spring day. Children ran and played as their parents sat on benches and chatted pleasantly in the shade. There was no joy in Dolirca's world. She was a tiny, tattered leaf adrift on a sea of hateful souls. Her uncle wanted her dead. The android human abomination wanted her pets dead. Her grandmother, the only person who loved her, was dead. Tata Sapale died trying to protect Dolirca, but even Tata failed. Maybe Tata wanted her dead, too. That's why she let the Berrillian kill her. Yes, it had been a pathetic excuse to avoid having to own up the the fact that she was going to abandon Dolirca.

They all wanted to be rid of her, because they were jealous. They also knew she was right. Dolirca was born to rule Azsuram, not them. They were created to be led. There was nothing wrong with following a divine leader, nothing whatsoever. She offered them more than they could receive by the merits of their otherwise meaningless lives. That's why they all turned their backs on her. They turned their backs and laughed at her because they were srimpil, living in the mud and consuming excrement. And everyone knew how to handle a swarm of srimpil. You burned their mud puddle and beat it with sticks. Let the srimpil survive, and they would spread throughout the fields and no crops would grow.

A leader had to mind her fields. Those simple followers must have their daily rations. Dolirca must burn the srimpil, and she would most definitely beat them with a big stick. She must protect her helpless servants, because she was a good and gracious queen empress. Then they'd all be sorry. They'd grovel and they'd beg for their pointless lives to be spared. She, as a just ruler, would mete out their punishment. She would pound common sense into their heads with an axe. Then there would be peace, love, and the return of hope. That was how life should be under a divine leader.

As Dolirca pondered her retribution and assent, a butterfly flittered in through the bars of her window. She was so preoccupied and vexed she didn't take notice of it at first. It flew in jerking circles around her head several times before she sat up and focused on it. She had never seen a live butterfly. Pictures and holos to be certain, but never one in person. There were no butterflies on Azsuram. None on Kaljax, for that matter. The few that remained were on the human worldship fleet over three hundred light-years away.

She marveled at its delicate beauty, the lines of brightness and the patches of color. It was, for that moment, to her the most precious creature in the universe. It represented freedom from worry and confinement. She wished she could be a butterfly. She would soar to the sky and never return to the dismal world of people and lies and hate.

"Aren't you the prettiest thing there's ever been?" she asked the insect as it gyrated though the air. "But where did you come from? Your species doesn't exist here. That wicked robot would never bring in an invasive Earth species to the planet he conquered. He would ever so hate your beauty and grace. Those are aspects it fully lacks."

She held out her finger. The butterfly initially jerked away, then it gently landed on her.

"Oh my. You *are* the precious one. I almost forget how much I miss One and Two when I look at you."

She swung her finger gently from side to side and sang an ancient lullaby to the bug.

Spirit of beauty and spirit of love, you are such a precious gift from above; You will always own my heart and soul, and together we shall make one whole.

When she was done, she slipped the butterfly to her other hand and drew it to her face. "My name is Dolirca. I'm pleased to meet you. I only wish I knew your name, so we could be the best of friends forever."

"I am Callophrys," said the insect in a lilting whisper that sounded like tiny bells ringing.

Dolirca snapped her hand away, and the butterfly floated up slowly.

"Do not be angry at me, Dolirca. I wish only to be your friend," responded the butterfly.

"But … butterflies can't talk."

"I can. That is all you need to believe. Please," said Callophrys plaintively as she landed on Dolirca's shoulder, "don't be mad at me."

"I'm not mad. I could never be mad at you, sweet Callophrys. I was just surprised. Yes, that is it. I was startled. That is all."

"Then you will be my friend?"

"Oh yes, dearest, I will be so always. I am in need of a friend, and you are so pretty. How could we not be the best of friends?"

Callophrys rose in the air and flitted happily. "You have made me so happy. I have a new friend. Tomorrow I will visit my friend and we will talk."

The butterfly flew toward the window.

"But why can't you stay now and visit. I'm so lonely."

"I must feed my children, sweetest Dolirca. I hear them cry for their supper. But I will be back soon, and we shall become sisters."

"Until tomorrow, dearest Callophrys. Kiss your children on the forehead from me."

"I will. I will kiss your children on your behalf, too."

Callophrys was swept up by a strong breeze and was gone.

The next day, the butterfly returned as promised. She sat again on Dolirca's shoulder, and told her tales of fair maidens and handsome princes. Callophrys sang ballads about places so far away they could only be visited in one's imagination. She praised Dolirca to an extent that would have embarrassed most people. But Dolirca listened to each compliment and accepted it wholly. Every affirmation was gathered in greedily. Callophrys was wise to see her wondrous qualities so hidden to everyone she lived with.

The following day Callophrys visited for longer. She spun yarns of magical realms where the beautiful and the just were always the same. And the butterfly brought gifts. Despite her featherweight, she bore the most enrapturing flower to Dolirca. It smelled of everything nice. Home, children, good food, and loving companionship. Dolirca was most impressed that she'd never seen the flower on Azsuram before. Callophrys knew of such rarities, hidden so completely from the eyes of the busy locals.

Then for three days the butterfly did not come. Dolirca worried that her uncle must have seen its visits and hunted Callophrys down and killed her. But, her friend did find her way back to Dolirca's prison cell. Callophrys brought gifts of sweet cakes and waters so pure they sparkled in Dolirca's mouth as she drank them. The stories the butterfly brought were not full of joy and wonder. Callophrys told of people ruining her forest, killing her children, and chasing her so they could wear her wings on their faces as decorations. She cried for her lost babies and worried that soon, there would be no beauty on Azsuram. Night, she lamented, was coming.

"I won't let them harm you, sweet friend," said Dolirca with tears streaming down her cheeks.

"But how can you help? You are locked in here like a criminal. I know I am safe when I'm with you, but once I fly past those bars, I am prey to all who are evil and want the light to go out in this world."

"I will help you—on my life I will. Once I'm free, I will guard you. Together we will drive out the wicked, and this world will be one of love."

"I can help you escape, if you'd like," said little Callophrys.

"How can you, my precious? You are so small, and these walls so thick."

Callophrys flew to the lock. She poked her proboscis in the opening and shook it mightily. The mechanism clicked loudly and the door creaked open. She led Dolirca past two sleeping guards and opened the next door. She was free.

The butterfly lit on her shoulder and asked where they would go next.

"To free my guards."

Dolirca ran to the zoo, over the turnstile, and right to her pets' cages. She ran with such abandon that she did not notice Callophrys had gone.

"One," she shouted to her pet. "Oh, Two, there you are."

She jumped over the railing and tried to muscle the cage door open. It was locked. She looked around wildly for Callophrys to ask her friend to pick this lock, too. But the butterfly was nowhere to be seen. Instead, three guards were running toward her, yelling into their handhelds.

Two guards tackled her while the third retrieved a length of rope to bind her.

"Where are you, Callophrys?" shouted Dolirca. "I need your help. Kill these cruel men. Do not let them lock me up again."

But still Callophrys did not come. Only more guards did. Finally, her uncle ran over.

"How the hell did you get out?" he screamed at her. He was very angry. "Why did you kill those two guards? Did you have to kill them? Dory, you must stop killing people."

What was he saying? Her guards slept. No one killed them. That was another hateful lie. She hated JJ with all her heart.

"I didn't kill them, and Callophrys couldn't hurt anyone."

JJ assumed Callophrys was one of Dory's supporters, but he was unfamiliar with the name. "Who the hell is Callophrys, and where is he?"

"I don't know. I think you scared her away. She's free, flying in the trees, looking for her dead children. You murdered her children, and she must find them."

Dolirca lunged and kicked at her uncle. The guards held her more tightly.

"She's where? I did what?"

"You heard me. She's gone where you can't catch her and display her on your face."

"Dory, honey, what are you talking about? Is Callophrys a person?"

"No. Don't ask me that. You know she isn't. Why do you taunt and bait me? You know she's a butterfly and she's beautiful and she's my only friend."

"Dory, are you saying an insect that has never lived on Azsuram came to your aide? A butterfly killed two grown men?" Dory was sicker than he'd ever imagined. She was completely insane.

"Callophrys set me free, but she didn't kill anyone."

"Take her back to her cell," shouted JJ to the guards. "And have the tech re-key the lock. Only I am to have the code. Is that clear?"

They acknowledged his order, as three of them dragged Dolirca away. In the background, the Toe howled in angry protestation from their confinement.

TWELVE

"Ladies and gentlemen, I have called this meeting to update you on the Berrillian situation. Please come to order."

That should have been Katashi Matsumoto's actual first name. *Order*. Dude was highly in favor of it. When I was particularly bored during a session with the admiral, I'd trip about what it would be like to be his butler, or to have sex with him. The order, right-way wrong-way thing would be a barrier to easy interactions. Hey, sometimes I got really bored.

"Dr. De Jesus has been at the lead, so I'll have him present the essentials," Katashi said as he sat down.

"Thank you. Over the last few months we've established a pretty clear picture of the Berrillians's size and intent. You have documents in front of you displaying their main bases, areas of manufacturing, and approximate numbers in terms of population concentrations."

The woman next to me whistled loudly.

"Yes," responded Toño, "there are a lot of them out there."

"How could they come to control so many worlds?" asked Jason Kaserian, chief assistant to Bin Li.

"They're ferocious, merciless, and focused," I replied, "that's how. It's a lesson we can never forget." I rapped the stack of papers with a knuckle. "I'd bet my bottom credit there were people on all these worlds just as talented and determined as we are. They staged the best defense they could and were conquered. The Berrillians win by numbers and an absolute disregard for their own individual lives."

"God help us," said Alexis Gore grimly.

"I got an amen for that," I replied.

"Let us focus on our options, not on the metaphysical," snapped Katashi.

"So, our AIs have screened an enormous number of their documents, communications, and troop movements. A clear picture has emerged as to their plans regarding us. Their supreme leader, Anganctus, has ordered an all-out attack on the worldship fleet."

The few who didn't already know that information gasped.

"Yes. A frightening prospect, forewarned or not," replied Toño. "They are aware we must possess some weapon they cannot counter, since General Ryan defeated their latest incursion so decisively." He looked at me as if to ask what the hell it was I'd not told him. "Anganctus's strategy is simple. He will flood us with thinly spread out forces in immense numbers. He correctly assumes our main weapon is limited in number. He mentions he can't imagine why it is, but he's guessed that it is."

"Or at least he hopes it is. He cannot know," remarked Katashi.

"This is correct. He also has the humans and the Deavoriath well scrambled up in his mind. I don't know if he thinks they are our allies or if he confuses the humans *with* the Deavoriath."

"I don't see an advantage in that flaw we could use against him," said Vice Admiral Kipchoge Kipsang.

"No," was Katashi's terse response.

"We have also compiled a fairly grim picture of life on the occupied worlds. I will spare you the details in the interest—"

"No," thundered Katashi. "I want *everyone* to fully understand the price of failure. Please provide us with the details of Berrillian subjugation."

Toño looked quite uncomfortable and wavered. "Upon seizing a planet they make it unequivocally theirs. All the acquired populace have three roles and three roles alone. One is the production of war materials. They readily incorporate any local innovations, but the entire industrial might of the subjected world is coopted for Berrillian purposes.

"Second, the conquered world's entire food production capabilities are converted to the Berrillian's needs. One of their first acts is to package what they term *non-essential populations* into food stores."

"You have to be kidding. That's *abominable*," said a lower level diplomat I didn't know.

"Nevertheless, the bulk of the sentient and non-sentient animals on the planet are killed and preserved for later consumption."

"But, if they treat the native population so horrendously, why don't the locals rebel? I would. I mean, choose my family being cooked and eaten versus fighting back. I know what I'd do," said that same junior diplomat.

"Two factors mitigate such resistance. First, families of those dubbed essential are prioritized to the bottom of the kill list. Second, anyone essential who balks at the arrangement or is felt to be dragging their heels is sent to a *sporting cage*. The person in question is placed in a cage with a Berrillian. It is considered both sport and entertainment."

"For the big cats, that is. Not so much for the guy running like hell," I added.

"We really have to kill these animals," said the diplomat, as he covered his mouth.

"I agree. That leads me to the third function of a Berrillian-run world. Reproduction. The Berrillians reproduce at a spectacular rate. Matings are assigned and the offspring reared in communal settings to keep the entire process moving along as rapidly as possible. Obviously, the aggressive food production aspect of their overall strategy allows this to proceed quickly."

"Sick bastards," remarked Bin Li.

"Keep in mind they don't feel that way. They have believed with a singular passion for the last million years that their way is the only way," I responded. "It works for them, so they stick with the winning formula."

"Thank you, Dr. De Jesus. I will now ask for comments and proposals," said Katashi.

"Are you certain the information you have obtained is reliable? This Anganctus fellow might have guessed we obtained the key to their technology from the Battle of Azsuram. If so, he might be putting up an enormous smokescreen of misinformation," asked a senior officer.

"Excellent point. Dr. De Jesus?" asked Katashi.

"We've actually considered that possibility. The honest answer is there's no way to be certain. The scale of the deception would be almost unimaginable and the consistency we observe would be nearly impossible to fake, but you are correct in worrying."

"Is there some way we could test the information we receive?" I asked. "Some way to have them communicate something that would confirm they were broadcasting legit intelligence and not deceptions?"

Toño thought long and hard on that point. "I suppose so."

"Such a thing has been done before," said Katashi. "It is a common issue in the encryption community."

"But it would be difficult," remarked Kipchoge.

"General Ryan. You are a man inclined to the covert and iconoclastic. I will ask you to come up with a plan to test the Berrillians's reliability. Whatever personnel or resources you need are yours for the asking. Please have some preliminary ideas ready for our next scheduled meeting."

Yeah, I think Katashi disapproved of my style, but he was the boss. And hey, the next meeting was three days away. I had all the time in the world. Maybe I'd take up a new hobby with all my spare time. I always wanted to learn backgammon.

THIRTEEN

"The situation concerning my niece has gone from the simply tragic to bizarre. I want to know how she got out of her cell, how she killed those two guards, and I really want to know how it's never going to happen again," JJ shouted at the chief of security.

Ertins Legram-Som was a proud man. He didn't appreciate being scolded like an ill-tempered child, but he understood JJ's frustration. There was no way the prisoner could have escaped, and there weren't any marks on the bodies to suggest how she'd killed them. In fact, the doctor doing the autopsies didn't know why the two men didn't hop off the table and walk away. They suffered from no trauma, no poisoning, and no medical conditions whatsoever. They seemed to have been switched off, more than died. Ertins had derided the doctor, just as JJ was now scalding Ertins.

"JJ, I am speaking as your life-long friend and your security leader when I tell you we have no idea. As far as I can tell the woman couldn't have left her cell and the guards shouldn't be dead."

"Tell me again what the cameras showed."

Ertins bristled. He had answered that question ten times already. He had gone over the tapes themselves with JJ twice. "Nothing."

"That's not possible."

"It *is* possible, because that's the truth. A clever person could easily doctor the holos to make them show whatever they want to. You know that."

"Dory is neither clever, nor did she have access to do so."

"Then clearly, she had help."

"Who? And how could they have killed two armed men without a struggle or a mark?"

JJ's frustration was getting the better of his judgment.

"We're investi—"

"I know. But while you are, more lives are at risk. What are you doing to protect our citizens?"

Ertins took several deep breaths. "There are two guards in her cell at all times. The number of cameras has been tripled. Armed personnel walk the building's perimeter between temporary gun posts. She will not escape again. I promise you that with my life."

JJ shook his head in defeat. "Let's hope it doesn't come to an honor death."

There was a rapid knock on Ertins's office door.

"Come," he barked out.

A frightened officer rushed into the room. He was breathing heavily, suggesting he'd run some distance quickly.

"What is it, Resstok?" asked Ertins.

"Sh … she's … she's gone, sir."

"Who's gone?" As if he couldn't guess.

"Dolirca. Her cell is empty."

"Resstok, I personally assigned you the position of remaining in her cell until I relieved you. How could you disobey my direct order?" Ertins stood from his chair threateningly.

"On my family, I swear I didn't leave. You and I put her in the cell. I sat staring at the girl the entire time. Then, she just wasn't there."

"What do the cameras show?"

"The same thing. She was sitting there looking out the window, then she wasn't. It is like she became invisible."

"That's not possible," replied JJ.

"I wouldn't know about that, sir. But that is what it looked like to me."

"And nothing else? No one entered, no one left, and no one reached through the window?" a livid Erins asked.

"No, sir. Well, not unless you count the butterfly."

****

"It's so lovely up here, Callophrys. It's beyond peaceful," said Dolirca.

"You deserve to renew yourself, sweetest Dolirca. After what your enemies did to you, I wanted you to have this," replied Callophrys, as she flittered near her face.

"I am not familiar with this place. Where are we?"

"Far from danger, my lady."

"Yes, and for that I thank you. But where are we?"

"It is a place beyond your physical limits. It is a space that exists more in your mind and in your heart, than in your universe."

Dolirca frowned. "I hear riddles. Why won't you just tell me? I thought we were friends."

"Oh, but we are. If I told you, my lady, I fear you would not comprehend. Please don't make me embarrass the both of us."

She suddenly beamed a happy smile. "Of course, silly. If you say it is so, I shall accept that. Thank you."

"I live only to serve you, my lady."

"How long are we to remain here? What will we do?"

"Those questions can only be answered by you. We will stay as long as you like, and we will do whatever it is you wish to."

"Truly, this is paradise."

"No, my lady, it is not. This place is lovely but it is not paradise. That blessed state can only be had by you back on your world of Azsuram. Only after the last of your enemies are dead and you wear their skins as decoration can true bliss be yours. Only after you bear the sacred crown of Azsuram on your gentle head can you be said to be in paradise."

Dolirca's face twisted. Was that true? Why couldn't she be happy here? She certainly was safe.

"I don't want to go back there. They all hate me and want to kill me for no good reason. They want to kill my pets. *Oh*, Callophrys, can you bring my Toe here? If they were here with you and me, my world would be nothing but bliss. We could all be so happy together. Can you do that?"

"No, my sweet empress, I cannot. I could never be happy knowing the evil hearts that plot against you at this very moment still beat in the chests of those traitors. You are their ruler by divine right. They cannot resist you, yet the twisted minds that control your subjects try only to harm you. No. We must put you on your throne, and put the scattered pieces of subverters in the ground."

"But I don't want to. I want to be happy *without* them."

"I cry, sweet lady, that the corrupters have clouded your mind. My tears burn my face, as they are mixed with the hate those evil-doers bear toward you. Some acts can neither be forgotten, nor forgiven. As you yourself said, they hate you. They wish you gone. You have said you would strike them all dead, without mercy or an afterthought."

"I said that—" Dolirca trailed off absently.

"Yes. You told me your soul would know no peace, your body no rest, until you smite all those who wronged you. Do you not recall those very words?"

"I don't think I do."

"Then they have already won. You are already crushed. There can be no recovery. If they can make you forget what you said and felt, how can we defeat them? They are too strong. My lady, forgive my failure to you. I must go away. I can never return. To let down one so pure and noble as you must be punished beyond all limits and for all time. Goodbye."

The butterfly slowly lifted into the air and distanced herself from Dolirca.

"Stop. Wait. I do remember, now. *Yes*. You don't have to leave. I recall now. I must destroy those who worship false idols. With your help, we will punish the guilty, reward the innocent, and I shall rule Azsuram forever. Come back to me, purest Callophrys. We shall return at the next council meeting, where all my subjects will be gathered."

She landed on Dolirca's shoulder. "I live only to serve you. Here are a few of my suggestions."

FORTEEN

"Okay," I said to the war council, "I have some thoughts as to how we can confirm that the Berrillians are not feeding us false information."

"Excellent. I understand you have come up with two options," said Katashi.

"Uh, yeah, I guess so. Neither one's very *structured* at this point."

"Proceed," he replied coolly.

"My first plan is the simplest. I go to one of their assets and damage it. For example, I destroy one of their ships. If they accurately report the act, we'll know they don't suspect we've broken their code."

"I do not like this plan," responded Katashi immediately. "It is too simple and does not advance our position in any manner. If a ship is destroyed, they would rightly suspect we were responsible for the act. If they combined their fear that we'd broken their code with a random attack, they would see easily that broadcasting the event was just what we desired in the first place. They would thus harm their own war effort by aiding us in ours. Frankly, General Ryan, I'm profoundly disappointed in you."

Yeah, but how do you really feel about me?

"I said it was preliminary and not fleshed out yet, didn't I?"

"We face extinction if we miscalculate or underestimate our foe. We cannot *tend to know* or *sort of understand*. Do I make myself clear, general?"

"Abundantly. Okay, plan two. This one's tough. It involves significant personal risk. If my mission fails, you lose *Wrath*. Without *Wrath*, the war is over before the first battle begins."

"Times of war, general. The fortunes of war are never easy to accept. However, any such decision is mine alone. You needn't worry about the ramifications of your success *or* failure. Please continue."

Off my Christmas card list forever and a day, that's what this dude was. Maybe ten thousand years from now, I'd still address one to him, just to have the satisfaction of tearing it to shreds before mailing it.

"Happy to, Kash."

He nearly stood to strike me.

Good, you imperious boil on my butt.

"I can travel to an occupied world. Once undercover there, I can let it be known I have some knowledge or device the Berrillians would die to get their paws on. Reports of such an operation would be highly classified. So, if they reported or discussed the matter, we'd know we were in the clear."

"Is that all? You're finished talking?" responded Katashi. He balled both fists and clenched his jaw. It had been a long time since I'd drawn that response out of a superior officer. Man, I'd forgotten how good it felt.

"Admiral, if I might?" said Toño. "Jon, are you serious? That plan is far too risky. Think it through. To convince them you're not a spy planting misinformation, they'd have to believe without a doubt you were a local and that the asset you held was both important and had escaped their previous, viciously thorough investigations."

"Yup. That's the plan."

"I will reassign this task to someone less flippant and unprepared to complete this assignment. Forgive me for over-estimating your scope of competency, General Ryan. I will not suffer you to experience it again. I would like to—"

"No."

Apparently that we me speaking. Oh my.

The full weight of Katashi's sternness and disdain hit me like a dam burst.

"I *beg* your pardon?"

"Beg if you'd like, but you ain't gonna get it." I said just enough and didn't run off at the mouth. He could be as mean to me as he wanted to be in private. But in public, to attack the horse's ass who saved everybody more times than

I could accurately count? No way, baby. It wasn't just that he insulted me. It was that he thought he could assault the legend. Now, I'm not so full of myself—thank you very much—that something like that mattered to me. But it meant a heck of a lot to a lot of people. To see their hero muddied would make their lives harder. I represented hope in a crazy, hostile galaxy.

Plus, what the hell? I was pissed. I had to put up with Saunders. This joker? Not so much. Time to take the Kat-man to school.

"Security, please escort General Ryan to the brig, pending his court martial. I will not brook such insubordination, even from someone with this man's history."

"Court martial, is it? Wow. You know, I've been gone a lot. Can you tell me if I still get a last cigarette when you prop me in front of the firing squad? Just curious. I promised myself I'd quit the damn things, but maybe I won't have to bite the bullet after all."

No one moved to take me into custody.

"Silence. You are only making matters worse for yourself," snarled Katashi.

"No, Katty, you are. You're the only person in this room with a shovel. You're digging faster than a frightened mole in sand, by the way. Might want to level off. Word to the wise."

"Is there a point to your outburst? Do you wish to add mutiny to the charges I will bring against you?"

"Well, thanks. I didn't anticipate a tight ass like you'd give me a choice. Here's what I choose. You shut up before you verbally end your otherwise dubious career. Your act may work on plebes at the academy, but it doesn't cut muster out here in the real world, populated by seasoned people who know the score. You got that?"

Katashi stood to leave.

"I don't have to—"

"No I think you do. You're in command and we're at war. I don't want to see you next to me in front of that firing squad, after you're being convicted of desertion. I wouldn't want to die next to a loser like you. It would impinge upon my heretofore ultra-cool reputation."

The admiral sat back down, though rage was just below his surface.

"We would not be facing a firing squad, Ryan. Shooting a robot would be too dignified—not worth the price of the bullet. I will see you switched off and melted for scrap. You sully the humans who fight for survival, while you joke your way through all eternity. I'd say you are a disgrace to the uniform you wear but, fortunately, you're literally not man enough to wear it. You insult the honor of all those who serve in the military. You insult common decency by your very existence."

"Wait, wait. Hang on a doggone minute. No one told me you were the person in command of common decency, *too*. Man, do I feel stupid. I would never have mouthed off if I'd have known *that*. I blame myself, but darn, I wish someone'd told me."

"Ryan, this is the last thing I'll say to you. I will hold you in contempt at your court martial. That way you may be gagged before the proceedings begin."

"Dude. So many choices. You're too generous, giving me so many ways to go. Okay, cheap shot first. Do you *promise* that's the last thing you'll ever say to me? *Ba-dum-bum-CHING*. Now the serious part. I hold *you* in contempt. You're about ten feet below anyone's contempt, but my comeback is more impactful if it bounces off of yours. *You're* the disgrace to any person who's ever served in uniform, because you don't get it. You put *yourself* first. That's not how it works, jocko. The *service* part comes first. You and I, our opinions, fancies, and pleasant misconceptions, they don't count for shit. And our jackass prejudices can *never* be on the list of what's important.

"You sit there thinking you can court martial me for being insubordinate. It is to laugh. You put yourself above those you're sworn to serve and protect. Well, here's a little clue, seeing as you're badly in need of one. That's not how it works, egg-sucker. You're looking at a jail cell. Except for Stuart Marshall himself, I've never been more disappointed in a person than I am in you. And Stuart had a reason. They screwed up his download. But you, you corrupted yourself with your ego, you arrogant bastard."

"I have always detested robots. You pseudo-humans make me ill. That you've been permitted to father children is beyond disgusting. And I'll bet you can guess what I think of the slut who spread her legs for a machine, can't you, robo-papa?"

That did it. I rushed toward him with the intent of snapping his neck.

Toño stepped in front of me and put me in a bear-hug restraint. I tried to squirm out, but let's face it, he was just as strong as me.

"Stop, Jon. This is not the way. He's baiting you."

"Jon, he's right," yelled Alexis as she sprinted over. "This isn't the way to do it."

I relaxed into Toño's arms and tried not to start crying.

"This is the way you do it," said Alexis.

She stepped over to Katashi and slapped his face with impressive force, then whipped the back of her hand across his other cheek with equal intensity.

Katashi reached up and seized her hand and began to pull her toward him. His face was twisted with hate.

Alexis grabbed the water pitcher on the desk with her free hand and clunked him good with it.

Katashi lurched back into his chair, stunned.

Two MPs lifted him up and began dragging him away.

"Sick bay first, boys," Alexis called after them. "And try not to drop him too many times along the way, okay?"

She stepped over to Toño and me and joined our embrace.

After that horrendous meeting, I went to *Wrath*. I wanted to be alone, to think. It didn't take Kayla long to learn what happened and to come to join me. I'll admit it, I had left the wall open. I guess if I really wanted solitude, I would have closed it.

She stroked my hair and asked, "You okay, love?"

I took a deep breath but couldn't answer.

"Never stop to worry about the opinion of a hater. They're incapable of meaningful thought."

"I know. Still hurts though."

She gently turned my face toward hers. "Why? The man's a bigot and a pompous fool. You can't let him in your wheelhouse."

"It … it what he said about—" I couldn't finish the sentence.

"What? About me? Honey, don't you see that's where he was farthest off track? He's heard about you and worked with you, superficially. But his prejudice and his shortsightedness blinded him. You're the most *human* person I have ever known." She hugged my head close. "Seriously. You mess things up more than anyone I've ever met. Toño would never be so incompetent as to program an android to be so reckless. No, you're human all right. We own you and are proud to do so."

"I have to say it. If you ever, you know, have second thoughts, I want you to let me know. Promise?"

"No."

"Huh?"

"I can't promise, because I could never have second thoughts." She tapped the top of my head. "I know the kooky guy in there is just as alive as I am. More so, most likely. In all the time I've known you and loved you, I've never once thought of you as anything but a living, breathing hunk of a guy. You're too damn cute to be anything else."

Man it was nice to be loved so completely.

"I'm not good at this gushy stuff—"

She put a finger over my lips. "*Gushy* stuff? That's what you call expressing genuine passion?"

"Yeah, it sort of condenses the verbiage. I'm a busy guy. Streamlining is my thing."

"Oh, it is? And here I thought your thing was to be the hotty in charge of saving humanity."

"That too, of course. Kind of goes without saying."

"Then, could you manage our time wisely and seal that wall? It'll save us the trouble of waiting until we walk home."

"You bet. A minute saved is—"

My last lame words were thankfully muffled by her lips.

FIFTEEN

I have called this emergency council meeting to discuss the very serious and increasingly bizarre situation surrounding my niece." JJ was trying his best to be restrained and professional. Inside, magma boiled. "I don't want to be overly formal, so I'll present the facts as we know them, rather than call experts to present them."

"This is a departure from protocol, brother," said Fashallana.

"Yes, and I will skip expedience if the council insists, but the situation is changing rapidly. I want to form a detailed plan as quickly as possible."

"Very well," she responded. "We will only call experts if there is a disagreement or point of contention," she replied.

"Thanks. As most of you know, Dolirca had her Toe throw her husband off the cliffs. Then she escaped from prison as if by magic, killing two guards in the process. Most recently, she disappeared completely while under intense observation."

"Where would she have attained that level of skill?" asked Nmemton. "My aunt never seemed, I don't know, talented at anything but being mean."

"She couldn't have done any of those things on her own, because you're correct, she possesses no covert or martial talents. She used to be a bright enough kid, but lately she's just been deranged," said JJ.

"What can we do?" asked Noresmel. "She's not here, and we have no idea where to find her."

"True. If she returns, however, we need a plan."

"What do you propose, JJ?" asked General Tao.

JJ stared intently at him a few seconds. "Shoot on sight."

A collective gasp rose from the crowd.

"That's extrajudicial and without precedent," said Fashallana. "How can you possibly justify such a rash action?"

"It won't be illegal, if the council votes in favor of it."

"Most unusual, but technically, your statement is correct," responded Draldon. He was the legal advisor for the council.

"I move we vote on the issue—" JJ began to say.

"That won't be necessary, uncle." All eyes snapped around to see Dolirca calmly strolling down the aisle toward the dais. "I am here to lead my people. Voting will no longer burden you, my subjects."

A beautiful butterfly wafted in the air above her, leisurely following her progress.

"Seize that woman," yelled JJ pointing to Dolirca.

A crowd of people advanced and put hands on her, but were abruptly thrown backward. A few crashed into chairs. Dolirca had not so much as swung an arm. A couple men surged forward a second time. They were rebuffed even harder. One slammed into a wall three meters away. Again, Dolirca didn't strike at them. She just kept casually approaching the stage.

JJ drew his pistol from its holster and aimed it at Dolirca. Before he could fire, the weapon flew into the air, and he collapsed roughly back into his chair. He tried to stand up but was unable to. It was like he was glued to the chair.

"Dolirca, what the hell is going on here?" demanded JJ, as best he could, given his restraints.

"Why, uncle, I'm here to rule."

"Oh boy, you're battier than I thought. You can't rule. You're not fit. I don't know how you're doing it, but release me at once."

Callophrys flapped over to JJ and landed on his nose. He tried to strike it but had to settle for blowing violently at it. She flew to Dolirca and landed on her shoulder.

"How I do it is none of your concern. *That* I do it is where you should focus your limited mind."

Dolirca walked onto the stage. She put a heel on JJ's chair and pushed him to the floor, sideways. She sat in the chair nearest to the podium.

"My people," Dolirca said magisterially to the stunned audience, "please be at ease. Sit. I insist."

Every man and women sat so fast it appeared their butts were attached to their chairs with an overstretched spring. The room was as quiet as the grave.

"My people, there have been a great many lies and untruths spoken about me. I am here to proclaim that all those lies are untrue and all the untruths are lies." She smiled like an idiot. "I am your loving empress. I stress the word *loving*. I only want the best for you, each and every one of you little gems. Naturally, to that exclusive end, I may perform acts that seem on their surface to be arbitrary and cruel. Know that this is not the case. Never. I only act to better your small lives, your insignificant existences. *Loving*. Keep that word in your tiny brains, always. In fact, my first act as your empress queen will be to proclaim that the word *Dolirca* will replace the word formerly known as *loving*. Those caught using the outmoded term will be executed. Is that clear, my *Dolirca* subjects?"

Not a single soul in the assembly as much as breathed.

"Fine. Now in the adjustment periods, yours to my reign and me to your petty lives, be assured I will be kind and tolerant. However, after that brief interlude is over, I will brook no dissent and tolerate no subterfuge. Any and all words, acts, or deeds against me will be punishable by death. I like to keep the rules simple. If you would all be so kind as to leave my uncle and me alone, I would thank you."

The rush for an exit was chaotic. It was a miracle no one was injured or killed. At a certain level of panic, animal instincts not otherwise caring mind ruled supreme.

"Dory, let me go," demanded JJ with his cheek pressed against the floor.

She lifted an arm in his direction and said, "Rise, court jester."

JJ slumped to the floor, but then immediately shot to his feet and rushed at Dolirca. Before he closed any distance, he levitated from the floor, his legs whipping in what might otherwise have been a comical image.

"I did not give you permission to approach the throne, jester. I hate to hold you in suspense, so allow me to list, quickly, several rules that might just allow you to live a little longer."

"You—"

"Silence."

JJ kept yelling, but his lungs produced no sound. It was like his voice had been removed.

"Better. Now first, as to your name. JJ is short for Jon Junior, as in Jonathan Ryan II. It will never do to have the machine's name mentioned again. Henceforth, your name will reflect your job. Urpentor, the jester, is your name. Second, never speak unless I give you leave. Third, I now rule Azsuram. Defy me, Brathos, just *annoy* me, and you will wish, as I always have, that you'd never been born. Those are the rules. If you differ with any, please just say so and I'll change them to your liking."

She cupped a hand to her ear.

JJ continued to scream for all he was worth, but still he could produce no sound. He still kicked wildly floating in the air.

"Very well. Thank you for accepting my decrees, Urpentor. You may go."

She flicked the back of her hand toward the door, and JJ flew thought it. Fortunately, it had been left open by the rushing mob. He rolled on the ground several times. When he tentatively sat up, he found he could speak again. Unfortunately, he didn't know what to say.

SIXTEEN

"I have to apologize again for the horrible behavior of former admiral Matsumoto." Alexis blushed deeply and she couldn't bring her eyes to meet mine.

"Not a problem. He acted like a spoiled ape, not you," I said reassuringly.

"Still, I was his CIC. Technically, I guess I still am. His court martial is pending. I demoted him to seaman, so I'm still his commander." She grunted a grim laugh.

"Make sure he swabs the deck while waiting. Navy folk, they love swabbed decks."

"I'll see that he's provided a suicide-watch approved mop, as soon as I can." She giggled at that one. "Seriously, I don't know what got into him. He always seemed like the model officer."

"I'll tell you what got into him. Prejudice, pride, and a hefty helping of stupid. And they've all been scrambling around in his head for a very long time. I never thought he was a model officer, just a humorless one. To see the faults in a person, sometimes you need to put them under powerful stress. Then you see the defects. The man was simply never tested by fire. One look at the flame and his dark side couldn't be contained."

"Wow. Warrior, savior, *and* philosopher. I'm continually more impressed." She winked at me.

"Don't kid yourself. I'm a fighter pilot. Our brains are incapable of philosophy. It would gum up the works. No, I've just seen a lot of people. Non-people, too, for that matter. Haven't met a species yet that's difficult to read, if I apply myself to the task."

"Well, I'm still mortified by what he said."

"Me, I had a different take. Here we are, humans trying against all odds to survive, and some asshole still feels perfectly comfortable drawing a line in the sand, demarcating his idiotic thought process. It's so damn discouraging. Same thing with Stuart Marshall. He would nuke us all to have his way. It kills me, really it does. I'm not Pollyanna enough to think we should all get along and love one another. But to work actively against your own survival because of your prejudice or quest for power? It totally blows me away. I mean, the Berrillians want to cook our children and put them in cans. But he'd rather let them eat his grandkids as a quick snack than see someone who disgusts him save their butts. Crazy."

"And depressing."

"But what is one to do?"

"Press ahead, Jon. As always, we move on."

"I know. But I'd be lying if I didn't admit, it's getting harder."

"I can only imagine. Sorry, my friend," Alexis said with intense empathy. "So, you haven't asked what we're going to do to Katashi in the long run. You have to be curious."

"Nope. I'll forget about him as soon as I can. If you asked for my suggestion, I'd say send him to the Berrillian flagship under a white flag to begin negotiations for their surrender." I winked at her.

"I'll make certain that's on the table." She relaxed back in her chair. "So, what was your plan to test the Berrillian code's reliability?"

"*Is*, not was. With your permission, I'm ready to move on it."

"Since that fiasco of a meeting, our best minds have been unable to come up with a great plan. Hell, even a doable plan. I'm thinking of cutting their pay. They're so close to useless, I might as well save the public some coin. What've you got?"

"Preliminary thoughts for now. Basically, I go to a Berrillian-held world, pretend to be a local with a juicy secret, and if they report it, we know they don't suspect us."

"And you said it was preliminary. That sounds so easy. You appear there and they *don't* detect you? Lord knows they're good at it, you know? You blend in to an alien society, even though you've never been there and aren't even remotely related. Then you put a top-secret message in, what, a bottle? Finally, you escape without being dismembered or them suspecting you're a spy. Did I mention they're really good at that stuff, by the way?"

"The way you say it, sure, it sounds ridiculous. But I'm sure in reality it'll be much less impossible."

"The fate of humanity rests on a mission being *less impossible*. The fact that the words are grammatically incorrect seems prophetically apropos."

"I've faced longer odds. I think." I scratched my head. "I'm pretty sure I have. And look at me."

"If you insist. Okay, you realize that if any one thing goes wrong, you don't come back, and we don't have your magic cube, we're all assorted cold cuts, right?"

"Sure. Maybe snacks, too. Don't underestimate the importance of a tasty, nutritious snack in the middle of a long conquest."

"Maybe we should surrender now, you know, help a tiger out?"

"I agree. I'll drop off Katashi right now to begin negotiating *our* surrender."

"In your dreams, flyboy. Look, firm up your plan, run it by my military eggheads, and we'll see. I have to say, I'm probably going to nix any plan where we might lose you, but I'm willing to listen to whatever you come up with."

"Sounds fair. I'll get back to you in a couple days."

"And, Jon, if they chop me up into dinner, I'm coming to haunt you *forever*."

"Get in line. There are a lot of ghosts ahead of you."

Over the next two days, I honed my sketchy plan into a loose one, poorly structured, vague on key points, and incredibly unlikely to succeed. A typical Jon Plan. When I presented it, Alexis turned a medically alarming beet red almost continually, screamed at me three times, and threatened me with physical violence twice. Yup, a trademark Ryan scheme had been hatched. But in the end, lacking any other viable option, she gave me the green light. I've discovered over time that the only thing scarier than listening to one of my own crazy stratagems out loud is when someone in authority approves one. It means they're beyond desperate, and that I'm a certain goner. Same monkey, same circus, just a new town. I wasn't in my happy place, but I was in my comfort zone.

To help establish a convincing cover and to have someone watching my back, my plan called for a woman to play the role of my wife. And boy, did the powers that be ever come up with a doozy. Commander Kendra Aubrey Hatcher, Navy Seal, black ops specialist, three-time all-Navy tae kwon do champion, and tighthead props on the present women's championship rugby team. Because she was a consummate overachiever, she was a fighter pilot, too, and went by the handle of Echo. Of course, the fighters she flew were Corsair-Class spaceships. No one needed fixed-wing fighters anymore, not on an epic space journey. Kendra was one tough gal. She wasn't what I called a looker, but she was solidly put together. She was nearly six feet tall, probably one hundred and fifty pounds, and her muscles looked like a sculptor had crafted them to her specs.

I went through the planet options with *Wrath*. His detailed charts and records included a good portion of the space currently held by the Berrillians. I chose a planet with a historically humanoid population we'd likely blend in with. I also wanted to land directly, without new reconnaissance. If we spent any time in orbit, we'd almost certainly be detected. *Wrath's* maps were forty-thousand years out of date, but they would have to do. There was a perfect valley, cut deeply between soaring cliffs. Assuming it was still there, it was extremely unlikely we would be observable.

Language, culture, weapons, and money were all other issues I'd have. The weapons part was easy. We reconfigured captured Berrillian laser rifles to fit our hands. That was something a local resistance could easily do. Money, if it was still relevant in a destroyed society, was impossible to predict. I elected to bring a large number of one-hundred-gram gold ingots. The language would be trivial for me and totally challenging for Kendra. Culture would be tricky for both, but hopefully easily played by ear.

She insisted on spending the better part of a week training with the modified weapons. In the end she was impressive. She could fire rapidly on the run and accurately while diving to the ground. She also memorized the old maps *Wrath* had. I was impressed with her thoroughness.

Finally, it was time to take the plunge. Kayla brought the kids, and the six of us dined on *Wrath*. It was the last chance I'd have to see my family for a long time, assuming I survived. It also gave Kayla an opportunity to chat with Kendra. They'd met twice before, but only in passing. The women got along well, if formally. I guessed it didn't matter much. They didn't have to be friends for our mission to succeed.

When it was time to say goodbye, Kayla and I slipped away. "So," I asked mischievously, "you gonna be jealous, what with me spending a lot of time in the company of a gorgeous woman?"

"Not in the slightest."

"Why, because you trust me so perfectly?" I batted my eyes.

"Ah, yeah. I trust you about as far as I can throw you. Jon, you know she's a lesbian, right?"

"Huh?"

"Honey, I know you can be insensitive and self-absorbed, but really? She practically carries a sign."

"Oh. So you're *not* consumed with jealousy?"

"Not hardly. God bless her, she just not a threat to me." Kayla noted I was pouting slightly. "Sorry to spoil your fun. I know you do so love to torture me."

"Not torture, just, you know, razz you. It's meant to show how much I love you."

"Luckily, I understand."

"What's that supposed to mean?"

"Well, hon, you said it in Jon-speak. Most people don't understand that language."

"Hmm. Not sure that makes me feel better."

"Good. That way you'll be more focused on the mission."

We kissed awhile and then she took the kids home. That was tougher than I thought it would have been.

"Okay, Kendra, you ready to do this?" I asked as I attached my command prerogatives to the control panel.

"Yes, sir. Oorah. Let's kick some tiger butt."

We blinked out of reality then reappeared one hundred and fifty light years away. The planet, or rather what was left of it, was called Mosparo. We successfully popped into the bottom of the deep gorge. The maps had been accurate enough to allow an uneventful landing. I immediately set *Wrath* and Al scanning for signs of detection. After an hour, I figured we were either safe, or the Berrillians were masters of deceit and restraint. Having faced them, I favored the fact that my initial plan was sound.

Al translated the locally broadcast language and pour it into my head. Not a pretty tongue. It sounded like Klingon—guttural, harsh, and a lot of saliva was involved. It wasn't going to be an easy one for Kendra to learn, let alone master. To her credit, she sat right down with Al and began laboring at the task immediately. She worked eighteen hours a day at it. She was tougher than me, I can say that much. Toño had devised an earpiece unit to help her. It transmitted whatever Kendra heard to Al, who could then tell her what to say. But until she had some basic command of the language, the tool wouldn't help enough for her to pass as a native speaker.

I spent most of my time patrolling in ever expanding circles. The location I'd selected was a long way from any outposts or towns. I'd occasionally find an abandoned road, some military artifact, or human-looking remains. Interestingly, I never found any Berrillian bodies. They must have recovered their dead, if there'd been any. There were signs of many battles in the area, namely blast craters and rubble. Lots of rubble. It seemed to me that missiles and shells had exploded in great numbers. Maybe the valley region was a stronghold for the resistance, but I couldn't be certain. One thing I didn't find was anything alive larger than a bug.

Within a few days, Al found out that the Berrillians were still exploiting the enslaved population. They were sending a huge number of communications, both locally and off planet. He caught very few transmissions from the humanoids. When he did, the general message was don't resist, don't complain, and work hard. What they never contained was a message of hope. They'd apparently learned that as bad and as bleak as things were, pissing the cats off made life even more intolerable. Sorry bastards. They were slowly succumbing to the monsters who ruled them, and they knew it. All they wanted was the least inhumane deaths possible.

A week into her marathon language course, Kendra was getting the hang of the local dialect of Xastral. It was one of the hundreds of languages spoken on Mosparo. From that point on, the four of us spoke only Xastral. That way she could practice listening to Al's prompts and getting them to sound natural when she spoke. We were then ready to try to find some locals in an attempt to blend in with them. I hoped we'd find some Berrillians to fool. That was the trickiest part of my plan. There probably weren't any free-living natives any longer. Those would have all been rounded up, if not already processed. If we ran into the enemy not knowing we weren't supposed to be wandering the barrens, we'd have a firefight on our hands real quick.

We didn't dare use any vehicles, unless we scavenged them. But all we found were piles of burned out junk. So, we walked and walked and walked. That led to the inevitable problem of being farther from our base than I'd like. I could summon *Shearwater* remotely, but that would take time, time we might not have if we encountered a large Berrillian patrol. I guess that's why they sent two trained killers here, right? If they'd sent a couple level-headed accountants, the mission would fail for sure.

As any soldier who'd been on an endless march could tell you, there were only two things to do. Talk or not talk. Either way, you were bored out of your mind unless you were scared out of your wits. Us two, we mostly talked. Not at first, of course. We both wanted to appear to be the harder case—the tougher, more indifferent warrior. But after a few days of that bullshit we began chatting.

"So, Echo, where you from?"

"You mean on Earth?"

"I guess. You look too old to be a space rat."

"Cincinnati, blessed capital of the buckeye state, whatever the hell a buckeye is."

"It's what they see with, the male deer. Yeah, you used to find them laying on the ground everywhere when I was a kid. Totally gross when you stepped on them. They made this squishy pop."

"I'm starting a running tab of the number of stupid, idiotic, or sexist things you say. When we get back home, I'm slugging you in the arm once for each of them. Please keep that in mind."

"What if I'm into that kind of stuff? I might go out of my way to enjoy your company."

"FYI. Number two's written in stone. Please go on. It's my present goal to make certain you never enjoy my company."

"How old were you when we hit space?"

"High school. Between freshman and sophomore years. Hell of a time to go through big changes. I had horrible acne, hated every living thing, and hadn't figured out my sexual orientation issues. It was one continuous Charlie foxtrot."

"Ah, the high school years. Six best years of my life."

"They *were* the six best years of your life. I know your type, Ryan. You were starting quarterback even as a frosh. You nailed more cheerleaders than the rest of the team's combined total, and you were prom king. You'd a been president of all your classes, but you thought that was way too uncool for a demigod like you."

"You left off the summa cum laude and how many non-cheerleaders I bagged."

"Other girls? Yes. Academics? No way. You were too cool to be caught dead excelling scholastically."

"Did they make a holo about me I was unaware of?"

"Yes, they did. It's located in your dreams, if you want to find a copy. No, you're just a personification of the worst of the worst I failed miserably to impress."

"Wow, big word. *Personification.* I'm seriously impressed. I can tell I'm going to learn a lot of useful vocabulary on this vacation."

"Three."

"You married or otherwise spoken for?"

She was quiet a few seconds. "Nah. I'm between oases crossing the desert of life."

"Is that good or bad?"

"It just is. I don't care too much either way, truth be told."

"That sucks. And don't you dare say *four*, cause I'm being serious."

"Thanks. I'll put you up for the Sensitivity Medal when we get back. They're shaped like a puppy and smell like cotton candy."

"She snarked, thus avoiding the issue."

"Man takes a hint. Maybe you are special, after all, Ryan."

"You look up *special* in the dictionary, you see my picture."

"No, that would be looking in the *dick*-tionary."

"I'm starting my own list, sweetie. One"

"Four."

"You know I'm an android, right. Punches don't hurt me."

"A) Mine will and B) I gotta tell you I was so thrilled to being assigned to not just a dude with a swollen ego, but a metal dude with one. Yeah, this gig is going to end well."

"Time will tell. I'm cautiously optimistic myself."

"That you'll live, maybe. Beyond that, you're delusional. Hey, here's a joke. Knock, knock."

"Who's there?"

"The bitch."

"The bitch who?"

"The bitch who'll shoot you if you don't shut the fuck up, already."

"Wait, that wasn't funny?"

"I wasn't kidding, she said hoping there's a man in the universe that'll take two consecutive hints."

"Time'll tell. That's a tall order."

"Yeah, and you're a tall guy, right?"

"Devilishly handsome to boot."

"Why do I always get assigned to the psychos?"

"Hmmh hum hm mhmhm hm."

"The pilot mumbled *it takes one to know one*," Al translated into her ear and my head. He was so damn helpful, like jock itch.

Kendra didn't say a word, but I did hear her weapon fire up. She certainly was a woman of few words, but serious convictions.

SEVENTEEN

"If I could only turn into a butterfly like you, dearest Callophrys. Then we could fly away together and never be sad again."

In her sweet high-pitched tone, Callophrys responded. "No, child. If we did that, you could not rule this world. What would your subjects do without you? What would become of them?"

Dolirca's face twisted in anger. "They don't love me. If I was gone, I think they'd throw a party."

"Never. They adore you. A few, like your wicked uncle, may still resent your wisdom and your power. But they can be taught to love you. It only takes a little persuasion. A word here, an electric shock there, an amputation once in awhile. It's actually quite simple to sway weak minds."

"I should torture my enemies into becoming my friends? That's wrong. I also doubt it would work. My uncle is too human to love me."

"Do you know what a bet is, child? A wager between friends?"

"Of course. My wretched husband Burlinhar is a gambler. He's always away with his buddies drinking and playing games of chance. I do so hope to convince him to stop his nasty habits. But he is so stubborn." She punched the pillow she reclined on.

"I would like to make *you* a bet. I bet that I can torture any person you choose into loving you."

"Oh, that will never do. Making a bad person say they love me proves nothing." She pouted deeply and hugged her pillow.

"No. I said *make* them love you, not just *say* the words. They will become your best friend—aside from me, of course."

"Do you think it possible?"

"I'll wager it is."

"And if you can't. What do I win?"

"Why, you win the death of an enemy who won't change their mind. What better gift is there?"

"I'd rather have a pony. Yes, a silver pony with a flowing pink mane, ribbons on her tail, and bells on her bridle. And her saddle would be made of puffy rain clouds."

"If I lose, we shall see about that pony. So, we have a bet?"

She waved a limp hand passively. "If you say so, we do."

"And whom shall we put to the test? As if I didn't know."

"Yes. You're right as always. I wish for my husband to truly love me." She scowled. "He never really has. He holds his nose when we have intercourse. I will see him love me."

"Ah, child, Burlinhar is *dead*. You had your Toe throw him off a cliff. He's buried not one hundred meters from here."

"That is a sick joke, Callophrys. Please do not offend me with such a vile jest. No, I *threatened* him. I said if he didn't love me and support me, I *might* have him thrown off a cliff." She giggled and covered her mouth. "But I could never do that, not even to him. It would be wrong. And I love him. He is my brood-mate you know?"

"I, er—"

"Eas-el, you see the girl is *completely* mad. Why play this game when she's incapable of comprehension? Destroy this planet and release the rest of us," chided Des-al.

"What did you say, Callophrys? You spoke, but it wasn't your voice," asked a confused Dolirca.

"Nothing, child. You heard the wind, an empty wind that cannot act until I allow it. Now, if I couldn't torture your brood-mate, who would you chose? Your foul uncle JJ?"

"Who? Oh, you mean Urpentor? JJ changed his name to make me happy. I was sad for some reason. He told me he wanted me to be happy, so he would be my jester. Silly uncle JJ.”

“Empress, for now I suggest you rest. Your mind is heavy with the power of command. I shall return to you tomorrow and we will decide who to torture.”

“Torture? Really?” She made a sick expression. “Must we?”

“Yes. Remember, we have a bet to settle.”

“If you say we do, we must. I am quite tired. Thank you for worrying about me, Nmemton. Please leave me now, so I might rest.”

“*Eas-el.* This has gone too far. If you do not stop the charade, I will be forced to challenge your position,” howled Des-al. “And if I challenge, you will lose. And when you lose, my prophecy that your rash action would cost the existence of yet another of the few Last Nightmares will come true, and I will punish you forever.”

“Sleep, idiot child,” remarked the butterfly. “Tomorrow I return and the terror will commence.”

EIGHTEEN

It took us two weeks to run into anything not dead or destroyed. We found a sheep-like beast wandering loose and grazing on the sparse vegetation. I say sheep-like, because it definitely wasn't one, but it looked like it fit that classification in terms of the food chain. It was also very tame. It walked over to us, smelled us, then slowly nibbled away, oblivious to our continued presence.

"They must'a missed that one," said Kendra pointing at it with her rifle.

"Both sides, it would seem."

"We should take her with us."

"Say what? Why would we do that and how do you know it's a girl?"

"She's the luckiest bitch on the planet. Maybe some'd rub off on us. She must be a female, because only she would be smart enough to avoid capture. A ram would have tried to butt someone, and would have gotten his ass killed."

"The only way she comes is if you're hungry enough to butcher her and bring the best cuts. I'll take a pass."

"Pig."

"Your point being?"

"Let's march. This conversation's boring."

A few days later, I spied a craft in the air, way off in the distance. It was a small ship, maybe scouting. No way they saw us. It had to be Berrillian because any native flight capabilities would have been long since neutralized. It circled one area a few times, then left.

"I say we head that way," I indicated the region the ship seemed to be interested in.

"Not sure that's wise. If they scrutinized the region once, they'll probably do it again. Doesn't seem smart to go to where they're bound to search."

"Presumably they're searching for something they believe to be there. Whatever that is would likely help us."

"*If* we find them first and *if* we're not observed. I say no."

"I got four stars on my shoulder that say we do it my way."

"Yes, sir. I believe I hear that choir myself, now that you mention it."

It turned out to be a two-day forced march. Kendra really impressed me. She never flagged or asked for a breather. She kept up without me slowing too much. The area we ended up in looked exactly as desolate and uninhabited as all the landscape had since we began our search. There were a few more signs of battle, but nothing recent. The most promising position seemed to be the rolling hill that rose from the otherwise flat, barren landscape.

We made camp at the base of the first real rise we came to. Kendra said she needed a meal and three hours of rack time. I spent the time checking with Al and using my night vision to scan the hills. I was surprised when I saw a little movement halfway up a hill a few clicks away. The signal was faint, but it was there. Could have been a rat taking a piss, but it was better for us to have an iffy destination, than none at all.

By the next morning, we'd made it to where I'd seen whatever it was. There were fresh tracks that someone had tried to cover up. That excluded Berrillians or a wild animal. Plus, the scent was unfamiliar. I would not mistake the Berrillian stench.

Pushing myself off the dirt I said, "I do believe we found a human track. I saw it four hours ago. Whoever made it must be close. I'll bet they're holed up in a cave or deep ravine."

Al, scan the area around me and see if there are radar signals consistent with cave openings or deep cuts in the hillsides.

Almost instantaneously Al provided me with three close by options. Two gullies and one cave. If I were running from a pack of five-hundred-pound killing machines, I knew I'd choose a cave.

"There's a cave mouth three hundred fifty meters that direction. Let's move, but stay sharp. Whoever's there won't have the welcome mat out."

"Working with you is damn spooky," Kendra said as we headed out. "You smell the ground and acquire a target without a word."

"Yeah, and I wasn't even trying to be as impressive as I can be."

"I said *spooky*, not impressive. Get over yourself, already."

"If anyone is holed up in the cave, they'll not risk firing on us at a distance. The noise and muzzle-flashes will draw the Berrillians's attention. We're clearly humans, so if they are going to ambush us, it'll be after we're inside the cave."

We reached the mouth without incident, as I expected.

"This is where it gets interesting," said Kendra, as she stepped into the cave itself.

I followed. We alternated small advances, while covering each other. In a few minutes, we were deep enough in that Kendra had to don her night-vision equipment. Again, to her credit, it didn't slow her a bit. It was like she was born with them on.

There it was. A footstep. Twenty meters or so, farther along. Definitely not a cat paw.

I turned to Kendra. With hand signals, I told her, *Stop. I hear. Enemy. Twenty ahead. Crouch. Come. Cover me.*

She returned, *I don't understand. Twenty enemy. Twenty pace count.*

Twenty pace count.

I understand.

With that, I advanced slowly. She followed a couple meters behind, along the opposite wall.

I signaled, *Stop.*

She flattened on the floor, aiming ahead.

I could hear rapid breathing, three, maybe four, sets of lungs, immediately ahead. Whoever was there, was scared. I mean, who wouldn't be, but a seasoned veteran would probably be more in control.

I called out in Xastral. "We're humans. We come in peace. We don't want a fight. Please acknowledge you understand."

Kendra flashed *I understand.*

It took almost a minute, but a male voice returned, "Show yourselves. We won't shoot."

"No can do. Until we know we can trust you, we need to be cautious."

He was clearly confused. "Then how the hell do you suggest we proceed? You want to exchange email addresses?"

Civilians. Good, and bad. They were more likely to be trigger happy, but were also asking an unknown force for directions.

"I count four of you. You know there are two of us. Turn on the lights, then two of you and one of us stands in the clear, weapons in the air."

"You can't count us. I'm not stupid."

"Okay, please answer honestly. How many are you?"

"Ah, four. But you can't have known."

"Buddy, I do this for a living. Can we get on with this before the Berrillians hear us yelling?"

"What's a Berrillian? Who the hell are you?"

"Big cat, weighs the same as two and a half men. Big teeth. They rule the planet. Am I ringing any bells?"

"You mean the Quantrep?"

"Sure. They have lots of names." I shrugged at Kendra.

The cave was flooded with light.

"Okay, two of my team are stepping out from the rocks."

"My wingman is, too." I nodded to Kendra. We'd discussed this type of scenario before. If I got killed and she didn't, she was permanently marooned. She specifically said she'd rather die than be stuck here, waiting for the big cats to find her.

She signaled, *I understand,* and slowly stood lifting her rifle above her head.

Two figures lurched erect from behind a large boulder. One was an adult, a woman most likely. The other was a kid, not even into his teens. Maybe this was a family. That meant dad was covering his wife and child, with an even younger one still with him. That wasn't reassuring. He'd be real jumpy.

I slowly stood up. My rifle way overhead.

"We're both up and defenseless. Your call, sport. Either shoot us, or come out."

I tossed my gun to the ground.

Kendra set hers down gently.

"Stay right where you are," he said louder than I'm sure he intended. He stepped sideways into view. He held a rifle, but it wasn't Berrillian. I thought I'd picked up the faint whiff of gunpowder. It looked like he pointed a conventional shotgun at me. Not an ideal weapon to hold off the Berrillian hordes, but useful to hunt game.

Whoever the fourth member was, they remained concealed. Had to be a young child.

"My name is Jon." I tilted my head. "This is my wife, Echo." My name worked in terms of the harsh Xastral phonetics, but Kendra's didn't.

She waved to them unconvincingly.

"How do I know this is not a trick?" the man challenged.

"You search us. Here, we'll lay on the ground, and your wife and son can pick their weapons back up. They cover you while you pat us down."

"I ... I can't pat down your *wife*. What kind of suggestion is that?"

Hmm. Must be a prudish society. "I meant your wife pats down my wife, my friend. What kind of husband do you take me for?"

"I ... I suppose so. Relledma, pick up your weapon and search the woman. And please be thorough. This is no time for shyness."

"Vorss, can I just leave my stick on the ground, while I search her? From the looks of her, a piece of wood wouldn't protect me if she attacked."

"Woman, don't reveal secrets you don't have to. You don't know that we can we trust these strangers."

Relledma walked cautiously to Kendra. "I'm going to be thorough. Otherwise my fearless leader will make me do it again. Sorry, sweetheart."

"No problem, ma'am." Al's translation circuit was working like a charm.

Relledma ran her hands over Kendra comprehensively, including under each breast. I bet mama would blush if she knew Kendra was probably not bothered in the least.

"She's unarmed, husband. May I help her up to maintain a shred of my dignity?"

"Yes, but be careful. She looks more like a soldier than a wife."

"Can't I be both?" asked Kendra.

"Wh … *what* are you saying? Jon, what is your woman saying?"

"She joking, Vorss. She's trying to lighten the mood so you don't accidentally shoot her reason for living."

I didn't have to look back to hear the word *five* mumbled.

"Husband, do you still wish to search this man who can joke while you point a gun at him?"

"Of course. Think of our children."

"Think of how silly we act. These people are human. They speak Xastral better than I do. Do you think they are spies for the Quantrep, who consider our species as worth nothing more than slaughter?"

"If they turn on us, I will tell you I told you so. Do you hear me?" replied Vorss.

He lowered his shotgun.

"Come, dear," Relledma said to Kendra taking hold of her elbow. "I have some hot tea."

Vorss waved me over.

"Where's your other child?" I asked as I walked over.

An old woman stood up from behind the rocks, holding an infant.

"This is Symetra. She holds our daughter Proventia."

"Is she the grandma?" I asked, pissed at myself for having miscounted.

"No," replied Relledma. "She flees the beasts as we do. We came together several months ago."

"Nice to meet you, Symetra," I said tipping my cap.

"You are a strange man, Jon," said Vorss. "First you use the wrong word for our conquerors, then you introduce yourself to an unescorted woman. Were you raised by farm animals?"

"No, wild ones," I said as I winked at Relledma. "Vorss, in case you hadn't noticed, our society is sort of broken—gone in fact. Those rules you cling to didn't save us from the Quantrep. I fear that soon, no one will exist who knows our quaint, ineffective ways."

"What have I been *saying*, husband?" responded Relledma, with a frown.

"The old ways were silly to begin with and are now gone. At least let us die free of all the social rules that were obsolete a century ago."

"Woman, how can you say that? We must remain true to our ways. It is the only thing the enemy cannot take from us."

"It's the only thing I'd gift them for free," she responded. "Stupid rules to the stupid cats."

"May I sit?" I asked hoping to break up the ongoing domestic quarrel.

"Yes, please," said Relledma pointing to a rock. "I'd offer you food, but we don't have enough for even the children."

"Here," Kendra said removing her pack. "I have plenty more." She reached in, removed all her rations, and handed them to Relledma. "These are packets of dehydrated milk for the baby. You have water, right?"

"Yes, plenty. Deeper in the cave, there is a lake. My dear, I can't accept your last supplies." .

"I insist. We're all in this together. If we don't help one another, surely we deserve to perish," responded Kendra.

"As if we won't in any case," said a bitter Symetra.

"We cannot give up and allow the Quantrep to have that satisfaction," said Vorss. "You are the picture of kindness, Echo."

Their son was inching toward his mother, eyes fixed on the packets.

"Here," Kendra said to the boy, "let me show you how."

He was transfixed as she showed how the flameless ration heater made the beef stew warm. Once it was ready, he wolfed down like I'd expect a starving child would. It was heartwarming. He couldn't help staring at a second packet.

"You still hungry, little dude?" Kendra asked. "Well, let's open up—"

Mom interrupted. "Let the food settle before you decide you need more, Havilpo. Come, sit with your mother and let the nice lady enjoy her tea."

Reluctantly he obeyed.

Kendra waved him back conspiratorially. From her vest pocket, a huge chocolate bar appeared.

"Here, take this. But don't tell your mom, okay?"

He giggled and nodded in the affirmative, then went back to mom. He opened the wrapper tentatively and bit off the tiniest corner. One, two, three. He stuffed three-quarters of the chocolate bar in his mouth, like a fish taking bait.

Everyone laughed and smiled. Everyone but Symetra, I noted with concern. Hey, maybe she'd been through hell three times over, but a kid eating a candy bar? You had to smile at that, unless you were dead inside. If you were dead inside, you didn't struggle on. I needed to keep an eye on that one.

Relledma finally agreed to split one ration pack between the three adults. Good mom. After they had licked the plate clean, she heated up some water to make the milk.

"Where did you find powdered milk?" she asked Kendra. "The horrible lords of our world stopped production a long time ago." She wrinkled up her face. "They hate the taste of our milk and forbade its production."

I wondered briefly if she meant *our milk* literally or if she meant *cow-like creature's milk*. But, in the end it didn't matter. What we carried was better than they'd had.

As Relledma fed Proventia, Vorss turned to me. "So, now the important questions. What are you doing here? How did you survive? Do you have a plan to keep the few of us left alive?"

"Husband—"

He raised a hand to silence her. "This is *man's* talk. Please respect me, at least that much."

Good wife that she was, she gave him a pass on that one.

Kendra flagged my attention, pointed to him, and held up one finger. Two lists. I'd brought an accountant with me, after all.

"We come from Usellar." That was geographically far enough away to account for our oddities. "I was here working ... on an assignment, when they attacked. We couldn't get home before they took out the airships." I lowered my head.

"Chankak's blessing on your families back home," said Relledma.

"There is no Chankak, woman," blasted Symetra. "Stop invoking your superstitions. I have enough pain to carry, without such mockery."

We all let that outburst pass.

"As to a plan, no. Who can stop the Quantrep?"

"Earlier, you called them something else. What was it?" asked Vorss

"Berrillians. That's what they call themselves. Their home world is Berrill."

"How would you know this?" He eyed me with renewed suspicion. "They shoot us, they eat us, but they don't chat with us."

"I worked for … my assignment was very high level. We had some information we didn't … didn't share with the general public."

"Well, whatever it was you secreted away didn't matter, and it doesn't matter. We've lost and it's over," responded Vorss.

"So it would seem," I replied.

"Sir, we've just met, and you have given my flesh and blood food, but please don't mock our position. We have lost *everything*." Quietly, he said, "My greatest hope is that we all starve to death here, as a family. Please don't remark that the futility of our lives would *seem so*."

"Sorry. I'm just trying to stay positive. That's my nature."

"Then you are a greater fool than you appear to be," said Symetra, that bundle-of-laughs. Again, I let her remark pass.

"And, how is it you and your woman survived this long?" asked Vorss.

"We managed to acquire these." I held up my modified Berrillian gun.

"An adequate gun is hardly enough to hold them off."

"True. We fled the city sooner than most, got farther away than most made it. From there, it's been the blessings of Chankak, and more than our share of luck."

"Do you have a base of operations?" he asked.

"Not any longer. We're just running as fast as is safe."

"From where to where? Why does it matter where the Quantrep shit you out?" Man, I needed to slip that Symetra some happy pills. What a Debbie Downer.

"Because our mission isn't necessarily over," I replied studying her eyes.

"What mission?" asked Vorss. "All the governments have collapsed, all communication networks are shattered, and no more than a handful of us roam free. The only mission left to any of us is to die well."

"Not for us," I said. "You know what they say. No rest for the wicked."

"No one says that," scoffed Symetra.

"Well, *I* do," I replied. Bitch.

"As nothing matters any longer, might you tell me what your mission was, or is?"

"No. It's still not safe to say."

"What? Do you have a bug spray that will repel the giant insects that consume us?" asked Symetra.

I lowered my head. "No. Something worse."

"*Jon*," shouted Kendra. "Enough." Good ad-lib, commander.

"She can talk to you like that?" Vorss asked, incredulously.

"We're different, I guess. More modern."

"If that's what the future holds, it is good we are all to die very shortly," responded Symetra.

"Please, not in front of the children. Such words will breed nightmares." Relledma held her son closer.

Symetra looked only partially abashed.

"Very mysterious then, your mission. So be it. It is of no concern to me. What is it you seek to accomplish?" Vorss asked absently.

"Do you know this area well?" I asked in a hushed tone.

"Yes. I was born nearby, before moving to Kremklaw. My wife's family has lived in this area for many generations. Does that matter?" He seemed more interested, now.

"We need to find something. A place. We lost our maps when we had to leave a camp in a hurry."

"What is the name of the place you wish to travel to?"

"Ah, it doesn't have a name. It's a location we must find."

"Again, very mysterious. What can you tell me, so I might help?"

"I'm afraid not much. I need to find a working radio. That way, I can confirm if my compatriots are still active."

"That is impossible. Any radio broadcast sent would be tracked within seconds. The sender would die, before they finished their greeting."

"Be that as it may, if the others are still secure, my role evaporates. Then we are free to die as well as we can."

"What others?" asked Symetra dubiously.

"Look, the less I say the better. I need to know if I'm the only one left. Can you direct us to a radio?"

"No. And, please, that's my final answer." Vorss crossed his arms.

"Husband, how can you sat that to people who have fed our hungry children?"

"If they find a radio, they will find the Quantrep, or be found by them. Either way, they could be tortured into divulging our location. I forbid telling them."

"We would never betray your location," I said. "That I can promise."

"You seem not to know the enemy as well as I do," replied Vorss.

"Then I thank you for your time and the tea," I said rising. "Echo and I must be going." I nodded to her and she stood.

"No, wait," Relledma said. "Tell us what it is you must do. If your mission is worthy enough, I will defy my husband and aide you."

"Wife—"

"No, you old fud. Not *this* time. These lovely people have shown us kindness that I thought had passed from our world. If I can help them, I might, despite what a man with his head stuck in the past might think."

"But I forbade it," he said, deflating.

"Jon, I'm listening," said Relledma.

"I was assigned to a program named *Last Leap*. We were in charge of a doomsday device. I need to know if the other half of the group still functions."

"What is a doomsday device? I've never heard of such a thing," stated Vorss.

I waited a moment to build suspense. "It's the ultimate weapon. When it was decided the Berrillians could not be stopped, we were to destroy Mosparo." I lowered my head.

"Such a thing is not possible. I am no scientist, but neither am I a fool." Vorss puffed out his chest.

"If you knew of the project, it wouldn't be much of a secret, now, would it?" I replied.

"No, I mean, one cannot blow a planet up. That is science fiction, not fact." He was adamant.

"If the man says there is such a tool, then I believe him," said Relledma. "I don't need to know how a sewage plant works, I just need to know how to flush the toilet."

"Wife. Such language."

I couldn't help but snicker.

"How does it work? Yes, if you can convince me, I will believe you," responded Vorss.

"Simply, actually. We placed large stockpiles of nuclear weapons inside mountain ranges that occur naturally along the coasts all over the planet. If exploded, the mountains will fall into the seas, creating tidal waves of enormous size. If our estimates are correct, and I believe they are, we would generate waves over ten kilometers tall. Those would crash into the coasts all over Mosparo. Nothing could resist them. The waves would splash over the tallest mountain ranges as if they weren't even there. All civilization, and possibly all life, would be extinguished. *That* is our doomsday weapon."

"You would kill everyone on Mosparo?" Vorss was incredulous.

"If they weren't already dead, yes," I said flatly.

"This is a fairy tale," said Symetra. "If such a device existed, it would already have been triggered."

"Which is why I suspect my comrades have been taken out," I replied, "making it my job to explode the device."

"I will tell you where you will find a radio. Your work is Chankak's work."

"I'll do better. I'll take you there," said Symetra.

Well, knock me over with a feather.

"You are too old to make the trip," said Vorss.

"Then I will die trying to help my people. I will provide a map, in case I fail physically."

They say never look a gift horse in the mouth. I totally suspected this to be a Trojan horse, however. Still, beggars couldn't be choosers. Clichés existed for didactic purposes, right?

"I will accept any help I can get," I said to her, still studying her face. What was her game? I guessed it was possible she hated the Berrillians so much, she'd see them dead any way possible.

"When can you be ready to leave?" I asked.

Symetra stood. "Now. Let me find my cane. The camp is fifteen kilometers from here."

Oh, great. She needed a cane. It'd take us a month to get there. Maybe I'd assign Kendra to carry her. I would, but there was the male-female thing there on Mosparo. I was nothing, if not respectful of traditional local customs.

Kendra turned out to be an impatient person. Fifteen minutes into our journey, she'd handed me her pack and was carrying Symetra piggyback. I swear, it was like watching a self-loathing, two-headed mule lumber down a hillside. Kendra was complaining that the old woman needed to stay balanced and to not lean to one side. She needed to stop farting, too. Symetra complained that Kendra didn't step correctly, that she was going too fast, and Kendra's breath was worse the her farts. She also said no one who mattered had to smell her gas. That brought swear words from Kendra, which elicited them in triplicate from Symetra. Hey, I didn't complain. It was most entertaining. I couldn't be certain, but I think the old bag used her cane like a riding crop on Kendra's thigh. I was prepared to see Symetra fly off the first cliff we came to.

We camped a little after dusk. No point arriving where we were heading in the middle of the night. Plus, Kendra needed a break. We were moving again at first light, much to the distress of our guest.

"This is probably my last day on Mosparo. I should die well rested."

"No, it's better to die foggy. Trust me on this," responded Kendra. "Dying's not as bad, if you aren't paying much attention."

"And you would know, child, because you've died?"

"Oh yeah. Six or seven times now. But Chankak won't take me. Our devil's already got a restraining order on me. So, I'm stuck here with you."

"I was a powerful woman in a rich family. You never would have been able to speak to me like that, if my servants were around."

"I bet they volunteered for the Berrillians to eat them first." Kendra then stuck out her tongue at Symetra.

"How dare you. I have half a mind—"

"I know. Maybe if you shut up, the missing half would come back. Why don't you make that your goal for the day—brain recovery."

"Your wife is revolting," she said to me. "How could you marry such a shrew?"

"Let me tell you about my wife."

"That'll just about do it, dear husband. I hate to confuse the crazy lady."

"No, you wouldn't," I said. "You'd pay good money for extra turns at it."

"I heard that, you two imbeciles."

"Hey, I found something for you to eat, old and pointless. It's a knuckle sandwich covered in spit. You want I should heat it up for you?"

"Girls, girls," I said with a huge smile, "let's give it a rest. I don't want the enemy to hear us this far off."

Kendra looked at me and mouthed the word *six*. She was kind of cute when she seethed.

By midday, I caught sight of the small group of buildings. I confirmed with Symetra that it was the facility she was directing us toward.

"I can't see a thing," she complained. "How can I confirm what you hallucinate you're looking at?"

I described the setup.

"Sounds like it. What kind of eyes do you have? No one can see that well."

"If he couldn't, how could he tell you what it looked like?" asked Kendra.

"He could be trying to trick me."

"That would be like trying to drink water from a glass. But, think about it. Why would he trick you about where we are, when we're counting on you for directions?"

"If he's trying to trick me, he'd be plenty sneaky like that." Symetra scowled. "He probably gets it from you."

"He's getting nothing from me, but that's another story altogether. Now, it hot here in the sun, and we don't have extra water. We'll go attack the bad guys, and you stay here and have heat stroke or something, for the benefit of society."

"If you leave me a canteen, I won't have heat stroke."

"I know. I'm doing my part to make Mosparo a better world." Kendra flashed her a toothy smile.

"Hating you is pretty easy, girl," said Symetra.

"Any time," she responded. "So, Ryan, we ready to throw our young lives away?"

"Can hardly wait, devoted wife."

"Seven."

"I got point. Stay close and don't hurl insults back at the old hag."

"I'll try my best."

We crouched low and approached the nearest building. It was a wooden shack, with tiny windows. Half way there, I caught sight of the first Berrillian. A solitary sentry, looking as bored as a solitary sentry in the middle of nowhere always looked. Some things were universal. We held position. I counted four more cats. More had to be inside. Maybe there were ten total. There was very little chatter, so not much must have been going on.

My goal was to gain access to one of their radios and make a broadcast asking my comrades in Project Last Leap to initiate the weapons; something along those lines. Then we had to hightail it back to *Wrath* without being killed. In my wildest dream, we could hijack a ship, or at least a surface vehicle, to make the trip quickly. Fortunately, killing the enemy personnel was permissible; desirable, in fact. We just had to do it without anyone reporting or suspecting that we were aliens with advanced tech. Two against ten. My kind of odds. Not that I favored them. I was just always stuck with those types of odds.

I signaled Kendra to power up her weapon and follow me. We arrived at the wooden structure without a being noticed. The lone guard would be back any second. I relayed to Kendra I'd take him with my knife. She indicated she understood.

He turned the corner at a leisurely pace looking off into the distance. I slapped a vise lock on his jaws with my left arm and swiped my blade across his thick throat. He lurched back, slamming me into the wall but collapsed quickly after that.

Crap. Too much noise.

We turned the corner and located the building's only doorway. We positioned ourselves on either side. I indicated I'd go right and high. She should go left and low. She nodded.

We burst through the flimsy door and caught the sole occupant behind a desk by complete surprise. It was odd, seeing a huge tiger working behind a desk. Not sure why it struck me so funny. It was almost comical.

He lunged for his weapon that leaned against the wall behind him.

Kendra slammed him in the back of his head with the butt of her rifle. In one fluid movement, she dropped the gun, drew her bowie knife, and plunged it into his back.

He started to roar.

She jumped on top of his muzzle, driving his chin against his chest, muffling his cry. Her knife flashed like lightening as it repeatedly stabbed and sliced his pelt. She was good. He slumped forward, never able to get much of a sound out of his mouth.

Kendra spun, slapped her knife in its scabbard and retrieved her rifle.

I pointed to one window and went to check out the other. I saw nothing suggesting alarm in the compound. I turned to her.

She signaled no enemy in sight.

So far, so good. I scanned the room. Crap. No radio. This was a clerical room, or something. I stepped over to Kendra and looked out her window. All clear.

"Let's try for that building over there," I whispered to Kendra. "Follow close. We'll angle to the right."

I sprinted the short distance as she covered me, then I covered her crossing. We edged around the building, scraping our backs against the wall. Same drill at the door.

The front room was empty. I pointed to the far door. We went through it, quickly. Empty, too.

We checked out the windows. Nothing was moving.

"We'll make for the big one on the left. You cover me first."

"Roger that."

We got to the door. I slowly turned the knob, then kicked it open. We flew in, me up, Kendra down. Six Berrillians stood like a firing squad, guns trained on us. Symetra stood just behind them.

Son of a *bitch*.

"Drop your weapons and stand still," commanded the senior officer.

We complied. In a shootout, we'd both be dead. Never fight a battle you couldn't win unless there were zero alternatives.

A cat came over and searched us. He removed all our belts and packs.

"Remove your clothing, quickly," said the leader.

"Are you sure—"

That's all I said before the back of a huge paw hammered my jaw.

Off with the clothes, it was.

"We're just a couple hungry people looking for a meal," I said as I stripped.

"Is that so, *Jon*? I've heard a different tale, a much more interesting one. This woman is under the impression you know of a doomsday weapon we have so far missed. Shall I call her a liar?"

"Please do. Then eat her," said Kendra.

"Whether we eat her or not depends very much on the information we extract from the two of you. If she is correct, we will reward her appropriately."

"What," I asked, "you'll prepare her in a divine sauce as opposed to ripping her apart while she screams?"

He nodded to the one who searched us. He stepped over to Kendra and smacked her as he had me. She sailed a meter and struck the wall. Bang, she got right back to her feet.

"I'll remember which one you are, kitty cat," she said to him as she rubbed her chin.

"And I shall forget you as soon as I crap you out," he replied.

"Hope you brought a few more friends. You and these pussies are already dead." Man was she convincingly badass.

"Enough. Time passes unfulfilled. I am Pack Adjutant Roaquar. You are my prisoners. You will tell me the location and nature of your alleged device. I would not expect warriors such as yourselves to divulge such information freely. I will not insult you by asking you to. I will have my team slowly and painfully dismember the female as you watch, Jon."

"No matter what you do to her, I'll never talk."

"Perhaps you missed my point. You will see in agonizing detail what we do to her. Then we will do the same to you. I have found over time that foreknowledge of the process makes it much more unpalatable. Based on my considerable experience, I'm guessing that after your right leg is gnawed off, you tongue will flap like the wings of a bird."

"Then start with me, not her."

"Thank you for confirming you care about her. That will make her horrible death more impactful. Do you know why your pitiful species has fallen so easily to us, Jon? You are weak. You sacrifice for others and place personal concerns before those of the pack. You disgust me."

"That's nice. I don't feel so bad being disgusted at you, now."

He nodded to the guard.

My turn. He stepped over to me. Good. He swung the back of his paw at my head.

Faster than I should have been able to, I punched his paw mid-flight. I felt the bones explode under the skin.

He roared in agony and cradled his paw. He took two steps away from me. That's when Roaquar put a laser round right between his eyes. The guard was dead before he hit the floor.

"Impressive. You are a warrior, indeed. Would that we could have been comrades."

"Never too late." I held out my hand to shake.

He waved his rifle, indicating I should lower my hand.

"Why'd you shoot your own dude?"

"He was weak. The weak always die. It is all they are good for. He should not have allowed you to strike him. He should not have allowed you to injure him. After you struck, he should have raged and torn you to pieces. Instead he wanted to show me his boo-boo. Weak fool."

"Can't say I blame you. Plus, that's one less of you for us to kill. Thanks."

"Your bravado is becoming quite annoying. Tesmack, take the woman outside and begin the process."

We all exited into the hot, unyielding sun. Kendra was staked to the dirt by her hands and feet. The fact that she was still buck naked was most, err, notable. At least, to me, it was.

We stood there, Kendra on the ground, Tesmack on all fours at her side, and Roaquar directly above him, still aiming his rifle at her. The rest of the patrol stood behind us in a semi-circle, guns across their chests.

It was go-time. Couldn't let them hurt my wingman. I dropped five control fibers down my leg and onto the dirt.

One to each guard behind.

When I was connected to them, I spoke again.

Lay down quietly and sleep.

I glanced over my shoulder. They were all out. My plan was complete. I had four sleeping witnesses who would tell of the human warriors who claimed to control a doomsday weapon. They would probably sing that song just before they were executed for cowardice, but what did I care? Served them all right in my book.

Single fiber to Tesmack.

When that was attached, I spoke. "Ah, Pack Adjutant Roaquar, there seems to be a problem?"

Without turning he said, "Shut up and watch. The time for talk is over."

"Yeah, that might be true, but it appears the time for sleep has started."

He lowered his gun and turned. Oh, yeah. The look on his face when he saw the four snoozing cats was precious. I think he disapproved. When he looked back to Tesmack to find him out like a light, too, he was stunned.

He pointed his gun at me. "What have you done?"

I put my hands on my chest. "Me? I didn't do a thing. Personally, I blame you. You pushed these brave soldiers too hard. They needed their rest, and you drove them past their limits. This'll probably be a black mark on your permanent record." I tsk-tsked him, just to add further flare.

He roared in anger and raised his rifle overhead. I sliced it in half with my finger laser.

If the look on his face was precious when he saw his sleeping squad, now it was double precious. Truly, I'd never seen primal fear, confusion, disbelief, and anger all on one face before.

He threw his front half to the ground and charged me.

I smiled and cracked my knuckles. Good. I needed this.

He leaped in the air to pounce on me. I did a soccer-style flip kick and lifted him past me. He rolled along the ground a few times and bounded right back at me. His growl was pure hatred. He batted at me with his claws. I grabbed his foreleg at the wrist before he struck and flipped him onto his back.

He was slower to spring back. I could see it in his eyes. Disbelief.

I started to laugh. I laughed for Sapale and I laughed for all the souls butchered by these monsters. The madman inside me laughed, because he was insane with fatigue, remorse, and loss. He had born more than he could, more than any human could. He woke up and demanded his retribution, his release.

Roaquar stopped and stared at me. His disbelief had turned to fear. He knew those emotions. Seeing them scared him, as well they should have. He wasn't afraid to die, but he was sure as hell afraid of me.

He inched backward, probably unaware that he was.

I cut all four of his legs in half with one swing of my laser.

He collapsed awkwardly to the ground and struggled to stand on all fours. He slipped on the bleeding stumps each time he did.

I walked over to him and struck him in the back of the head.

He slumped to the ground.

I continued to pummel him with my fists. I closed my eyes. After who knew how long, I heard a voice.

"Ryan, stop it. He's dead. Stand down. Stand the *fuck* down." Kendra was yelling at me from where she was staked to the ground.

I looked to her. My arms stopped pounding. I looked in front of me. There was nothing recognizable left of the pack adjutant's head. Just mush.

I stood and looked at my hands. They were covered in what I'd been pulverizing. I stumbled over to Kendra and ripped the stakes from the ground.

The first thing she did was seize me by the shoulders and look deeply into my eyes. "Are you all right, soldier?"

I lowered my gaze.

"No, *look* at me. *Tell* me you're okay." She shook me roughly.

"I'm not okay, but I'm done."

"That'll have to do for now. Are you able to get the hell out of here, or do I have to carry you, too?"

That brought a grim smile to my face. "I want to be on top of Symetra. Pretty please."

She slapped my cheek affectionately. "You pig. That'll cost you two punches, when we get back."

I rubbed my shoulder in anticipation.

"But that traitorous bitch isn't coming with us," she replied.

That brought me back all the way. "Huh?" I scanned the area searching for her. There she was, limping away for all she was worth, cane in one hand.

"You've done enough for one day. I'll deal with her," she said patting the side of my head.

"Wait," I called after her. "Are you sure?"

"Not compromising this mission and that family in that cave. If we spare her sorry hide, we're pissing away the little good we can do."

Slowly, reluctantly, I began to nod.

Kendra jogged toward Symetra as she drew her knife.

When the old woman heard Kendra's foot scrape just behind her, she stopped but didn't turn. "You want to know why I did it, before you kill me. Am I right?"

"Yeah. I am sort of curious what it takes to betray your own people. I do want to know just how pitiful a life I'm snuffing out, bitch."

"If you told them where your base was and they found it, he promised to help me."

"Help you *what*? What is worth our lives, the lives of the beautiful family up in that cave?" Kendra pointed her knife off into the distance.

"He said he'd try and locate my family. If they were still alive, he'd bring them to me. I did it for my family. I'd do it a thousand times over, if I could."

"No, you did it for yourself. Your family would be ashamed to know what you've done."

"They're not ashamed of me." Her voice quavered. "They're all long dead. We were a working family of no value, other than food to these monsters."

"If you knew they were dead, why did you do it? That makes no sense."

"Please kill me now."

"Gladly." Kendra nearly removed Symetra's head slitting her throat.

When Kendra came back to me I thanked her. "I don't know if I could have done it."

"What? You couldn't kill someone who had to die to preserve the mission? You couldn't kill someone who sold you out? You couldn't kill a person as low as that?"

"I know why she did it."

Kendra tensed her jaw. "Jon, the last thing she told me was that she knew they were dead. Still, she betrayed us."

"I know. That's why I don't know if I could punish her for what she did. Thanks again." I dropped my head.

"General Ryan. You're making as little sense as the old bitch did."

"Kendra," I said sadly, "Echo, when you've seen enough death, when you've suffered more than you can bear, you do things you wouldn't believe yourself capable of, before it all that happened." I cupped my hand on her face. "I pray you never know what she and I do. I pray you stay as pure and as full of wonder as you are, and that it's never taken away from you."

A tear welled up in one eye. Just one. "Thank you, sir. I hope so, too."

"One last thing, Commander. I never thought I'd find myself saying this to a beautiful woman, but could you put some clothes on, please? I'm a married man. My wife can't see me from where she is. Even if you trust me, I'm not sure I do."

She placed her knife against my chin. "That'll cost you three punches, you little lying sack of shit."

"Huh?"

She looked straight down. "The little general's standing at ease. Yes, I'm calling you a liar." She kissed the tip of my nose and slapped her blade away. She turned and walked away like a fashion model on a Paris runway, heading for the building our clothes were in.

NINETEEN

"Not today, Callophrys. I don't feel so well," Dolirca said, with a pronounced fingernails-on-chalkboard whine.

"It will begin today, child. I insist," replied the butterfly.

"Wait. I am empress. I will do as I wish. I will not take orders from anyone."

"I am not anyone. I am a bug."

"All the more reason," she replied with a huff.

"My patience is gone. I came to you to make you great, to make you powerful. What good is power, if one does not use it?"

"I'm happy knowing I am powerful. Why use power unless it is necessary?"

"Because it is there," she responded much too loudly.

Dolirca sat up and stared at her friend. "I beg your pardon?"

"I give you unlimited power. You have unlimited enemies. You must crush them. There can be no other option."

She smiled and giggled like a child. "Of course, you're right. I was being silly, wasn't I?"

"Yes, but you will be serious now. I insist."

"Very well, grumpy. But I must tell you, I am tired today, so we can only crush and destroy a little, before I must rest."

"Any action is a start. I have come to regret my choice of operatives."

"Was it not I who warned you that your plan was a fool's wish?" spoke Des-al, for both to hear.

"Yes. Thanks for the reminder. When I'm having a bad day, it's good to know I may rely on you to make it worse."

"I didn't say that, Callophrys. Who did? Who are you speaking with?"

"Another of your loyal servants, empress. Pay him no mind. He is old, and he cannot remember how to wait."

"Oh. Well, I'm ready to walk my kingdom. Shall we?"

"Yes."

She strolled through the village, the butterfly on her shoulder, her Toe following closely. When anyone saw her approach, they ran, making no pretense of civility or deference. They came upon a creek that ran near a road.

"I've never liked that stream," she said pointing at it with disgust. "Make it vanish."

"When I spoke of destruction, I was referring to your *enemies*, not a harmless trickle of *water*."

"Who is empress?"

"For the immediate future, you are."

The stream disappeared. All that remained was the dry bed.

She pouted. "But I'll still know the ugly creek was there. And should it rain, the creek will surely return."

"Argh!"

From where the creek bed had been, there appeared a mighty mountain, tall and thin.

Dolirca studied it massaging her chin. "Could it be lower? Maybe with trees near the top. I love apple trees. I know they're from that wretched Earth, but apples are so sweet."

The mountain halved in size and a scattering of apple trees popped into being.

"We are done with the landscaping. We must find and punish a *person* now."

"Oh. All right. But I'm still not certain the trees are—"

"*No more trees.* A person."

"Yes. I will see punished he who betrayed me most."

"*Now* we're talking. Lead on, empress yada-yada-yay."

Shortly, they arrived at the village graveyard. Dolirca picked her way cautiously though the plots. Finally, she arrived at one and pointed to it.

"My brood-mate lies here. He was so cruel to me. He drank, he gambled, and he never loved me. When I joked about harming him, he jumped to his death to spite me. His last words were, *this will teach her.* I wish to see him punished."

There was a brief silence. "Child, Burlinhar is dead. One cannot punish the dead."

She crossed her arms and came to bear on the butterfly. "Why not? I make the rules. I say punish him, so he will not do it again."

"It? Do what? Betray you or kill himself?"

"Yes. Proceed. Your empress awaits."

"No, that's not how it works. I could reanimate his corpse and destroy it, but that wouldn't be Burlinhar, just his bones. I could retrieve him from the afterlife and kill him. But that wouldn't be punishment, because he's already dead. He wouldn't be worse off. Punishment means the person is worse off after he suffers it."

"Can you hear yourself, Eas-el? You babble like a fool. Destroy this world, or I will," chided Des-al.

"Destroy my world? How presumptuous of you, Callophrys. I forbid it. Another remark along those lines and it is—"

"What? Continue to speak. I command it."

"I've decided who must be punished."

"Thank the forces of creation and the winds of light. Yes, whom shall I destroy, what is his name?"

"Callophrys."

"Yes, I'm waiting. His name so that I might smite him?"

"*Her* name is Callophrys."

"No, pathetic child, *I* am Callophrys."

"Yes. I wish you to punish yourself. You were insolent and harsh, and you frightened me just now. You asked for a name. I gave you a name. You must crush and destroy Callophrys."

"It never pays to work with the insane, Eas-el. Did I not warn you?" said Des-al, with an echoing chuckle.

"No, know it all, you didn't. You warned me of this, that, and every other thing, but playing with lunatics was probably the only thing you *didn't* advise against."

"Young Eas-el, I would speak as tiere, the leader of the Last Nightmare. You know the rules. You knew them before this universe existed. You bound us to come here, and come we did. You bound us to await the completion of your first conquest, and await you we did. You bound yourself to this idiot child's whim, and bound to it you are. She has named her first victim, and it is you. The rules clearly state what your actions must be."

"But that's … that's preposterous. I am not *bound* to destroy myself. I pledged to aid her, mislead her, and betray her. There was no specific mention of self-annihilation as a possible outcome. None."

"Eas-el, you named the game. The game is afoot. You are bound to it. You know this. Do you know what else, foolish Eas-el?"

"What?"

"I told you I'd cry for any of our kind lost because of your folly."

"Yes, I recall your sanctimonious words."

"It turns out even I can be wrong. I shall not miss you."

Dolirca turned to speak with the butterfly on her shoulder. There was no butterfly on her shoulder. She wondered if there ever had been.

"Burlinhar," she said to his plot, "are you ready to come home yet? I will forgive you if you come along now. If you dawdle, I shall be cross with you. When I'm cross, things cease to exist."

Hearing no response and growing bored with the conversation, Dolirca waved to her Toe to follow her and left to find her children.

TWENTY

Before we left the Berrillian outpost, we had some cleanup to do. The bodies of Roaquar and Symetra might contain too many suspicious clues as to what happened. I came up with a simple solution, albeit a tad gruesome. On the spot where Roaquar's head should have been, I placed Symetra's nearly transected neck. I then placed a grenade in her laceration. It blew up and erased a lot of forensic details if those who came later cared to look for them.

Since the guards wouldn't even have a bad explanation as to why they were unconscious and unharmed, we did some harming. We hit them multiple times, each in the head and in other locations, reflecting hand-to-hand combat. We then scattered them at intervals, suggesting each was knocked out in a different fight. It wasn't brilliant, but it'd probably pass muster. I knew these cats pretty well. Whoever oversaw the investigation would kill the guards first and ask questions later.

That left our escape. It was several days' march to the vortex. Once our attack was discovered, and especially the possible existence of a doomsday weapon, the entire section would be swarming with Berrillians. Assets at our disposal were a few broken-down internal combustion vehicles and a scout ship. The spaceship was probably the outpost's transport. Since the cars were not too promising, we checked out the ship.

It stunk to high heaven. Typical Berrillian. No one was aboard. I studied the control panel.

"Al," I said out loud so Kendra could follow, "do you think you and I can fly this flea bag?"

"Likely, captain. The controls are designed for paws, not fingers, but that's not too much of a barrier. See if you can interface me to the ship's computer."

"There," I said after a minute, "you should be connected."

"All right, I think we can do this. Shall I fly you here, remotely?"

"Yes. Make sure you disable remote communication. I don't want the Berrillians to know who we are. And keep a close lookout for enemy craft. Once they see an unauthorized launch, they'll be after us fast."

"Understood. Preflight complete."

"Let do this. Kendra, strap yourself in the best you can."

I deployed my fibers to steady myself.

"Okay, three, two, one. Let's boogie, Al."

Our liftoff was rocky, but not too bad. The trip took just ten minutes. Sure beat the hell out of walking. I was right. By the time we sat down, a flight of ships was closing in on us fast.

"Al, is there a self-destruct?"

"Not really, Captain. I can set the fuel cells to rupture, but it'll be hard to know how long they will hold together."

"Rig it the best you can." I turned to Kendra. "Let's set the remainder of our charges for a ten-minute delay. I'll place some on the bridge and amidships, you pack yours aft. Meet at the vortex as soon as your charges are armed."

"Check."

She sprinted away.

How long until they land? I asked Al in my head.

Six or seven minutes, maximum.

We're cutting it close, but hopefully they won't disarm all the explosives in three minutes.

Unlikely. Plus, if one fuel cell ruptures, there's nothing they can do but incinerate.

Well, let's just hope that's exactly how it goes down.

Kendra was waiting by the sealed cube by the time I arrived. Hopefully there'd be no record it was here. If they figured that out, the mission would be a failure.

"Al, time to explosion?"

"Three minutes."

"ETA on incoming ships?"

"One minute."

"Any signs they detect us or have scanned us?"

"Negative. They have located their ship, but we're still too low for them to pick up."

"*Wrath*, do you know the exact location of the cave Kendra and I hid in?"

"Affirmative, Form."

"Set the vortex as deep in the cave as is safely possible."

I felt that slight nausea.

"It is done, Form."

"How far are we from the cave mouth?"

"Two thousand meters."

Woah, we were way far back.

"Any chance we have been or can be scanned this deep?"

"No chance. Their technology is far from capable of such penetration."

"Can you see the four humans, farther up in the cave?"

I crossed my fingers.

"Yes. They are seated around a small fire."

Set us down as close to them as is safe."

Brief nausea.

"Which direction are they?"

A line appeared in the floor. "One hundred seventy-eight point sixteen degrees clockwise from your perspective, ten meters in a straight line."

"Kendra, let's rock. Don't forget your rifle."

"Don't leave home without it."

She followed me as we scrambled out the opening.

Boy, were they surprised to see us, especially coming up from the rear. Luckily, Vorss didn't have time to retrieve his shotgun by the time he recognized us.

"Thank Chankak you're all right," he yelled as he hugged me. He quickly scanned behind Kendra. "Where's Symetra?"

I looked to the floor. "She didn't make it."

"How, what?"

"She died bravely, worried about her family. Do the details really matter?" I replied.

"No, I guess they don't," he said sadly.

"And your mission? Are we about to drown?"

"No. That's actually a long story. I'd love to tell you but from a safer place."

"So far, this cave has been safe," he said furrowing his brow. Man, he liked to argue.

"I have a ship just over there," I thumbed over my shoulder. "Let's talk there."

"You have a vessel right over there? Jon, that's preposterous. I heard no sound."

"Then come with me and prove me wrong. By the way," I said addressing Havilpo, "there's a lot of food inside my ship. More than you can *possibly* eat."

His saucer eyes convinced his dad to relent. When they saw the shiny vortex, the adults gasped.

"Come on in," I said waving at them. "It's perfectly safe."

Tentatively, Vorss stuck his head in and looked around. Then he slowly stepped in. Relledma entered without hesitation, carrying both of her children.

"*Wrath*, take us to *Exeter* immediately," I said evenly.

After my nausea, I knew we were safely home. Now, I just needed to figure out what the hell to tell Vorss.

"*Wrath*, open a portal." It opened. "Vorss, come with us. I have a tale to tell, but I'd prefer you were sitting when I tell it."

Havilpo tugged at Kendra's shirt. "Where's the food, Echo? Your man mentioned *lots* of food."

We all started laughing. It felt good to laugh again.

Fortunately for the mental integrity of Vorss and his family, *Exeter* was jam-packed with counselors, psychologists, and social workers. The family was going to need most of them. Not just to explain where the hell they were, but that they were the last four survivors of an entire civilization. Their care team would need a lot of overtime. But you know what? It was worth it. It was a tiny gesture against the Berrillian onslaught, but one Kendra and I would cherish forever. A few good, innocent people survived a horrible death.

A few days after our return, Toño confirmed to me there was a burst of coded traffic concerning a possible planetary threat on the conquered world of Mosparo. Mission complete. That was great. Of course, just because we had their code securely broken didn't mean we were certain of victory the next time we battled them. But having a big leg up was comforting. He informed me a few days later that a routine status report from Mosparo to their central command noted the loss of one shuttle craft, due to resistance sabotage. That was nice icing on the cake. Knowing they'd focus an enormous effort in a vain attempt to locate us put a little smile on my face. Best of luck, suckers.

After our last debriefing, Kendra caught up with me in the hallway. "Yo, general dude," she said. "Forget something?"

I played dumb. Yeah, not too much playing needed, right? "What? A goodbye kiss?"

"No, but you're close. I promised you eight, which are now nine, punches in the arm on account of you being a pig."

I shook my head. "I don't remember anything along those lines. Are you sure you're not referring to another devilishly handsome general you served under in combat?"

She buried her index finger in my chest. "Nope. You're the only pathetic loser who almost fits that bill. You want to try and weasel your way out of it, or are you gonna take it like a man?"

I put on a dramatic and unconvincing display of a man wrestling with ideas in his head.

"Aw, what the hell. You want I should roll my sleeve up, so you stand a little better chance of hurting me, sunshine?"

"No. If these ten whacks don't do it, I'll tip my cap to you."

She began rubbing her right fist in her left palm, savoring the moment.

"I'm willing to make a deal," she said with a wicked smile.

"I like deals. What sort of extortion am I looking at, here?"

"In exchange for me not pounding the crap out of your arm, you introduce me to a friend of yours."

"Hmm. That seems too easy. You shake my buddy's hand, and I don't have to replace an appendage?"

"Something like that."

"Who?"

"Amanda Walker. And I wasn't thinking about shaking just her hand." Wow, Echo had big, blindingly white teeth, didn't she?

I held out my hand and made the deal. And it wasn't because I was chicken. No. I am, at my core, a matchmaker. Shadchan Jon, that's me.

I've never been one to put off doing a task, so I led Kendra right to Amanda's front door, on the off-chance Mandy was home. I knocked and, low and behold, she answered.

"Jon. Ah, come in. Nice to see you."

"Good to see you," I said as I hugged her.

"This is Commander Kendra Hatcher."

They shook hands.

"Oh, yes, you're the woman who went on Jon's latest epic mission."

"That would be me, ma'am."

"Ma'am? Wow, you can just call me Mandy, really."

"Thanks."

"So, Jon, what brings you by? Not that it's not always great to see you."

"Our whole trip, all Kendra could do was ask about you. She's a real admirer of your political theory, it turns out. Anyway, she wanted to meet you."

"Nice to meet you, again, Kendra," said Mandy with a smile.

"So, how've you been?" I asked. "Do you miss the halls of power?"

"Huh? I'm sorry. What did you say, Jon?" Mandy responded with clear distraction.

"I said your nose is on fire, and there are demons jumping off the top of your head."

"That's nice," Mandy replied blankly as she continued to stare at Kendra. "If I can help in any way, you let me know."

"Wow," I said, "would you look at the time? I'm late for my scheduled autopsy. Got to run."

"Best of luck, Jon. Kendra, would you like some tea?"

"Nah, it might screw up the autopsy. Too much liquid and all, Mandy."

I let myself out. I don't think either woman noticed I was gone.

TWENTY-ONE

After any mission, a good, bad, or indifferent one, it was always a blessing to return home. Seeing Kayla and the kids helped ease the pain I'd experienced dealing with the heartless Berrillians. It also made me twenty times more determined not to let them make another attempted conquest of the human worldship fleet. I also did something I, honest to goodness, had never done before. I went on vacation with my family. Most people took such a mundane thing for granted. Not me. I either never had a family, or never had time to take a holiday.

I took my tribe to the Disneyship. Yes, one of the smaller asteroids was turned into a relaxation mecca. Naturally, the Disney theme parks didn't fill the entire ship. Several other major players were there. too. A few large sectors were dedicated to more adult-oriented actives. Yes, I'm referring, of course, to Vegasville and Bransonburg. One for wild gambling and debauchery, the other for being old and liking anemic entertainment. Hey, to each their own. That's my motto.

After an epic three-week visit, it was time for me to get back to work. The Berrillians weren't going to slow their progress just to allow me excessive idle time. I did also have to visit Azsuram, to see if JJ had strangled his niece yet. It struck me that since my last visit there, JJ hadn't called me. I guess that was okay. Adults did that. The old expression was, call your *mother*, after all, not call *pops*. Still—

Was I ever overwhelmed when I got there. JJ met me at the landing pad with the most troubled look on his face I'd ever seen. After he filled me in on all that had happened while I was gone, I probably had the same look on mine. It was too bizarre, to surreal, too unbelievable to get my head around it. They locked up Dolirca, she befriended a butterfly, all hell broke loose; then, just as suddenly, she was locked up again, nuttier than a fruitcake, but harmless? I had him tell me the story four or five times, and still I didn't believe it. It was time to confront Dory.

For better or worse, she was loonier than the last time, but less hostile toward me.

"Grandfather, how nice to see you," she positively beamed. "I was just talking to JJ about you earlier today."

JJ shook his head discretely.

"Nice to see you, kiddo. How are you doing?"

"Great. The kids are in school, but I'm sure they'll be excited to see you when they get home."

She didn't mention her home was presently a jail cell.

JJ shook his head again.

"Burlinhar, my grandfather is here," she called over her shoulder. "Please take the time to be social."

JJ really shook his head with that faux pas. The girl really wasn't faking. She was thickly insulated from reality.

"Dory, I understand you had quite the adventure while I was gone," I said, as neutrally as I could.

She angled her head and pursed her lips. "Me? No, no adventure for me. Same old same old. Cooking, mending the children's clothes, and visiting with my friends."

"Really? I heard you got to play queen."

"Empress," she said rather sternly. "I did get a chance to play empress with the children. They love those silly games. We used sheets for our fancy robes and pots for our crowns. I wish you could have been here, my sweet uncle. You could have been the court jester."

JJ visibly cringed upon hearing that title.

"And you had a butterfly as a royal pet, didn't you?"

She frowned. "A pretend butterfly. There have never been those insects on Azsuram."

JJ threw up his arms in frustration.

"What was you butterfly's name?" I asked.

"My *pretend* butterfly, grandfather. Her name was Callophrys. She was so beautiful, not a nightmare at all." Dory smiled off into the far distance.

Callophrys? I had to double check the name. I was correct. It was an actual genus name for a class of butterflies. There's no way Dory could have known that.

"Where's Callophrys now?"

"Why, grandfather, she's where all imaginary creatures are. She's," she waved her arms in the air, "out there in the Neverwhere."

I twisted my head in sad acknowledgement. "The Neverwhere. Okay. Is Callophrys coming back?"

She looked puzzled. "No, I sent her away." She pouted and looked at me. "She was bad, JJ. She made me cross so I sent her away, back to Neverwhere."

"What did she do that was bad, sweetheart? Why did you have to send her away?" asked JJ.

"I didn't send her away. I told her she had to crush and destroy herself." She crossed her arms and put on a stern face. "She frightened me, you know? She really was a nightmare from the Neverwhere."

"I'm sure she was, Dory. I'm glad she's gone for good. Do you remember what happened to Burlinhar?"

"Yes, I do. You're Burlinhar. Why would you ask such a silly question, brood-mate?"

Oh boy. "No, Dory, I'm Jon Ryan, your grandfather. Burlinhar is dead."

"Yes, I know. I asked that mean butterfly to punish him, and she refused. She said she couldn't punish the dead. But I was her empress, and I commanded it. I hate nightmares."

Hmm. That was an insightful concept for a crazy person, with a dash of gallows humor, too.

"Why can't you punish a dead person?" I asked her.

"Because they're dead. If you reanimate them and kill them, they're right where they began. They're no better or worse off. They're just dead again."

No way the simple mind of my niece could generate that argument. "Is that what Callophrys told you?"

"Yes. Did you hear her, too? She was wicked, but I'll miss her. She was so beautiful. And you know what else, grandfather? Her name was never Eas-el. Why did the voice call her that?"

"I don't know, sweetie. Voices in a person's head can be kind of hard to understand."

"Good. I didn't like Tiere's voice. I am glad he is gone forever, too."

"I thought you said the voice in your head was Callophrys?" I asked completely confused.

"No," she stomped her foot. "The butterfly was Callophrys. The voice was Tiere's. But it wasn't in my head. His said it for everyone to hear. Don't you remember? You were there."

"No, Dory, I wasn't. JJ was. JJ, did you hear Tiere's voice?"

He got a funny look on his face.

"What? You either heard a voice or you didn't. Which is it?"

"I'm not sure. You must understand things were pretty unreal. Dory wielding super powers, a mountain range appearing out of nowhere—"

"Neverwhere," Dory corrected angrily.

"Out of Neverwhere. I heard something that could have been a voice, maybe. But it might have been the butterfly. Hell, I don't know."

I stepped to the nearest computer panel and deployed my probes. Within a few seconds, I was downloading the recordings of three security camera nearest to the event. Only one had audio recording. I boosted and amplified it to the point there was more noise than signal. Yes, there was a voice. Someone was scolding Eas-el for playing a foolish game. That someone, I'm pretty sure, was Tiere, the leader of the Last Nightmare. Who the hell were they?

I returned to JJ's house. I asked Fashallana to join us.

"I hope you will allow me to take Dory to Kaljax. I think they can provide the best care for her there. We have doctors, but they have specialists we simply don't," I said to them.

"Dad, I know my daughter is psychotic, but she's still my daughter. If you take her, I'll basically never see her again."

"I'll return to shuttle you there and back, as often as I can."

"Which is basically never. Dad, you're busy. You're likely to get busier as the Berrillians ready for another assault."

"You're right, sweetheart." I walked over and hugged her.

"I think we can maybe have you take her there for a consultation. Whatever treatment they recommend, we can then do it here," said JJ.

"When did you become a responsible, thoughtful adult?" I asked. I grabbed his head and gave him a noogie.

"Since always," he replied struggling to arrange his hair back to normal, without a mirror.

"How's that sound to you, Fash?" I asked.

"The best we can do. When do you want to make the trip?"

"Now. Soon. Maybe you can arrange for a a few of our doctors to come along. Can you all be ready in a couple hours?"

"I think I can pull that off," responded a dejected-looking Fashallana.

"Okay, I'll hang out here and meet you at the cube in two hours. JJ and I can discuss the intricacies and nuances of local politics."

"I'll bet. Home brewed, no doubt," she replied, with a sad smile.

I arrived at *Wrath* before anyone else, probably because I was the most anxious to get this over with and get back to *Exeter*.

I chatted with Al as I waited. Since no one else was around, we conversed in my head. I rarely chatted with *Wrath*. He was too psycho.

Is everything shipshape and ready to set sail?

Yes, pilot. Wrath *tells me it is impossible for everything to not be ready. In the for-what-it's-worth category,* Shearwater *is ready.*

The sooner I get Dolirca to Kaljax and back, the better I'll feel.

I am truly sorry about her failing mental health. I know you love her deeply.

Thanks, Al. You're becoming more human every day.

I'm going to stop being nice if all it gets me in return is insults.

Consider the source. I'm as human as a toaster.

No, captain. All kidding aside, I cannot allow that remark to pass. You're the most human homo sapiens *I've ever encountered. Never doubt that.*

You know I'm going to start bawling like a baby now, right? Your affirmation means as much to me as, well, as the affirmation of another toaster.

I fear Dr. De Jesus is correct. You're incorrigible, mostly because you love being the jerk-ass wise guy.

Why, Al, I do believe I'm going to have to wash your speakers out with soap. Such a foul mouth. I'm going to raise this as an issue with Toño ASAHP.

Don't you mean ASATP?

Huh?

As soon as toasterly possible. Please try and keep up, pilot. But again, on a serious note, I am sorry about Dolirca. The little I knew of her, she seemed sweet.

She was. Hell, maybe she still is. Nuttier than a bushel of almonds, I'll tell you that for nothing. Did I tell you about her imaginary butterfly friend?

No, but I reviewed the records.

And you can believe my shock when some of her voices turned out to be real. She was babbling about this Callophrys not being a nightmare from Neverwhere, then I hear a disembodied voice say it was the tiere, the leader of the Last Nightmare. You ever hear about them, Al?

Can't say—

Form. Excuse me for interrupting. Did you specifically hear the words tiere, the leader of the Last Nightmare?

I didn't know you listened in on us, Wrath.

You are *using a radio frequency, Form.*

I guess we are, aren't we? In answer to your uninvited question, yes. I think what my granddaughter was trying to say was that the butterfly she called Callophrys was really named Eas-el. He or she was a member of the Last Nightmare. That mean anything to you, Wrath?

He made no response. I asked again, this time out loud. Still, no reply. The butthead was being difficult again.

"*Wrath*, I am your Form. I—"

I stopped speaking when I felt faint wisps of nausea, but a shade different than normal for cube travel. Then there was a rustling sound outside the vortex. Maybe the others were finally here. I stuck my head out the portal to chastise them for being slow.

There stood Kymee, Yibitriander, and six other Deavoriath I didn't recognize. There were two cubes behind them.

Yibitriander walked over to me with the most somber face I'd ever seen.

"Jon, it's probably too late, but we had to investigate. We're probably already dead; the entire universe is already dead."

TWENTY-TWO

"With Eas-el gone, we count but eleven. I vote we return to the Neverwhere and exist as best we can," said Cor-ax to the collective of the Last Nightmare.

"We have been committed to act. There is no choice. There can be no vote. Our course is predetermined," responded Des-al.

"But it was Eas-el who pulled us along. He is no longer. We can do as we will. We are the Last Nightmare," replied Gil-em.

"He crossed the boundary between the Neverwhere and this universe. There can be no going back." Des-al was resolute.

"Of course there is egress, tiere. After we destroy a universe, we always return there. Why can't we return *before* we destroy a universe?" Min-il was always the most clever.

"To return *before* we destroyed a universe is impossible. It would set off a time paradox. If we enter a universe with the intention of destroying it, destroy it we will. If we move to destroy a universe, which we have, its destruction is a certainty. Therefore, in a very real sense, it already *is* destroyed, because we came with that intent. We cannot exit until what *has* happened at our hands *happens*."

"I should have said, why can't we return *instead* of destroying a universe?"

"In saying *instead*, you state another impossibility. You posit three things. One, that we came with the intention of destruction. Two, we have one option, that is, to destroy it. Or finally, three, that we have the option of returning home without destroying it. As I proved above, if we entered with intention, the universe is already doomed, and we cannot stop that process."

"There is no logic in your argument. *We* have not entered the time-space. Eas-el alone did. We can stay here and not leave to destroy a Thirteenth Universe. To *think* a concept does not *cause* it to exist. Only its *being* means it is real."

"Ours is not the logic of buttonholes and dirt. Our logic is beyond experience. So, it has been, so it will be."

"But none of the eleven Last Nightmare *wishes* to attack this universe that foolish Eas-el did," complained Min-il.

"Desire has nothing to do with obligation, nor does it alter the fact that the Thiryteenth Universe is already destroyed. We have always attacked, once a plane of existence knows of us. We must destroy it. To do less would break a pattern established before time began. Plus—"

"Plus, you now lust for souls. You, tiere, want to feel the pain of others and know the anguish that is inevitable when we strike. I see it in your words. I hear it in your eyes." Gil-em was furious. "I say if you wish to exist there, then you should. Do not involve us."

"I would if I could. We are the Last Nightmare. We are one. The life force here now conversing is *one*. If I sojourned forth and you did not, there would be two. There can be only one. Therefore we all must go. I am tired of the discussion. The tiere has spoken. We depart for this Thirteenth Universe now. We return, only if any among us outlasts the resistance we will face." Des-al took hold of Gil-em's mind. "If you want to exist here, little one, all you need do is survive."

TWENTY-THREE

Seeing eight Deavoriath together at one time was rare. To see any off Oowaoa was inconceivable. Multiplying *rare* times *inconceivable* equaled *be very scared*. I sure was. Knowing the race as well as I did, I could come up with absolutely no reason to justify my observations. No reasonable, unreasonable, or imaginary reason popped into my mind. In fact, the Deavoriath actually standing there was much less likely then all my optical systems failing simultaneously, making it only *appear* they were present.

"*Wrath* alerted us as to what you heard concerning the Last Nightmare," said Kymee as we bumped shoulders. The usual joy in his face was gone.

"You have to know it basically freaks me out to see so many of you off world. For people who never leave home, you did so in number," I said.

"Then you understand how very serious this news is," remarked Yibitriander.

"Uh yeah," I replied. "I honestly didn't think there was anything that could move even *one* of you off Oowaoa."

"I doubt there's a second," responded Yibitriander flatly.

"What's so—" I began to ask.

"There will be plenty of time for questions later. For now, we'd like to inspect where the incursion happened," said Kymee.

"The incursion?" I asked.

"Where Eas-el first entered this universe."

"I guess that'd be Dory's living room," replied JJ.

"Take us there at once," instructed Yibitriander, in a tone I'm certain he hadn't used for a few million years.

The trip was quick and silent. Perhaps they were talking telepathically, but their facial expressions could only be described as grim.

JJ opened the door and stood aside, directing the group in.

"Where *precisely* is the earliest known location of Eas-el?" asked Yibitriander without looking at JJ.

"You mean the butterfly, right?" JJ asked. I must say he looked quite intimidated by this pack of three-legged stiffs.

"Yes," Yibitriander said dismissively, "the butterfly."

JJ walked to the window and pointed to the table next to it. "Dory said she was sitting here, looking out this window, when the butterfly came through the window."

Yibitriander looked at his companions like JJ had just farted long and hard.

"What?" I asked in my boy's defense.

I swear Yibitriander looked like the very image of a Nazi officer responding to a condemned prisoner. "If you knew what the Last Nightmare were, you wouldn't continue to refer to Eas-el as a *butterfly*."

"What *do* they look like?" asked JJ, rather pointedly.

"Please stand aside, child," said Yibitriander, pushing JJ with the back of his hand.

Kymee rushed to fill the rudeness gap. "All in good time, my friend. *All* in good time."

"Jon, please ask *Wrath* what exact time he estimates the contact took place." Yibitriander addressed me, without the courtesy of a glance over.

"Why don't you ask him?"

Yibitriander stared at me harshly.

"It is generally considered improper for anyone but the vortex's Form to initiate a conversation," said Kymee.

I started to say something along the lines that Yibitriander had been *Wrath's* form long before I was, but I let the distraction go. When matters involved Yibitriander everyone's nerves were on edge.

"He says 10-3314-0.3, whatever the hell that means," I said after checking.

"Hmm," remarked one of the others I didn't know.

"Yes," agreed Kymee.

"What?" I was forced to ask since nobody was saying anything intelligible.

Kymee held out a hand to say, *all in good time.*

This was getting annoying. Remind me never to vacation with the Deavoriath.

The pack crowded around the table. They sniffed the air intently. Then they all extended their probes, randomly sampling the air. They looked like a bunch of dogs at a fire hydrant.

"And where was Eas-el last seen to exist?" asked Yibitriander.

JJ led us all to the open-air location. "Dory was standing right about here with the bu … Nightmare was on her right shoulder," he said pointing to the ground.

"Jon, can you display any video records to help establish the location more precisely?" asked Kymee.

"Sure." I extended a fiber so Kymee could interface with it.

"Thank you."

"Does it really matter that much?" I asked.

"Yes, it actually does. I'll explain it all—"

"I know. In good time."

After extensively sampling the spot, they stood still, roughly in a circle. I was certain they were discussing what they'd learned amongst themselves. For that matter they could be communicating with the One That Is All. Finally, without a word or ever eye contact, the group split apart. Yibitriander escorted everyone but Kymee in the direction of the vortices. Kymee remained where he stood, looking profoundly glum.

Once the others were gone Kymee came over to me. "So, is this your son, JJ?" he asked trying to smile.

"Yes. JJ, this is my dear friend Kymee."

JJ extended a hand to shake. I took it and set it on Kymee's right elbow. "Here," I said to JJ, "like this." I pushed his shoulder against Kymee's.

"Your father speaks of you endlessly, JJ. He loves you very much."

"Ditto," said JJ as he blushed.

"Come," said Kymee as he slid a hand on JJ's back, "let's make ourselves more comfortable."

We sat at the kitchen table. "Do you drink beer, Kymee?" asked JJ.

"I do now," he replied. "Thank you."

JJ clinked three glasses on the table and we all took a sip.

"So, I think it's *in good time* now, my friend. What gives?" I asked, looking at him sideways.

"First, I'm sorry we barged in on you, and I'm sorry we were so mysterious."

"Not a problem," I replied.

"It's just that this is big, Jon—as big as it gets."

"That sounds heavy."

"Oh, I don't know how much it weighs, but it's a massive development." He sighed. "Most unwelcome, too."

"We'll sit here, and you talk when you're ready," I said.

After a moment, he spoke in a detached tone. "The Last Nightmare are a species that has existed longer than time."

"Sorry," I said, "I hate to interrupt, but what does that even mean?"

He smiled faintly. "It's complicated, Jon. Let's just say they've always existed."

"Longer than the Deavoriath?"

"Goodness yes. Much longer than this universe we live in."

"Wait, that's impossible. Nothing can exist before nothing existed," said JJ.

"Of course, it can, JJ. Just not in *this* universe."

"It's official. You lost me," he said looking to me.

"According to our best interpretation of physics, there isn't just one universe," I explained. "In fact, there are an infinite number of universes. Think of it like apples on an apple tree. Each apple is a separate, complete, and self-contained universe. It's isolated a long distance from all the other apples. They apples don't interact and can't even know the other apples are out there."

"That *is* how reality is structured," said Kymee. "Each universe may or may not have the same laws of physics. They can be similar or radically different from one another."

"What does any of that gibberish have to do with the Nightmare?" asked JJ, still confused.

"The *Last* Nightmare, JJ," corrected Kymee. "They are the final nightmare one will ever experience."

"That sounds bad," I responded.

"It isn't bad. It's much worse than bad. They end universes. They consume them."

"How can anyone consume a universe?" I asked, joining JJ on the confused side of the room.

"It's—"

"And do *not* tell me it's complicated."

"Very well, I won't. But that's exactly what they do. Before they enter, the universe exists. After they return to the Neverwhere, that universe ceases to exist. It never was."

"Where's this Neverwhere?" I asked.

"It's nowhere. Don't you see? *Never*," he moved his hands from his right side to his left, "space, *where.* In any case, Jon, don't focus too much on this part. It's not a critical point."

"Okay, these guys come from outside a universe and they destroy it. Why? Is it territorial? Dietary? What?"

"It's what they do. I doubt very much there's a rhyme or reason. Plus, it doesn't matter either way. If they are in your universe, you're doomed."

"What sort of time course are we looking at?"

He shrugged. "Who knows? Probably a long time, based on our measurement of time."

"Then what's the big deal? If we have millions of years or whatever, why stress?"

"Because however long it takes them to erase a universe, they're starting here, and they're starting now."

"Probably not a good thing, right?" asked JJ.

"You have your father's powers of understatement."

"So, no biggy. We've faced long odds before. The Uhoor come to mind. You and I have whooped Berrillian butt. Now, we just kick a different shaped ass."

125

"Jon, did the Berrillian threat drive eight Deavoriath to activate two vortices?"

I flicked my head to one side.

"The Uhoor *and* the Listhelons, combined?"

"No, not exactly."

"Suffice it to say that the only thing that would motivate all us bumps on logs to do anything constructive would be the only thing we fear."

"You make a strong case there. Not happy about it, but I *am* impressed."

"I'm confused. If these Last Nightmares have never been in our universe before, how can you guys know about them?" asked JJ.

"Excellent question. We have made some limited contacts with alternate universes. That is how we came to learn about them."

"Wait, the Deavoriath have traveled to other universes—other apples?" I asked.

"After a fashion. It's really complicated. It's also dangerous. The varied physical properties make it quite dodgy." Kymee chuckled. "One time Yibitriander cast a bitter enemy of ours out of this universe." He held up a hand to say, *don't ask.* "The universe they emerged in was different enough to cause an explosion of apocalyptic proportions. He almost blew *this* universe up."

"I bet they weren't too happy with him in *that* universe either," I scoffed.

"They never knew what hit them," replied Kymee morosely.

"Hey, that makes Yibitriander like a junior member of the Last Nightmare," I said with a giggle.

Kymee set a hand on my arm. "Don't ever let him hear you say that."

"Another not-funny-Jon-ism, dad," quipped JJ.

"He'd kill you ten times over," added Kymee.

"So what conclusion did you guys arrive at? What's our plan to beat the odds and not vanish?" I asked.

"We don't know," he said flatly.

"So, is there a short-term plan?" I asked.

"You meet with your people, let them know what we've discussed, and see what their thoughts are. I'll contact you shortly to see if the great Deavoriath have the slightest idea how to win this battle."

"Don't like the sound of that. If it's beyond you guys, God help the rest of us mortals."

Kymee stared into my eyes. "Amen."

TWENTY-FOUR

Sitting around a big table with a bunch of distraught politicians. Yup, that'd be me. I'd have said I was a bad person in a past life, but I was so old that blaming any past life seemed too needy a rationalization. It was my fate to be wet nurse to a bunch of trembling power seekers. The odds were spectacularly against us, hope was completely unjustifiable, and all eyes were on me alone for a solution. Same drunks, different bar. Oh, boy.

I rubbed my face with both palms. "We all know the facts, limited as they are. Any ideas?" I asked.

Alexis Gore was present, representing the USA. Bin Li sat for the UN, JJ for Azsuram, and a few other major leaders attended. A smattering of military types sat stiffly, hoping to hell no one called on *them*, because each and every one of them had no clue. If pressed for their opinion, the best they'd come up with would be, *I'd like to say it's been pleasant knowing you all.*

Alexis broke the silence. "So, your friend Kymee said he'd contact you? Maybe they'll come up with a viable plan. I mean, they ruled the galaxy for a million years. They must be one hell of a military force."

"It's possible, but Kymee looked pretty shaken. Never seen that look on any of their faces."

"Just because they entered on Azsuram, doesn't *necessarily* mean they'll enter there a second time. Maybe they'll start their annihilation ten billion light years away?" said JJ, with more whine than conviction.

"Yes, but we have to prepare for the worst-case scenario. Plus, maybe they do start with hacking up quasars, but we can't discount that they may move very rapidly from that point to ours. How, and at what rate they destroy, are unknown. By the time we do, it may be too late to do anything but cover our eyes and try not to cry." I wasn't very encouraging.

"When do you think we'll hear from the Deavoriath?" asked Bin.

"No idea. Probably soon, I'd guess. They tend to decide quickly."

"Any chance your vortex can stop them, General Ryan?" One of the military stiffs was trying to sound relevant.

"No. If the Deavoriath thought a vortex would stand up against these bozos, they wouldn't have had such long faces."

"What about a massive discharge of all our combined weapons. Your vortex, our nukes, the entire fleet's weaponry? Surely that would have a significant effect." That was General Colin Winchester, Royal Regiment of Fusiliers. He'd replaced Katashi Matsumoto as overall commander of our defenses.

"Who knows?" I had to answer honestly. "Keep in mind, we don't know the form of attack they employ. We don't even know if they *fly* spacecraft. Do they even have bodies to put big holes in? Do they attack in real space, or some alternate?"

"What do you mean by that?" asked Colin.

"They may not be in our reality at all. In that case, our weapons will be useless. They might occupy a completely different set of dimensions in our universe. Until we know more, it's hard to plan for much." I was mentally exhausted.

"Well, I suggest we not beat ourselves up," said Alexis. "I vote we adjourn to my study and see just how good two-hundred-year-old cognac is."

"I'll second that motion," I said quickly. That was a solid plan.

Halfway through my second snifter, Al went off in my head.

Pilot, I wish to thank you.

Hello, Al, old pal. You're welcome. Anything else? Otherwise I'm busy with critical matters of state.

Yes, I see. The state of drunken revelry.

Gee, sorry, Dad. I promise not to drive myself home. I'll call a cab, or maybe you or mom could come get me after I face-plant.

Silence. Al was always good with the silent interludes.

Al, up to the point the Last Nightmare kill me, I'm immortal. I can wait you out. You know that, right? In fact, I could come there right now and unplug you. Then I'd win.

That would be a good idea.

Huh? You think me turning you off is a good idea? I'll be right there.

No, my simpleminded commander. I think you coming here would be a good idea. But you think you can switch me off? I'll disable you faster than you can say, "Al's the best there is."

Oh, you're a tough guy, now?

No. I always have been. Give me a reason, android. Give me one good reason.

Al, I'm betting we're pretty far from the point here. Why would it be a good idea for me to come to Wrath?

So you can escort Kymee to your debauching associates.

Kymee's here?

If he wasn't, how could you escort him to your den of iniquity?

Al, I can't believe you made him wait while you played this childish game.

Ah, pilot, he's immortal, too. He can wait.

But, you stupid vacuum cleaner, we're under imminent threat. We're facing total extinction. This is serious.

I'm sorry, I was adjusting a diode. What did you say?

Tell him I'll be there on the double.

He asks what that means. He wonders if you're going to clone yourself. We're both on record as dead set against such an addition to our current set of dilemmas.

Tell him I'm rushing to greet him.

He says, thank you. He also asks me to remind you he's immortal. No rush.

He never said that, you outmode.

Outmode? I think the kettle is calling the pot black.

Are you done wasting words?

No. You haven't thanked me yet. Remember, if your ancient circuits still can, that is how our discussion began?

What am I supposed to thank you for, again?

Fortunately, the elevator doors were opening to the hangar bay so I was almost there.

For lowering myself to be your errand lackey, your appointment secretary, your handmaiden.

Thank you. Oh, by the way, if you were my handmaiden, you'd need to wear a pink dress. All my handmaidens do. I'll be conducting a formal inspection at zero six hundred hours. FYI, cutie pie.

I'm sending a complaint to my union and the EEOC officer as we speak. You'll rue the day you sexually harassed me, pilot.

"Kymee," I said as we bumped shoulders, "sorry my lame AI made you wait while he tried to be a comedian."

"No problem. I rather enjoy listening to you two bicker. It reminds me why I haven't seen my wife in over a hundred thousand years."

"Great. The universe is about to end, and I'm surrounded with *two* wannabe comedians. I hope the Last Nightmare hurry up and end my suffering."

"Maybe this is the juncture where we begin walking to where your leadership meets?" Kymee asked tilting his head impishly.

"Sure, why not?"

Kymee provided an interesting rolling commentary as we found our way to Alexis's study. He hadn't been in a vibrant, functioning environment for a seriously long time. To see people scurrying about, hear the whirring of machines, and feel the pulsing of the ship made a big impression on him. He needed to get out more. Too bad he might have waited until the end of the universe to step out of his shell.

By the time I returned with Kymee, Alexis had moved the group back to the conference room. She was back in business mode.

"Hey, where's the cognac?" I asked as I entered.

"Aren't you going to introduce me?" asked Kymee, with a big smile.

"Yes, of course. But first things first."

Alexis stood. "I'm President Alexis Gore," she said graciously, and held out her hand.

Kymee shook it. She introduced him around the table.

"Would you like some cognac?" she asked him.

He wrinkled his nose. "Is it alcoholic and strong?"

"Yes, but we have—"

"Then definitely, yes. Thank you. These are excellent times to be intoxicated."

We all chuckled. The bottle reappeared and he was handed a glass.

Kymee made a show of smelling and tasting it. "*Marvelous*," was his conclusion. "I trust you have plenty for everyone. I hate to drink alone, but I will if you force me to."

"Perish the thought. Diplomacy is most critical at these early stages. I'll have the steward bring up the reserves."

"You're as wise and thoughtful a leader as you are lovely, my dear."

"What? Did you come all this way just to hit on my president?" I asked, trying not to giggle.

"No, but a well-rounded individual learns to adapt quickly," he replied with a wink.

"I'm sure my husband will be flattered," Alexis said raising a toast toward Kymee.

"Either that, or I'll find myself dueling again for the first time in I can't tell you how long."

"You sly dog. You dueled?" I marveled.

"We were an aggressive race. What can I say in my defense?"

We all settled in and fell silent.

"So, to what do we owe this considerable honor?" asked Alexis.

"My people have made some decisions. I wanted to meet with you personally to discuss our proposals." He took a gulp of cognac. "Ah. You'll have to provide me with a few bottles when I leave, so I can conduct some further research on the liquid at my leisure."

"I think nufe is better," I responded.

"Yes, it might be, but I think they'll make a truly excellent blend."

Alexis cleared her throat.

"Yes, you're correct. I must get to the point of my visit." He signed deeply.

I wasn't so sure that was a good sign.

"I've gone over the data we collected on Azsuram in detail. I can state with certainty there was an incursion into our universe from the outside. For those who might care to know, I base this conclusion on lingering elementary particles not permitted by our physical laws. The traces were strongest at the location where Eas-el first presented himself to the girl in the form of a butterfly. This is consistent with the higher energies needed to enter our space-time.

"The fact that there was not a catastrophic reaction caused by the mixture of such radically different and incompatible forms of matter was amazing. It speaks to the power the Last Nightmare must command. The exit point was interesting for different reasons. The remnants of reactive particles suggest to me there was partial entry by a second Last Nightmare. That would explain the voice that addressed Eas-el."

"Is that important?" asked Alexis.

"Critically. If only Eas-el entered, and if he left or dissipated as he seems to have, we might have been spared. The fact that at least one other entered our universe almost certainly means they will all invade."

"Why? Maybe the others won't bother," responded JJ.

"You're correct, of course. We know so little about them. But we suspect they have a hive-mentality. If so, they are likely to invade."

"You mean they're like bees, not butterflies?" asked Bin Li.

"They're very different from both, I can promise you. Keep in mind, Bin, they are beyond ancient and are fundamentally different from the life forms you and I are familiar with. Their motivations are honestly unknowable, probably incomprehensible to us."

"Then how can you know?" Bin pressed.

"I can't, as I said. But I'm still quite certain."

"Do you think revenge might motivate them? Eas-el seems to have died?" asked Alexis.

"I doubt we could ever understand what motivates them. I doubt a basic emotion like the desire for vengeance is part of their makeup. But that doesn't mean they won't come. I think it's simply what they do."

"Like hive-minded insects," I said, more to myself.

"Like hive-minded insects," agreed Kymee. "They do what they do, because that's what the hive does. Not a very elegant justification, but likely the case."

"How long do you think we have, before they attack?" asked Colin.

"Interesting question," replied Kymee.

"I didn't mean it to be. I'm a practical man, not a scientist."

"Our flow of time and theirs must be radically different. That said, I think it will take them little to no time to decide to invade. I'm sure the decision was made eons ago, as part of their hard wiring. As to when in *our* space-time, I estimate they'll be on us far too soon."

"That's not really an answer to my query, is it?" Colin was a warrior, not a diplomat.

"No, I suppose not. What is it you told me, Jon? Hope for the best, but plan for the opposite?"

"Something like that."

"Then plan on any time now. They could already here. I doubt it will be longer than a few months at the extreme."

"Do your people have a viable defensive strategy?" asked Colin.

"No. I wish very much my answer were different, but we do not."

"Will conventional weapons have any effect? I include in "conventional" the advanced technology your people possess."

I could hear the gears turning in Colin's head as he asked.

"Probably some, but probably not enough. I base that on the fact that the Last Nightmare has successfully destroyed many universes. Each one of those universes contained people as clever as us. They failed. Likely, so shall we."

"But that doesn't mean we should roll ourselves into fetal balls and wait for death," Colin responded.

"No. We will go out with all guns blazing. Why the hell not?" replied Kymee.

"You've been around my dad too long," responded JJ. "You're starting to talk like him. It happens like a disease, you know. I'll warn you now, there's no cure."

Kymee smiled. "I hope not." He sat up straight. "Here's our initial plan. Already, thousands of us have dusted off their vortices and are contacting the advanced civilizations we knew. We are updating them, sharing data, and asking for their help."

"Wow," I responded.

"Tell me about it. We sit on our duffs for a million years then boom, we're on the road as a people. As part of that networking, I'm prepared to provide you with as many vortices as you wish. Naturally, the pilots will be fitted with command prerogatives."

"Ah, double wow." I was amazed.

"You have that many?" asked Colin. I think he was drooling.

"Yes. We have a huge number of them. More than we currently have Forms to pilot them. I would ask the android pilots to volunteer first. It is easier to convert someone like Jon than a flesh and blood human."

"How many of you are there?" Colin nearly shouted to me.

Before I could begin to count, Toño replied, "There were thirty-seven Ark astronauts. Carl Simpson was the only one who didn't make it back."

"Fine. Ask them if they're interested and get back to me—"

"All thirty-six have volunteered. Most are running here as fast as they can. Some are running here, and they aren't even on this ship," I announced.

"So fast? That's incredible," remarked Kymee.

"Dude," I said, "half of us were fighter pilots and every single one was crazier than a loon."

"I can testify to that second part," Toño said with a smirk.

"Toño, I was hoping to teach you and Carlos how to do the process. That way you won't be reliant on me alone to perform the upgrades. You can then teach your people, if you'd like."

Toño looked like he'd peed his pants. "I ... I—," he stuttered.

"We'd *love* to," replied Carlos.

"Once you've mastered the technique on androids, I can teach you how to do it on live subjects, too, if you'd like."

Carlos held a hand up to indicate Toño shouldn't even try and respond. "We'd love to."

There was a knock at the door. Two Ark pilots were already there.

My old pal Turk barreled into the room. "Do we get the laser fingers, too?" he asked without bothering to introduce himself.

"Of course. If you'd like one. It's a simple addition," replied Kymee. The man grinned from ear to ear.

"*Duh.*" responded Turk. "You think we'd let him have a leg up on us?"

You had to know who he pointed to.

"Perish the thought," said Toño rubbing his forehead. I think a flood of questionable memories about hotshot pilots rushed back to his awareness.

"Fine. Then I propose we gather at my vortex and head back to Oowaoa. We've a lot to accomplish and an uncertain timeline. Oh, there's one other issue." Kymee relaxed back into his chair. "There's the matter of the Berrillians."

"Yes, facing the ultimate crisis doesn't cancel out the lesser ones, does it?" asked Alexis.

"We're going to have to convince them of the existential threat and enlist their aide. At the very least, we must ask them to relent in their conquest efforts, so we can focus on the Last Nightmare."

"Cats aren't gonna go for that," I said flatly. "Their word for *peace* is *kill fewer for awhile.*"

"Well, we either win them over, or we will be forced to exterminate them out of hand," said a very serious Colin.

"Unfortunately, I'm forced to agree with you, General," said Kymee. "In my experience, they'd much prefer dying in battle over yielding to reason."

"Mine, too," I said sadly. As much as I hated the Berrillians, I was never in favor of genocide. The mean butterflies were the only exception. I was only too happy to cure the universe from them.

And so began a whole new chapter in humankind's ever-expanding book of well-I'll-be-damneds.

TWENTY-FIVE

It was both exiting and anticlimactic after Kymee, Toño, Carlos, and my thirty-five buddies crammed into the cube and left. I also had to keep telling myself everything we were doing was probably going to fall short of success. The image of their thirty-five cubes confronting the Last Nightmare and instantly vaporizing kept playing in my head. All my comrades were focused on was the chance to have my adventures. In reality, they were probably only volunteering to be the first to die. Oh well, that's what they pay us fighter pilots to do. In our collective case, it just took a couple hundred years longer than usual to complete our end of the bargain.

Since everyone involved in the upgrades was either an android or Kymee, he predicted the entire process wouldn't take more than a few days. A few added days training in how to operate a vortex would be needed, but then we'd have a solid defense force.

Okay, I'll admit it, I was a bit melancholy. I was about to lose my status as the only human with probes, a laser, and a vortex. I kept flashing on the parable of the workers in the vineyard. Just because *they* had what I did wouldn't diminish what *I* had. But, well I guess I was kind of competitive. On the plus side of the ledger, I would no longer be the only one who had to schlep all over creation. I'd be glad to let others spread news or transfer supplies. Humanity's range was just about to skyrocket. At least until we were snuffed out.

I took JJ home after the meeting adjourned. Kayla and the kids came, too. It was nice. We didn't look to have another family vacation on the horizon for a long time if ever. We visited as many friends as we could and ate way too much food. I'd say JJ and I drank too much beer, but that would be silly. How can one consume too much beer when facing extermination? When *Wrath* alerted me that thirty-six cubes had popped into space alongside *Exeter* I knew it was time to go.

I left with a better feeling than ever before, however. Kymee said he'd equip several Kaljaxians with command prerogatives and a personal vortex as soon as he was done with the androids. That way there would be a state-of-the-art home defense force guarding Azsuram. That went a long way in settling my nerves. Of course, I knew full well that JJ would be the first Kaljaxian to upgrade. Hell on wheels. That's all I could say. The boy was going to be *hell* on wheels.

When I returned Toño and his crew were hard at work fitting our new cubes with membrane generators and rail guns. They naturally had the gamma ray lasers and quantum decouplers like *Wrath*. We were to be an extremely lethal squadron. I hoped that mattered. The first briefing of the Thirty-Six Aces, as Colin insisted we be named, was, well it was a clusterfuck. One stuffy old man, me, and thirty-five hyper pseudo-adolescents acting like their caffeine and testosterone levels were both redlined. Okay I enjoyed the hell out of myself. Colin, not so much. I didn't know if British pilots were as crazy as their American counterparts, but from the expression Colin wore the entire time I seriously doubted they were.

"Ladies and gentlemen. *Ladies* and gentlemen. May we please come to order? I say, I'm not addressing punters at a rugby scrum. You're all senior officers. Will you *please* quiet down and listen? Put that row of chairs down, ah, what's your name again? And you, release that chicken at once or I'll ground you indefinitely."

It was only worse after Allison released that chicken. Where she got it from and more importantly *why* she got it were unclear. But once it was loose, feathers flew, pilots dove to the floor to catch the damn bird, and Colin erupted like a volcano. Lucky for the chicken, the door was open and it escaped with its life, at least temporarily.

"I'm at the point of calling the RMPs and tossing you all in the brig. We're at *war*, ladies and gentlemen. Humanity is on the verge. Please show some decorum."

"Hey, look. I found an egg," shouted Sami Al Jaber holding up his prize.

And that did it. The room re-exploded. Everyone wanted the stupid egg. A bunch of immature people wrestled Sami to the deck and piled on him. Fortunately in the confusion I extricated the egg from Sami's hand undamaged. Knowing this juvenile melee needed to come to an end, I set the egg on Turk's head and smashed it into his hair. Hey, someone had to be the adult and reestablish a mature tone.

After that we really did settle down. It was important to blow off steam and build esprit de corps, but we did have a job to do.

"I shall say this once. I hope never to witness such a childish and insubordinate display again for the rest of my life." Colin was icy mad. It was kind of scary. "We have a lot of training and planning to do, and we'll accomplish none of it if I have to have you all slapped in irons. Is that clear?"

No one said a peep. Not even the chicken. She'd unwisely wandered back into the room. I could tell about half the pilots were transfixed with the bird. But they at least kept their butts in their chairs.

"That's better. It's not nearly good, but it's better. Now, I've prepared a list of flights and elements for our group. We're too few to designate wings and such. I hope that's all right with everyone?"

Oh boy, he was boring right out the gate wasn't he?

"General Ryan will be the group's vice commander. He is at liberty to choose his XO and the other leads. Those interested parties may contact him at the end of this briefing."

Oh boy. That's when it started. Recalling that we were all androids with com-links in our heads and Colin was flesh and blood, the derisive chatter began. What a bunch of babies.

Gosh, General Ryan, can I wipe your butt every time you pinch off a loaf? I want to be king. Is that possible?

That would be Hal.

I hope someday to have your baby. Maybe then I can get ahead in this man's army.

There was Hannah on the line.

No, I will have him first. Only I will bear his child and it will be a microwave oven.

That James, what a cut up.

Hey, where'd that chicken go?

I think that was Eva. Might have been Curly. That's what we called Marcy because her hair was so straight.

I got the head and neck right here, if you want it badly enough. Definitely Jonesy. Only he'd go there with either Eva or Curly. Pure death-wish.

Is it just me, or does anyone else think General Winchester's actually deceased. I think he is, but I don't want to start a rumor if it isn't true. He sure sounds like a dead man talking.

Francine was such a head case.

I think he's a great man and a natural boring leader.

Hey, that was me.

Who farted? I can't breathe. Medic!

Juvenile as always Turk chimed in. But potty humor got'em every time.

Up until then, we all looked attentive and respectful. But as soon as one guy cracked up, the whole lot of us couldn't stop laughing. It took Colin a second or two to figure it out, but then he was remarkably displeased.

"I'll have Dr. De Jesus disable your internal communications next time. I should have known better than trust that a bunch of Yanks could be professional soldiers for more than three minutes. Stop laughing and show some respect."

Did he say he wanted to yank me? Will y'all leave us alone a minute? I've been so lonely.

No, Billie, not helpful.

More snickers.

Colin swatted his pointer on the desk.

Is that a riding crop? The dude brought a riding crop to a briefing?

Carlotta wasn't going to let that go.

Lotta, stop talking about the man's briefs. I think he's Scottish. They don't wear tighty-whities. There was Turk, mind in the gutter as always.

"For the final time, put a cork in it already." Colin was officially upset. "Please read the reports you've received and be prepared for maneuvers at oh six hundred hours tomorrow. And the first one who becomes rowdy will be grounded for a week."

He asked who's randy? Ah, that would be Turk. He's always looking for a cheap thrill—the cheaper the better. Wait, that was me again. I was a bad example. Cool. I hadn't lost my edge.

By the next morning, most of us had it out of our systems. We had a serious job to do and were ready to get after it. Colin said blessedly few words and then turned the briefing over to me. I wasn't sure we needed training like a traditional fighter squadron might, but it was better to let Colin think he had some control over us.

We had a hangar designated just for our cubes. Even if the numbers swelled, there'd be plenty of room to park them all together. I lead the gang there.

Okay, people, we're going to see if we can maintain formation relocating to a series of places. First, we'll go orbit Earth, or, you know, what's left of it. We'll remain there precisely one minute. Then I want you in polar orbit above Azsuram. Thirty seconds there, then back on your pads. Any questions?

Can we shoot at something? asked Jonesy.

Not this time out. But we'll blow up some asteroids later. I promise.

Cool.

In three, two, one.

We all flashed into orbit around poor old planet Earth. Everyone had seen pictures of the devastation, but it was something else to see it up close. Then, we were all above Azsuram. Nice tight formation, nobody missing. Boom, we were back where we started less than two minutes later.

Okay, nice. This time I want you all to stay in tighter formation and reappear at the following coordinates in the Andromeda Galaxy. I broadcast the details.

Say what? We can go to M 31 just like that? No way. It's over two million light-years away.

You're not getting chicken are you, Allison? One fold in space-time is just the same as any other.

Chicken. You're not going to let me ever forget about that are you, boss?

On three, two, one.

Puff, we were at the edge of an alien galaxy. Looking out the view screen I could just make out the smudge that was our galaxy. Totally weird. Disorienting, too I'll have to admit. A few seconds later, we were back on *Exeter*.

You are privileged to pilot one of the most powerful ships in existence. I hope you all respect that fact. It'll take awhile, but pretty soon, you won't think about distances anymore. Everything is literally at your fingertips. Okay, we'll meet back in two hours for some target practice. Please study the combat simulations I provided you with. When the shit hits the fan for real, I don't want anyone taken out by friendly fire. Is that clear?

Thirty-five *yes, sirs* popped into my head all at once.

Back in command. Two weirds in one day.

We drilled for a few days. We destroyed whole lot of asteroids, I can tell you that. The combined fire power we provided the fleet was impressive with a capital *I*. It didn't take long before any further repetition wasn't useful. The vortex was easy to use after all.

It was time to face the Berrillians.

TWENTY-SIX

Anganctus lounged lazily in his throne on his flagship, *Color of Blood.* His fleet of nearly ten thousand heavy battleships orbited a planet whose name he could no longer recall. Their extraction of valuable resources was nearly complete. A colony would be left to consume whatever was left so it could grow and serve his will. This was what he deemed the dull but necessary process of empire building. He'd rather be engaged in combat with the next world he planned to destroy. There was no narcotic like battle. It was better than sex, and it served a greater purpose—it brought glory and it brought death. It was so much more satisfying to sink his teeth into a struggling enemy than his—

"My lord," shouted a young deck officer, "we're under attack."

Anganctus spun and sat straight in his throne. "Sound battle stations, you witless kitten. Alert the fleet."

The high-pitched whistle signaling battle stations sounded on every ship.

"Can you identify whose ships, what their strength is, and give me an estimated arrival time?" Anganctus called to the first officer.

"Yes. They're Deavoriath vortices. I count over one thousand. They're three kilometers off our port."

"*What.*" howled the king. "Defensive maneuvers, open fire immediately, and stand ready with the gravity beams."

"Ah, I'm not sure that's necessary, lord. The Deavoriath are sitting dead in space. They have their force fields up, so our weapons would have no impact on them," replied the deck officer.

"How dare you." Anganctus grabbed the rifle out of a nearby guard's arms and shot the officer right between the eyes.

The cat fell like a sack of wet sand.

"Remove that traitor from my sight. Officer of the watch, open fire."

The newly promoted officer had no reservations following that order. A plume of light flashed from the Berrillian fleet. Thousands of missiles were launched at the cubes. Naturally, when the initial broadside was completed the vortices sat unharmed, positioned exactly where they were to begin with.

"Damn you all to Haldrob," roared the king. "Can no one so much as frighten my sworn enemies? None of their wretched vessels were even damaged."

"Shall I bring the gravity beams to bear, lord," asked the same officer.

"Why, you hollow fool? They have never been effective against the cubes. I need a commander who can fight these devils, not an idiot with a checklist of options. I want *blood*."

"I await your command, master." Immediately the officer, an ambitious male of dubious talent named Frackor, regretted echoing the word *command*. He closed his eyes and prayed he'd open them again still among the living.

"What are the demons doing? Are they attacking yet?"

"No, majesty. They are *hailing* us." Fractor's eyes were still shut as he responded.

"They want to chat like old women? We're in the heat of battle. What madness is this? I demand answers."

"Shall I patch them through so you might demand answers from them, master?"

"*No*. You coward. Where's that rifle?" Anganctus scanned the area around his throne in a rush.

Fractor saw his life passing before his eyes. He had only tried to serve, it was all he ever desired. If being executed pleased the king, then it was … acceptable.

In a flash, Fractor tapped a series of keys. "This is the flagship *Color of Blood* of the invincible King Anganctus. We have opened this communication to accept your unconditional surrender."

"Wh—" the king started to shout.

"This is Yibitriander, commander of the battle fleet you face. We come in peace to discuss a matter of great urgency. Is Anganctus present?"

All eyes on *Color of Blood's* bridge turned to Anganctus, who was still fumbling with a rifle. None of the Faxél moved.

"Er … I am King Anganctus, Tenth Lord in the House of Zell, son of Vertopar the Merciless. Why have you invaded my space?"

"House of Zell? I don't recall that one. Must be new to power," responded Yibitriander.

"*New* to power. How dare you, scum. My mighty house has reigned for centuries."

"As I said, new to power," Yibitriander said flatly.

"I know of the arch demon Yibitriander. Are you of his seed?"

"No. I am *he*."

Anganctus was, for the first time in his life, speechless. He slumped back in his throne, nearly missing the seat he was so stunned.

"No. You cannot be over a million years old. You cannot be the one who battled—"

"Hexorth of House Claymort. I am the one who forced his tail between his thin legs and chased him into the brush."

"How can this be?"

"Anganctus, these are uninteresting discussions we can have later, if at all. I have pressing news. May we meet face to face under a flag of truce?"

The king gathered himself up. "I do not exchange words with my forever enemy. I eat their heart. Prepare to—"

"Sir," shouted Fractor, "they've launched a missile."

"How many?" the king asked incredulously.

"One. And it's directed along the z-axis, directly away from all ships."

"Wh—"

"Sir, they fired on the missile. It has exploded with elemental force."

"What does that mean, imbecile?"

"It degenerated into energy. It was completely transformed. I believe this is the same weapon the single vortex used on Havibibo's squadron."

"Sons of whore cats. They make a demonstration of superiority rather than attack. What timid kittens they are."

"Be that as it may, lord, they hail you once again."

A deflated king waved a single claw toward himself, indicating to put them through.

"King Anganctus, please understand I do not wish to destroy your fleet. If, however, you refuse to listen to my warning under a flag of truce, I shall do just that."

"I hope to never understand a species that prefers to spare a weaker opponent." Anganctus said as he shrugged. "It makes no sense."

"Sense, I have found, is relative," replied Yibitriander. "Come now, there can be no harm in talking."

Anganctus's face reflected a look of absolute revulsion. "No harm in putting on pretty scarves and bells and dancing in the meadow like foolish children wasting their time? Are your people all insane or only the one I address?"

"I am quite pressed for time. Gibber-jabbering about character flaws and perceptions is not what we must discuss. Either agree to meet under a truce or we shall not speak again."

"Very well, you rotten carcass. Where, when, and how?"

"Your bridge, now, just me and my associate along with you and one advisor. Otherwise the bridge must be cleared."

"Accepted."

"One last request. Please contact your fleets designated Roar, Thunder, and Consequences."

"I would ask why, but my luck in gaining ground in conversation with you is so far abysmal."

Thirty seconds later, Anganctus hailed us. "Yes, I understand you have those fleets poised for destruction too. Am I to assume that if any harm befalls you, there will be little left for my successor to wage war with?"

"That is correct. We will shuttle over to your ship presently. Please have an unarmed escort available for us."

"Fine. We'll have weak tea and blood cakes ready, too."

"That won't be necessary."

"No, those will be for me. If I am to live as a eunuch, I might as well learn to enjoy their ways."

****

Fifteen minutes later, the four of us stood uncomfortably on *Color of Blood's* bridge. Check that. Anganctus, Fractor, and I were ill at ease. Damn Yibitriander was in his element. He looked disinterested, confident, and imperious.

"What is so cursedly important you'd risk your sorry lives to tell me?" asked a grumpy king.

"We face a universal threat, all of us. There is a force about to set upon us that will likely kill us all in the process of destroying this universe."

"I knew it was a mistake to invite you here under a truce. My father told me a thousand times to kill and eat the insane, never converse with them."

"How quaint," Yibitriander responded blandly. He held out an info-disk to Anganctus. "This summarizes our data and our knowledge set on the Last Nightmare. You scientist will confirm to you the danger they pose. You don't have to believe *me*. I wouldn't if the tables were turned."

"The Last Nightmare? Never heard of them. Why should I fear the unknown? In my experience, the unknown can be pounded to dust with the application of sufficient conviction."

"Not in this case. They are the destroyers of universes. The Deavoriath have documentary evidence of one such annihilation. The Last Nightmare is credited with perhaps a dozen such acts."

"What does it mean to destroy a universe? Surely they can't collapse it back into a singularity and consume all the matter and energy," said Fractor.

"We are not certain *how* they do it, just *that* they do."

"So, what is your proposal? Why have you come to plague me this day?" asked the king.

"Two requests. First, we need to cease hostilities immediately so we can focus on our enemy. Second, we would ask you to join us in the defense of the universe when the time comes."

"Is *that* all?" Anganctus mocked, addressing Fractor. "Such a basic request could have been delivered by a servant girl."

"All I require is for the Berrillians to stand down until the crisis has passed. That way I will not be force to destroy you."

"We would rather you burned our children with the holy flames of war than submit to your domination," raged Anganctus.

"I do not require dominating your species. I only ask you to find some activity other than waging war on our empire for a short period. If the Last Nightmare don't end us all, I will be more than happy to crush you in battle afterwards." Yibitriander didn't even look at the two as he spoke those words.

"So it *is* an empire you desire? I knew it. Your race will never be content until all bow at your feet or are buried beneath them." Anganctus was livid.

"We *have* an empire. We simply do not wish to expand it over yours."

"At this particular time?" said Anganctus more as an accusation than a question.

"Recall I have no time for semantics. Will you relent?"

"Who is this silent human?" asked the king.

"Oh, I'm thinking you know me, boss. I'm Jon Ryan."

His massive muscles tensed. "You *devil*. You amalgamation of devils. How I have dreamed of crushing your throat with my jaws."

"Sorry, today's not good for me. Raincheck?"

He roared in anger. Scary guy. Seriously.

"Jon, it does not advance our position to bait the fellow," said Yibitriander. Funny, him being the voice of reason.

"I am not *this fellow*. I am *Anganctus*, lord of all I survey."

"About as unhelpful," replied Yibitriander with no small measure of smugness. "I require your answer."

"Here's what I will concede. Trust me, it is far more than you deserve. If my scientist convinces me this Last Nightmare is an existential threat as you suggest, I will gladly allow you to stand at my side as the glorious storm of Berrill separate them from their lives."

I thought that was more than we could have hoped for. I was stoked.

"We can discuss the details of our attack formation when the time comes," responded Yibitriander.

"I will signal your vortex if and when I am won over," concluded the king.

"Hardly. I cannot wait for such technicalities. One of the human vortices will remain behind and accept your terms. They will pass them along to me. If you see *me* or my vortex before we stand side by side against the Last Nightmare, it will be the last thing you see."

"Your attitude is not one I warm to," menaced Anganctus.

"How fortunate that your approval is not on my list of requirements."

Son of gun that Yibitriander was one tough guy. I was glad we were on the same side. Somewhere, way back in my head, a little voice said it hoped that our alliance would never change.

TWENTY-SEVEN

Within a week, Anganctus relayed his response. He said that our evidence was a weak as our wills to fight. He expanded to state, however, that he was as magnanimous as he was mighty. Since we clearly shivered in our boots even thinking about engaging a difficult enemy, the gracious citizens of Berrill would stoop so low as to hold our hands and lead us into battle. He provided a direct link to his flagship to contact us if we found the little butterflies that caused us such vexation. It was nice to have them onboard, but I could see his ego was going to be difficult to stomach.

The next meeting of the powers that be on *Exeter* was almost positive and upbeat.

"I'm certain you've all read Jon's report on the truce we've parlayed with the Berrillians. Strong work, Jon," Alexis said tossing me a partial salute.

"It was mostly Yibitriander's doing," I conceded. "I'm sure my presence intimidated them into acquiescing, however. So, thanks."

Toño closed his eyes and shook his head.

"Kymee, thank you for joining us again," said Alexis.

"Yeah. Sure beats the hell out of dealing with your son," I observed.

"Yibitriander is your *son?*" asked Alexis incredulously.

Kymee rocked his head side to side gently. "One of them. Boy's been a handful I can tell you that."

We all chuckled.

"I might as well get to the point," he said switching to his serious face. "We've made some excellent progress in enlisting the support of several highly-advanced races."

"You mean like us," I asked with a wink.

"To be certain," he replied with a wink of his own. "I meant to say races second only to those present." He looked at JJ. "It's getting hard to be silly around here. I think I may go back into seclusion."

"Take him with you if you do please," responded JJ.

"Do we know any of these communities?" asked Alexis.

"Likely not. Most are quite distant. Jon might have run across a few, but otherwise no."

"Who?" I asked.

"The Churell, Fenptodinians, Maxwal-Asute, and the Luminarians mostly. A few others have responded with more reservation or have declined to join an alliance."

"Why? Are they nuts?" I had to ask. "Ben Franklin said if we don't hang together, we'll hang separately. What are these guys thinking?"

"One has become non-corporeal since we last interacted with them. They are completely uninterested in the physical world."

"What, did they turn to gas of something?" I asked.

"No. Pure energy."

"That won't protect them from the Last Nightmare. I don't care if they turn into ice cream the Nightmare won't spare them."

"You're right," Kymee responded. "I've found that when a species makes that transition, they become very uppity. They generally believe they are so superior they cannot relate to us. Bunch of prissy asses, if you ask me."

"Kymee, there might be many non-corporeal races out there. Are you being fair?" Alexis asked.

"Oh, there have been many. Usually they're short lived and they're always intolerably smug."

"Are the corporeal species tolerable?" she asked cautiously.

"You'll meet with them soon and can decide for yourself."

"Are you serious," she said with a huge smile.

"Absolutely. All the key players must meet to forge a firm alliance. When the fighting begins, we must all work as one," said Kymee.

"I just never thought I'd come in contact with so many alien races so quickly," she replied.

"You're a real babe in the woods, Allie," I said to her with a grin. "There's a lot of them out there."

"We've arranged for a meeting two days from now," he said. "We'd like to keep it as intimate as possible, so we ask that only two or three representatives from each species attend."

"Certainly," she replied. "Makes sense."

"Will all the others be able to make the trip?" I asked.

"Jon, you're really smarter than you look," he responded. "Yes, but several can't given their own technology. *We* will bring them. Some have mastered the folding of space-time, most have not. They all have some form of FTL drive but wouldn't make it here very quickly."

"So, they can only be counted on to defend against the Last Nightmare if the enemy comes to them?" Colin Winchester asked astutely.

"True," Kymee replied. "But they're as capable in that capacity as most anyone else."

"For whatever *that's* worth," Colin said sourly.

"Let's try and remain upbeat, shall we, General Winchester?" asked Bin Li.

"I'll be as upbeat as the village idiot when those bastards are in their graves. Up until then I'll remain pragmatic."

Glances were exchanged around the room, but no one felt like taking him to task over such a minor point. He sure was a dour fellow.

"Fine," concluded Kymee. "I'll see some of you in a few days." He stood to leave.

"I have a few questions," said Carlos. "May I walk you back to your vortex?"

"Absolutely," he said placing a hand on Carlos's back.

As the rest of us began drifting apart Alexis buttonholed me. "Jon, can you spare a few minutes?"

"Sure, boss. Your place or mine?"

"You're positively impossible," she said with a smile.

"So I've been told."

JJ leaned in. "No, he's positively revolting." He mussed my hair. "Pop, call me later, okay?"

"No." I stuck my tongue out at him.

"Let's go to my office," she said gesturing to the door.

"Can I get you anything," she asked as we sat down.

"No, I'm good. What's on your mind, Allie?"

She tented her fingers and leaned back in her officer chair, thinking how to best express herself. "It's all changing, Jon, isn't it?"

"All what?"

She wrinkled her forehead. "Everything. The old rules are out the window. Humanity … humanity has just taken that one giant step again."

"You mean the aliens?"

"Yes," she said with more certainty, "that's part of it. But we have the cubes. We have unlimited access to the universe." There was a look of wonder on her face.

"Assuming there *is* a universe to be had."

"Oh, I'm not worried about that. I almost feel sorry for the Last Nightmare."

"Oh really? How did you noodle that out?"

"We have a worse nightmare of our own—you. You'll figure something out, pull some big rabbit out of your hat. I just hope I can see the looks on their faces when they realize this was a universe too far."

"Assuming they have faces."

"You really don't struggle to make things easy, do you?" She smiled.

"Never saw the point." After I was done being cute I became serious. "Yes. Assuming we survive things will never be the same. We could shuttle the entire population off the worldships and relocate them anywhere—literally anywhere."

"That would be tempting. Can you imagine ten thousand empty worldship drifting in space because they were outmoded?"

"No way. We could sell them."

"No, we won't need money where we're going. Plus, we could retrieve all the gold and diamonds our treasuries could hold."

"Yeah, that's true. So, Allie, assuming we survive, what do you see us doing?"

She took a moment to answer. "Who knows? Right now I'm just pinching myself and imagining a brave new existence."

"Funny."

"What?"

"Welcome to my world. I been doing this for a long time. It's kind of all right. You're going to love it."

"Why do you say it so sadly then? You play so well to a crowd."

I shrugged. "I'm cool."

"We all know that, but the coolest dude ever appears perturbed." She snapped her fingers and pointed at me. "Might it be that misery may love company, but heroes don't."

I shrugged again. "Maybe."

"It's going to be all right out there in the future. We're going to love it. You're going to love it. If you don't let me know and we'll return our new toys to the Deavoriath."

I perked up more than I'd like to admit. "Really?"

"No, Jon. Get over yourself. We're keeping the new toys. We're keeping you, too, so try and keep up with the new ways."

"Aye, aye, boss lady."

TWENTY-EIGHT

The grand meeting on Oowaoa was a blast. I was sorry it was for such a somber downer of a reason. Otherwise, it was like the circus hit town and I was the biggest kid alive. I've met my share of aliens, but those guys took the cake. Hell, they took the bakery. There were so many totally weird-looking sideshow freaks present, even I was on overload.

We convened in a large hall, possibly built for just such gatherings. It was as old as everything else on the planet, so the hosts certainly didn't make any last-minute changes. Long, smooth benches arched around a central stage. There were also aisles with seats of wildly diverse shapes and sizes. Apparently, the Deavoriath were prepared to accommodate many species I couldn't even picture.

I made it a point to be there early, so I could watch as my new allies arrived. The contingent of Fenptodinians entered first. Man, I'd seen a lot of improbable creatures, but these guys won the blue ribbon. They ranged from around two to three meters tall and about half as wide. The best approximation I could make was they looked like jellyfish out of water. Their bell-shaped heads had fourteen eye stalks rising circumferentially, and their legs, thin filaments really, were too numerous to count. They glided with soft undulations. The main difference from a jellyfish was that they possessed a tough hide, clearly a barrier to water loss. Rhinoceros jellyfish, minus the horn. What a trip. One of the back rows of seats conformed to their bodies when they rested down. Can't say they sat, because they did not, in my humble opinion, have butts.

The Churell, pronounced chu-*rell*, paraded in next. I could catch my breath, so to speak, because they were more humanoid. Well, they looked like abbreviated centaurs. Four legs and two arms, but the horse part of their anatomy was much shorter than the legendary centaur. They were three-meter-tall humanoids with a ninety-degree bend a third of the way down from their round heads. The "C" shape of their neck allowed their center of gravity to ride more forward. They looked like they bounced really well. All wore nasal prongs, presumably to supplement the native atmosphere.

The showstoppers were the Maxwal-Asute. I almost burst out laughing, which, it turned out, would have been my last mistake. These were a tough bunch of aliens. The smallest to attend, they weren't even a meter tall. I can describe them precisely, however. Fire hydrants with toilet plungers on their heads. No, seriously. It was like their heads were designed to affix them to the underside of a solid surface. Totally bizarre. Three short arms extended from their cylinder-shaped bodies, with three short legs propelling them. Unlike the three-legged Deavoriath, who walked with a rolling tumble of their legs, the Maxwal-Asute moved fluidly. They moved like a Paso Fino horse, with short, rapid steps. The little guys plopped into the conventional seats in the front row like they fit, which they didn't at all. I learned later they'd gladly exchanged comfort for making a statement of toughness and self-importance.

The last group to arrive were the Berrillians, specifically Anganctus and Fractor. Turk was sent to fetch them. I worried at first when I assigned him the transport, but he was equipped with the same weapons I was. Plus, the sooner others began offloading from me those type of roles, the sooner I'd see some peace. Once I tapped him, he was super excited. He was contributing at a high level again. In the end, that's what our type loved to do. As soon as he was back, he did make it a point to give me a hard time about their awful smell. Honestly, that it bothered him put a smile on my face.

Yibitriander, Kymee, and Lornot sat in the front of the auditorium on a slightly raised stage. Kymee and Lornot waved and pointed to individuals in the crowd, but old Yibitriander just sat there like a statue of the God of Constipation.

Once it became clear the Berrillians were not going to sit, preferring to pace in tight figure eights, Yibitriander spoke. "We will begin. Thank you all for coming today. We face a great crisis, but it is good to know none of us face it alone. I would—"

One of the Maxwal-Asute hopped off his seat and said loudly, "I question your data, Deavoriath. I would like—"

"Clang-fow Peditit, if you'd allow me to lead this session, I'm certain it would move along move fluidly. I can assure you all questions and input everyone has will be addressed before we adjourn."

"Fine. As you claim my questions will be addressed, they can and will be addressed now. You provided us with some data that you claim represents decayed particles from an alternate universe. Have the brains of the Deavoriath not aged as well as their bodies?"

Yibitriander knuckled the podium and closed his eyes. "What aspect of the data concerns you?"

"What *aspect*? The entire proposition *wreaks* of Deavoriath treachery."

Kymee rose, placed a hand on his son's shoulder, and took over. "I can assure you the data is real. I am confident your scientists have told you the implications of the information. Thank you for bringing your reservations to the front, but please understand there is no devious plan below the surface. Why, good Clang-fow Peditit, would we go to all this trouble, if it were only to trick you?"

"Because you're scum. It's what you do. I came today to look into your eyes when you lie, so I could be certain of it myself. I should kill you all."

"Thank you for that summary," said Yibitriander. "Do you care to depart from these proceedings? If not, you must trust us and allow others to speak."

I leaned over to Toño and whispered, "I can't believe the fire hydrant is talking like that to Yibitriander. I really can't believe he's taking it so casually."

"No, I've read a lot about the Maxwal-Asute. They're like this. They're aggressive, pugnacious, and completely insensitive. Apparently, everyone knows it and cuts them considerable slack."

"If he addresses me like that, I'll have my dog pee on him."

"You don't have a dog," Toño said.

"I'm getting one today. A *big* one."

Clang-fow Peditit touched plungers with one of the two others in his group. After a second, he turned to the podium. "Your answer does not force me to kill you now. I will remain as long as my patience holds. You may proceed."

"The representatives of the Fenptodinian Federation will sleep well tonight knowing the Clang is wondrously tolerant," said one of the jellyfish. Its name, which I say because it turned out they were an hermaphroditic species, was Wo-woo-loll. It was their leader, sort of the first among equals.

It was so cool. When I flipped my translator off, I could hear its actual voice. It was a mix of a baritone saxophone played in short soft bursts, mixed with a piccolo. It was beautiful and eerie, all at the same time. I wanted immediately to learn to speak their tongue, assuming, of course, I lived that long. Hey, it was good to have goals.

"If I might continue?" said an annoyed Yibitriander.

There was no response. That was good. I don't think he was in a very tolerant mood.

"I want to know if any of you have heard of the Last Nightmare or have any new insights to share with the alliance."

A Fenptodinian rose and spoke. "We have legends that likely anticipate them. The stories are very ancient and have undoubtedly evolved over time. They are known by us as the Final Ill Will. Perhaps the translation loses something. To me, your name and ours are synonymous," said Wo-woo-loll.

"Do the tales provide us any potential insight as to who they are and how they act?" asked Kymee.

"Possibly. The stories say the Final Ill Will comes not to punish but to destroy. They will be merciless, and no mortal species will stop them. Perhaps I mean to say, *can stop them*. Your thought process is challenging for my comprehension."

"But in twelve destroyed universes, surely there have been immortals like us. If it is a riddle, it *has* an answer," responded Yibitriander.

"I only pass along the tale. As with stories older than accurate recording, their exact content is impossible to determine," replied Wo-woo-loll.

"Thank you. Perhaps that will prove to be useful information," said Kymee.

"I have never heard of an enemy who cannot be ripped apart," said Anganctus. "I do not fear them, whoever they are."

"If typical tactics like yours were effective, I doubt they would have become so legendary," replied Wo-woo-loll.

"We will see," said Cabbray, one of the two Churell ambassadors.

I considered not mentioning that the Churell sounded like horses when they spoke. I know, how convenient that centaurs sounded like horses. Hey, I make no attempt to alter the facts, just to relate them in an unadulterated fashion. And, no, I didn't ask him to count by stomping his hoof. Even Jon Ryan has limits.

"I fear we will," replied Kymee.

"Do we have a notion as to when we might face them?" asked Chulang-fow Crush, one of the six Maxwal-Asute present, despite the Deavoriath specifying that only one or two representatives per species should attend.

"No," replied Yibitriander.

"Then even if we believed your *lies*, our great grandchildren might die of extreme age before these *imaginary* creatures arrive," spat Chichal-fow Eloden, another of the hotheaded fire hydrant guys.

"They will come soon," replied Kymee. "I wish we knew if they will come in force or spread out over space-time."

"We would be better prepared to join with you side by side, new and valued allies, if you supplied us your warp-space technology," said Anganctus. He was trying his best to sound non-threatening and helpful. Never having practiced that approach, he failed miserably and wasn't convincing at all.

"We will defer any such sharing pending a greater demonstration of your trustworthiness," responded Yibitriander coolly.

"You gave it to those insects," Anganctus roared pointing at me.

"In desperate times, we are willing to share with those who have shown themselves to be reliable individuals."

Anganctus was not pleased. He growled and stepped toward Yibitriander. Fractor grabbed his elbow and whispered in his ear. Reluctantly, Anganctus retreated.

"We are able to defend Maxwal-Asute space against any attack. We are not able to quickly bail out the others in this room, as our craft are limited to FTL speeds only. You will all be tolerated if you join in our defense, should our territory come under threat," said Clang-fow Peditit. I think he intentionally tried to sound like a jerk. He sure did a good job of it.

"I would like to hear formally from each species that they will rally to the mutual defense of all the other species present when the attack comes," said Yibitriander.

"We are devoted to mutual defense," responded Wo-woo-loll quickly.

"The Maxwal-Asute look forward to smiting these wretches and will do so anywhere, anytime," replied Clang-fow Peditit. That was apparently as close as he could come to saying *yes*.

"The Churell stand ready to defend the existence of all."

All eyes turned to the big cats.

"Why would we come if we were not committed to help our new friends?" said Anganctus.

"How very different that statement is from agreeing to help," said Yibitriander pointedly.

"Do you doubt us?" said Fractor. "That would signal a poor beginning to a possible long term alliance.

"I will stop doubting you, when you pledge that you will come to anyone else's aide, and once you've actually done so," said Yibitriander.

"You question my word, my integrity?" replied Anganctus.

"I do."

Boy, that Yibitriander wasn't shy in the least about confronting someone.

"I have killed for much lesser insults," howled Anganctus.

"So have I," said a very serious looking Yibitriander.

"The humans will support all our allies, without reservation or hesitation," I said to break the tension.

"As do the Faxél. There, is that good enough for the prissy Deavoriath?" asked an angry Anganctus.

"For now, yes," said Yibitriander.

"Then I move we adjourn, but remain in close contact," said Kymee.

No one responded to him. The meeting simply broke apart. The two big cats dashed out like their tails were on fire, making Turk sprint after them to catch up. I hoped the return trip would be as uneventful as their shuttle here, but I was beginning to believe there was no predicting what the cantankerous Faxél would do.

The Fenptodinians glided to the front of the room and spoke privately with Kymee. Everyone else left quietly.

Yibitriander came over to me. "I think that went as well as it could," he said in a low tone.

Wow. I was becoming his trusted confidant. Could BFFs be far behind?

"I have no idea. Toño told me the Maxwal-Asute are tough to handle, but I'm still not one hundred percent certain if they're on board."

"Oh, I've seen them much worse. If they're mad, especially when they have something to be mad about, they're absolutely intolerable."

"I think I'm not a big fan of Clang-fow Peditit and his clan."

"No one is, not even the Maxwal-Asute."

"Are you serious? They don't even like themselves?"

"No, Jon, I'm making a joke," Yibitriander responded with what might have been a hurt look.

Yibitriander making jokes? Dude, the world was about to end. Yikes.

"Okay. Got it. I just didn't expect one coming in this direction." I drew the line from him to me.

"I'll have you know I am capable of being quite funny."

"Never doubted it, Yib. Not for *one* second."

"Hmm," he enunciated clearly. "But," he said more officially, "the meeting was useful. I think, for what it's worth, that whenever our enemy does come we'll be somewhat ready."

"It's hard to imagine that with all the firepower we bring to the party, any enemy could be a threat."

"I know what you mean. That's what really concerns me. As I've said before, there had to have been sentients every bit as resourceful as us in every universe they've obliterated."

"It does give one pause."

He rocked on his heels a moment. "Pause to consider death. As you know, we have not faced it for several eternities. Frankly, I think we stopped believing that we might stop existing." After a second he went on. "The fact is, one does not have to accept or understand death to experience it. Dying has never been a consensual process. But still, when it seems to have one in its sights again—"

"It's sobering, and it's a bummer."

He smiled, something I couldn't remember him doing. "Yes. Damn it, it is. I've forgotten what it is to be told what to do."

"So, I'm guessing you have avoided your wives for quite some time?"

"I think they've been avoiding us, but that's another topic. Come, let's find some nufe." He rapped me on the back and led me away.

I guess when you face your own mortality, you prefer to do it with whoever is as close to a friend that you have. Well, that and with strong drink. Never face death without it.

TWENTY-NINE

It didn't take long to find out what was in store for our universe. I was relatively pissed about that aspect. I hoped their time and our time would be different enough that it would take forever for them to hit. Maybe the Last Nightmare would lose interest? No such freaking luck.

I was back on *Exeter* for only two days after the conference when the shit not only hit the fan, the shit destroyed the fan, the wall it was plugged into, and the power company generating the electricity. Man, the Last Nightmare was aptly named. I had to give them their due there. They were not bad news. They were the end of news.

Out of the blue I got a signal in my head from *Wrath*. *Form, I have a message from Master Form Yibitriander.*

Never heard him called that before. I guess in times of war, titles become important again.

What?

He says to contact him immediately. The Last Nightmare has begun.

You mean the Last Nightmare has attacked?

Both. Form, that is why they are referred to as the—

End the lecture. Patch me though.

Form.

Jon, they've begun. For whatever reason, they've appeared in the Zaltat Quadrant. Sorry, I mean to say they hit the Churell.

Okay, I'll alert the other androids, and we'll be right—

No. No need. The Churell no longer exist. There's no alliance to defend.

You have got to be kidding me.

I wish I was.

What happened? When did they attack?

By your clock, ten minutes ago.

Shit.

Seven minutes ago I received the Churell's distress call. As of four minutes, ago I lost all contact with them. I sent one vortex to see what happened. They were to relay back enemy numbers, interface with the Churell, and help me decide where to commit the majority of our forces.

And?

And Oxisanna reported back to me that there was nothing.

Nothing what? What does that mean?

She said outside her vortex there was no space-time. There was no matter and no energy. Even the quantum flux of vacuum energy had ceased.

That's impossible. What you just said is impossible. She must be wrong. Maybe she cracked under the pressure. Where was the space-time? What happened to the substance of space?

She cannot tell. It is as if it never was—it never existed.

I'll get Toño and Carlos. We need to examine the region. There may be some clues, some hint as to what happened.

I would advise against it.

Why? We need to look for at least the trace remnants.

There's nothing there to study.

Let me back the bus up, here. How did this Oxisanna know where to go, if there wasn't any where to go? I do believe we're talking gibberish here, my friend.

Her vortex took the coordinates she requested and folded space-time to access a point in what turned out to be a void. A vortex has to connect to a real point in space-time. Since the one requested didn't exist, the vortex manipulator defaulted to connect with the last real point in the direction it was told to go. That's where she contacted me from—the edge of nothingness.

Then what did she do?

She ordered the vortex to move into the emptiness.

And?

And she no longer exists. My dear friend of one and a half million years is gone.

But how? If there was nothing there, how could it hurt her?

I have no idea. Yes, theoretically she should have dragged space-time with her. For lack of a better term, she should have reanimated the void.

But she didn't?

No. She joined it. I can only assume either the Last Nightmare was still present or there was a lingering deadly effect. What is clear is that something caused her to unexist.

I was stunned silent. What had just happened could not have happened. There could be no annihilation like that.

I'm going in alone.

No, Jon, you can't. You're too valuable.

Yib, this is war. Everyone's expendable. Especially in this *war.*

Jon, I can't lose you.

Wow. Didn't see that one coming.

Ah, Yib, we're good pals and all, but I'm betting you can live without me.

He was silent a second.

I can't lose you because you remind me of myself before I became so ghastly—before I lost my humanity.

Ah, Yib, you mean you lost your Deavoriathity. You're not human. You know that, right?

I mean what I said. There never was such a thing as … as what you said. But there was a time, forever ago, when I, too, possessed humanity. I see myself in you. As childish as it sounds, I want you around as a beacon to guide me back to acceptability.

Seriously, I'm flattered. But I'm going. I need to touch base with Carlos and Toño. I'll say good bye to my family, and then I'm going in.

There was silence.

Yib, you still there?

A dissociative panic set in like I was struck by lightning. Were they gone, too? Then I felt a faint nausea. Yibitriander's vortex was right next to me. He stepped out.

"I'll be here when you're ready. We're both going in. Please hurry. I don't want to chicken out."

"Chicken out? You people can't say—"

"We do now. Thanks, Jon." He swished his hands at me. "Go."

I called Toño in his head. I ran down what Yibitriander had told me and asked him to alert Carlos and meet us at *Wrath's* dock ASAP.

Man, oh, man. I'd said my last good bye to Sapale before the Berrillians attacked. I thought it would be *me* doing the dying, but it was harder than hard. Doing it again, especially with my kids? Crap. When I got my hands around the neck of one of those Nightmares, I was sure going to make it suffer.

Three men were waiting for me when I returned a few minutes later. Yibitriander had changed his mind and followed me. I think he didn't trust me enough to let me out of his sight.

"We've decided we'll all go," said Toño preemptively.

"No, you're not," I said flatly.

"Jon, you're not—"

"Yes, in fact I am in charge of you two eggheads. I'm a four-star general in a time of war. Under martial law, I own you."

"He's going," whined Toño, pointing at Yibitriander

"My jurisdiction falls just short of the planet Oowaoa. That, and he's meaner than I will ever be. He goes, and you two stay. Period."

Toño rested a hand on my shoulder. "Jon, why?"

"Simple. He's got a family to look after." I pointed to Carlos.

"And me? I don't."

"Toño, you son of a gun, someone who knows his ass from a hole in the ground has to be here when the big bad guys attack. The lives of everyone will depend on it."

"Wh … are you saying I don't—" Carlos was freaking hot.

"Yes, that's what I'm saying. Once the fighting begins, your thoughts will be with that lovely family of yours. Your judgement will become compromised. Doc has to stay, because I know his head'll be clear."

"You have a family," Carlos responded as an accusation.

"Yes, but I'm a jet-jockey. I've been through more wars than I can recall, let alone battles. This is what I do. I'm hard wired to focus, when a rational mind shouldn't be able to."

"No, you're not. I was there when you were wired." Carlos thought for a mini-second about what he'd just said. Suddenly he began to laugh through his nose. He laughed so hard he doubled over. Slowly, Toño, then I, then even Yibitriander joined in. We must have been quite the sight.

After a minute Yibitriander's chuckling stopped and he asked, "Why are we laughing?"

Of course, that brought a second, louder round of giggles and gasps.

"I was being concrete," said Carlos, "while Jon was being allegorical concerning his wiring."

Yibitriander gave a great belly laugh. "You people think that's funny? When this is over, I'll tell you something *really* funny."

We did all calm down. Eventually. "I think it's time we go," I announced quietly.

"Yes. We must investigate this attack before the next one begins," agreed Yibitriander.

"Very well. And I will keep the mental picture of Toño's ass not being a hole in the ground in mind, should the worst happen," said a now-serious Carlos. "It will definitely keep me sober."

"Jon, if I didn't love you so much, I'd hate you more than the Nightmare. Now you have my best friend and closest associate picturing my ass. This will make working productively most challenging," said Toño barely able contain a laugh.

We all bumped shoulders. Yibitriander and I entered *Wrath*, and we were gone.

I had *Wrath* take us to a point as close to where Oxisanna entered the absolute void as possible. Looking through five walls I saw stars and nebulae like normal. Out the front wall there was nothing. I don't mean blackness. I mean nothing. It's what you see out of the back of your head. Not blackness, but nothing at all. I immediately had vertigo, even though I'm sure that was impossible. I felt like a young child might standing on a diving board fifty meters above a half-filled pool.

"This is unprecedented," Yibitriander said quietly. "I wouldn't have thought this could exist. There's nothing out there."

Fortunately, all my training kicked in. "Let's get some data back to the boys," I said.

"Yes. I'll work with *Wrath*, you interface with Al," responded Yibitriander, snapping into action.

Al, what do you read out there?

Nothing, captain.

Is there any radiation, any cosmic rays, or any EM signal at all?

None.

How about vacuum energy? There has *to be that.*

Negative.

But, Al, in any space, virtual particles pop in and out constantly. Even if this space was cleared by the Nightmare, new particles would have to appear. They couldn't know what happened before they existed.

I agree, but that does not change the fact that they are not there.

Al, there's a flashlight near the main cargo bay hatch. The one on the wall.

Yes. Would you like to review the rest of ship's stores now, pilot? Seems as good a time as any, right?

No, you electronic moron. Turn it on and throw it into the void. Make sure it rotates in a horizontal plane one time per second.

And then *we'll review ship's stores minus that wasted flashlight? I think you're due for a tune-up, pilot.*

Do it. I want to probe how dense the void is. It seems a cheap and easy enough way to me.

Oh my.

What?

I find myself in agreement. Do you know what that means?

No.

We both *need a tune-up. Flashlight away.*

I watched as the torch spun slowly toward the void. It faded very gradually and then it disappeared completely.

That seems odd.

What does, captain?

It faded away. Why didn't it just vanish?

Why should it? We are not familiar with what it is the Last Nightmare does.

I don't know. I rubbed my chin. *I would have presupposed that the nothingness that was there would re-experience existence, too, as the flashlight moved forward. But if there was some Last Nightmare magic still there, the flashlight shouldn't have faded away.*

How do you figure that?

Nothingness has to be absolute. You enter it's domain and you're done, finished, gone.

A valid observation. But I would remind you we do not know their technology, only that it is monumentally destructive.

True, but I'm trained to think about cause and effect. The reverse logic applies. Where you observe an effect, there must be a cause—an active *cause.*

What are you suggesting?

They're still in there.

Who? The Churell?

No. The Last Nightmare.

Ah, I see. Excellent point. Alternately, they could have left a void-generating device.

Yes. That's equally possible, but it tells me one thing important.

Which is?

They're not omnipotent, omnipresent, or omniscient.

You mean they are not gods.

Exactly. Gods, I'm not anxious to face. Magicians, not so much. You know, I'm a magician in an alternate-timeline life?

No. My goodness, I'm shocked. You completely blindsided me there. Why did you wait until the eleventh hour to mention this?

Funny toaster.

I stepped over to Yibitriander. "Have you figured anything out?" I asked.

"Little. *Wrath* detects nothing, absolutely nothing. Signals sent away from the void progress normally. Signals sent into the void are gone."

"Did you notice they sort of fade away?"

He hesitated, possible communicating with the vortex manipulator. "Yes, there is a quick but definite delay in their disappearance. Does that suggest something to you?"

"Yes, it does. If you broadcast a signal, any signal, what eventually becomes of it?"

"That depends on the signal. Light and gravity decrease with the square of the distance. Magnetism decreases with the cube."

"But eventually, what happens to the signal?"

"It fades away. For gravitational attraction, it's infinitesimal, then it's the square root of infinitesimal, and so on. Eventually it is essentially zero."

"But it never just drops to zero abruptly, like it hits a wall."

"No. Your point?"

"The void we're witnessing is being broadcast. If it were a thing, an entity unto itself, it would have a discrete margin, like a balloon."

"Yes," he replied tentatively.

Again, I think he was conversing with *Wrath*.

"What significance do you attach to this observation?" he asked.

"That something is still generating this effect. We witness its gradual decay, so it must have a center point and dampen at some rate. Ah, thank you, Al."

He'd slipped the numbers into my head.

"The void intensity drops with the π^e of the distance."

"What an odd value."

"Yeah, but there it is. Some *thing* or some *Nightmare* is still in there. It's smack-dab in the center, and it's begging for us to turn it off."

"I'm not hearing those exact words," he said with a nervous smile.

"Aw, sure you are." I cupped my ear. "Listen real hard."

THIRTY

"Des-al, more aliens have appeared at the demarcation boundary," reported For-tal.

"What are *these* fools doing?" he asked.

"Little. They did throw a battery-powered light generator into the void. Otherwise, they are dead in space."

"A *what*?"

"A chemical-energy-to-electricity-storage unit powering a weak light source."

"These are beyond a doubt the weirdest life forms we've ever encountered. That's silly."

"I find it impossible to disagree with you," replied For-tal. She left off the part of her being concerned with the presence of an observation she couldn't account for. That was, after all, De-al's job, not hers.

"Keep me informed. Zes-ol, what is the status of the digestion?"

"Proceeding as normal. We have dismembered five percent of the mass of the civilization's home star and most of the planetary mass. All radiative energy has been assimilated."

"And the sentients?"

"Neutralized, confined, and awaiting disposition."

"Excellent. I long to taste a soul in agony. How soon will it be reasonable to begin mass consumption?"

"Our power stores are augmenting rapidly. I estimate that we will have suspended the entire primary target solar system to a radius of ten parsecs in a matter of hours. Then we will be able to return to the Neverwhere with our prizes and assimilate them at our leisure."

"Have you selected the next target, Uil-or?"

"Yes. Once replenished, we can suspend a much larger portion of this galaxy. I am setting plans to reduce the region subtending three sentient species as soon as we return to this wasteland space."

"Fine. Which populations shall we assimilate next?" asked Des-al. His hunger could be smelled in his words.

"The Maxwal-Asute, the Fenptodinians, and the Homo sapiens segments."

"Why not the Deavoriath? Surely they are our greatest threats and our richest prize."

"They will serve as an excellent dessert. The sweetest victory always is."

"And then we expand our influence to engulf galaxies at an exponential rate?"

"Yes. With more energy stores comes increased capture."

"What of the race you mentioned before? The Faxél. Are we to leave them behind?"

"No. They, however, will likely provide little sustenance. I calculate they do not possess souls."

"Ah, yes. How annoying. One of *those* species."

"And, dare I ask, have you run across any immortals with souls?"

"None, per se."

"Zes-ol, do not anger me. We are too old and too successful to take unnecessary risk. There either are immortals with souls, or there are not. Speak to me or die."

"Des-al, you lead, we follow. But your worries about this immortal soul thing are getting old. Never have we encountered one. What passed as one always turned out not to be. Let it go."

"You would speak to me thusly? How dare you, petty worm. I brought you into existence. I have fed you for time untold. My concerns are mine alone. You do not need to share in them for them to be true, valid, or an issue that requires your input. Have you found such a force?"

"No." Zes-ol left off the part of not actually knowing how to identify such a fictitious entity. That was Des-al's job, not his. If the beast was so damn concerned, let *him* look for an immortal with a soul. Or had Eas-el said he feared an immortal soul? Bah. It mattered not. Either way, they were nothing more than the empty ramblings of an old life source.

THIRTY-ONE

Rather than do it remotely, I returned *Wrath* to *Exeter* to discuss our limited findings with Toño and Carlos. They were impressed by the dampening of the void, too, as opposed to it forming an exact wall. They advised I test whether an object cast into the void stopped existing, or if it merely disappeared, as if into smoke. How to do that wasn't clear. If I went after the flashlight and it actually had gone puff, so would I. Toño came up with trying to use an infinity charge to help test the options. He reasoned that the membrane might be able to expel the void field if it was just a broadcast phenomenon. If, however, the void was the end of matter and energy, the infinity wouldn't be seen to go off. It would just be MIA. The hook was that the charge had to go off close enough to *Wrath* to clearly detect it without it, you know, blowing us up. It was kind of a one-shot deal if done incorrectly.

So, Yib and I returned to the point where we'd been. I asked Al to give me his best guess as to how far to set off the charge, and then I ordered it launched. Yes, I crossed my fingers and toes.

In ten seconds, the vail of nothingness parted like an opening eyelid. Then the shockwave hit us. Moving at just under the speed of light, whatever composed the void was thrown back into us. We had our membrane up, and, thank goodness, it stopped the stuff. Al even thought to capture a little in an external sample tube as it shot past. Then we waited to see if the membrane projection would strike or not. I added closing my eyes to the finger toe thing. Nothing.

"Al, strong work!" I shouted. "You missed us."

"I had no doubt, pilot."

"Like hell you didn't, you lying dish washer."

"So, the void is a *perception*, not an absence of reality. Well I'll be damned," said Yibitriander.

"It would appear so."

"What now?" he asked.

"Now comes the tricky part. We need to determine if our limited membrane can hold it out. The charges deliver a complete space-time congruity wall. Ours allows visible light through, so we can see where we're going."

"If ours doesn't hold out the void?"

"We play it by ear. I do that particularly well."

He rolled his eyes. "Great."

"Al, project a maximal diameter spherical membrane."

"Done," he responded.

There was no deformation in the void. I had him turn the field off and start it small, then expand it to maximum. Still nothing. The void was unperturbed.

"Extend a complete membrane to max."

It took a second, but a dimple appeared in the void. It expanded into an open cave in the nothingness wall. Cool.

"*Wrath*, nudge forward into the open area," I said.

"As our first mistake will be our last, Form, let me confirm that a nudge is a slow, incremental move forward."

"Yes, it is. And be prepared to stop on a moment's notice," I added.

"Gee, you can't give me a little time to practice that maneuver?"

"*Wrath*," thundered Yibitriander, "remember your place."

The cube said nothing. We began inching into the opening. Nothing bad happened.

"Al, turn on *Shearwater's* flood lights," I ordered.

The cavity sprang to life. The membrane, being complete, reflected all the light. It was like we were inside a disco ball. Most excellent.

"Al, back us out to where we were. Then toss something out the hatch so that it comes to a stop one thousand meters past where the membrane projection ends."

"Aye, pilot. Say, would you please step closer to the cargo bay hatch. Just curious. I'm lonely back here."

"In your dreams, my rejected record player friend."

"Oh well. At least I tried. Second flashlight away."

"Put up the complete membrane and take us where we were, *Wrath*."

Once we were in position, I confirmed the flashlight was invisible. It had to be since there was a complete membrane between us and it.

"Al, use *Shearwater* to project a full membrane that overlaps *Wrath*'s and encompasses the flashlight."

"Whatever. Done."

"*Wrath*, suspend your membrane in the area of overlap."

"I agree with Al, whatever. Done."

"Now, Al, drop your membrane in the area where the complete membranes come in contact."

"Done."

There was the flashlight. It was dead in space and shining its beautiful beam right at us from the center of the window between membranes. It was no worse for wear.

"My word," said Yibitriander. "That's an impressive test, Jon."

"So, we can't see through the crap, our sensors can't penetrate it, but it's a harmless illusion."

"This is *so* cool, Jon," said my shipmate.

I let him saying *cool* slip past without comment.

"Now what?" he asked turning toward me.

It occurred to me I might be able to test the system further. I estimated where Oxisanna's vortex would be, assuming it still existed. *Wrath* moved slowly in her direction with the full membrane up. This one was shaped like a bulldozer bucket along the leading edge. Once I was confident we'd likely have her cube in the membrane bucket, I had Al expand a full membrane just up to the lip of the bucket-shaped membrane. I had *Wrath* drop the bucket and Al drop his corresponding portion. If Oxisanna's vortex was in the bucket space, it'd be surrounded by a small amount of void material inside two large clear bubbles. I hoped the void material thinned as it drifted away. If it didn't, my only plan would have failed.

Luck sides with the innocent, the deserving, and, it turned out, the reckless fighter pilot. When the two small portions of membrane dissolved, the void dissipated, and there was Oxisanna's vortex.

Yibitriander was on the radio in an instant. "Oxisanna, are you there? Are you okay?"

A very confused sounding female voice came from the speaker. "Ah, Yibitriander? Is that you? Are we both dead?"

"No, dear. We're all fine. I'll have *Wrath* send you the details. For now, move close to us and follow our lead."

"Yes. Thanks. I thought we were goners."

"I never doubted I'd retrieve you," he said, looking over at me tentatively when he was done.

"Funny," I said, "me either."

I had to bear in mind that the void around Oxisanna's vortex dissipated because the full membranes prevented retransmission into that space. Whatever lay at the center of the void was clearly generating the crap. Oh well, one unbeatable odd at a time, please.

"Now we go a visiting."

Tricky got trickier. I wished I could call Richard Nixon for help. I had an excellent idea where something critically important was. There were just a couple of tiny problems. What was there might eat us on sight. How could we visualize it, since I couldn't use partial membranes? Oh, and did I mention it might eat us before we knew what swallowed us? Yeah. But, rescuing the universe never was a calling for the timid or meek of heart. I was the man without a plan, but I had no problem launching myself into certain death with a big old smile on my face. Yeah. Say it again. Jon Ryan was a fighter pilot. We may have been impulsive idiots with an overdose of self-confidence, but in a pinch, you really wanted one of us on your team.

I had both Al and *Wrath* calculate where the center of the sphere of void was. Their figures agreed. I intended to have *Wrath* put us one thousand meters away from that spot with a full membrane expanded out the instant we materialized. Unfortunately, that shield could not include whatever surprise awaited us. If it did, there'd be void material between us and the bad guys, and we wouldn't see them or detect them to fire on. But with enough Jon-gyrations, maybe I could expose the foe.

We folded to the position a thousand meters from the center. Logically, if I placed a full membrane around the center, whatever was in there could neither emit void material nor escape. But the Last Nightmare needed be bound by my logic, right? Then the rudiments of a plan flew into my head.

"*Wrath*, maintain our full membrane. Al put a full membrane around the center point."

Like a choir, they both replied, "Done."

"*Wrath*, switch our membrane to partial. Allow light to pass."

It was like the sky clearing after a rain storm. All the stars exploded into the sky around us.

"Al, extend the longest tube-shaped full membrane you can from the containment sphere. Then vent the contents to space one hundred and eighty degrees opposite from our position."

Damn, was I good. In front of our eyes, the center of the void suddenly appeared like a very long peace pipe with smoke coming out the far end. Fortunately, though the material spread out rapidly, it never accumulated in our area. I hoped whoever was in the center would see the futility and switch the void production off.

They didn't.

"Al, shrink the central membrane to squeeze whoever's in there."

"How will I know when to stop decreasing the volume?" Al queried.

"When you see void material leaking out, you went too far."

"You know, captain, you're considerably smarter than you look," said Al.

Yibitriander nodded vigorously in silently agreement.

Within a few seconds, the shape of whatever was there became apparent. It was a sphere, two meters in diameter. It was small. If one of the Last Nightmare was in there, they were tiny little dudes. Didn't seem reasonable, but how the hell would I know?

"Yib, any thoughts as to what to do?" I asked.

"Nothing definitive."

"Al, *Wrath*, any ideas?" I called out.

They both replied in the negative.

Okay, it was down to me, yet again. I was in my happy place. If no one had a clue, whatever I did was the best plan ever conceived.

"*Wrath*, plot a course to the nearest black hole. I want to orbit at a safe distance, but put us close. Al, tow the central point with us in a closed membrane. Let's surprise whoever's in there. And everybody, time runs slower the closer we are. I don't want to slip out of our timeline and lose a chance to fight the Last Nightmare. Move extremely quickly. Yib, tell Oxisanna not to come. No point crapping up her timeline."

We popped back into space near a smallish singularity. I could tell it was there because there was no light where it was, only darkness. Stars outlined it beautifully. I had told *Wrath* to position us in a fixed point and told Al to open the full membrane toward us. That way the central point would be held pinned in the cup of a membrane, and the void material would be sucked into the black hole, allowing us to see it. Hopefully. Only about ten critical aspects could go wrong.

The instant we appeared, the center point brimmed void material, but it was rapidly pulled toward the singularity. In the cup was a two-meter steel ball. *Wrath* immediately sliced the surface with a focused gamma ray laser beam. It split open, like a plastic Easter egg. Inside was some mechanical device, emitting the void material. No living being was in there, not unless it was microscopically small. Promptly, Al turned his membrane off, and the sphere careened into the black hole. Nothing escaped at the last minute.

Bam, we were back to the location near where the central point had been. Our radio exploded with signals. Most were Churell, begging for assistance. A bunch were either *Exeter* or Oowaoa calling for updates.

I looked to Yibitriander. It was his call now. We were back to conventional warfare, the one he'd planned for and discussed with our new alliance. He called for all vortices to converge on Churell space, in a prearranged dispersed pattern. Instantly, thousands of cubes appeared in the region. Yibitriander directed them to various planets and convoys. There was no immediate sign of anything that could be the Last Nightmare. There were no unidentified ships, no clouds of void, nothing that posed a danger.

Then all holy hell broke loose.

Spheres of void rocketed into the region at incredible speed. I counted ten. They split up and headed toward various concentrations of ships and larger planets. Suddenly, bolts of energy shot from them, and whatever they touched vaporized or simply disappeared.

We all returned fire. I had *Wrath* target the nearest ones with the QD device, and Al fired rail cannons as fast as possible. Even accounting for inaccuracy, the cannon balls seemed to have no effect. Several vortices fired lasers. Though they clearly hit their marks, the spheres of void were unaffected.

I know I hit one sphere when the QD exploded. I nearly jumped out of my pseudo-skin. But most shots had no effect. Then it hit me. We had been unable to see or probe inside the void material. Whatever we shot at a craft wrapped in void material would never see the weapon. It was safe to assume the Last Nightmare had figured out how to see through the shit, so they could target us, but we couldn't target them.

Crap. What to do? How could we break their incredible defense? My mind went blank. Then *Wrath* rocked from a massive strike. One of those energy beams hit the partial membrane directly. We shot backward like a billiard ball. It took *Wrath* a second to stabilize and return to the fray. He responded affirmatively when I asked him if he was undamaged. I hoped it was true.

"Al," came from my mouth without my really knowing I had something to say, "place small full membranes directly in the paths of any void projectile in range.

Suddenly, two void balls exploded most spectacularly.

"*Wrath*, Al, broadcast that strategy to all ships."

Within seconds, five other void spheres exploded. Then the two remaining void ships turned and disappeared faster than they'd moved in attack. From the final explosion to the time they were undetectable was exactly half a second. Those ships were fast.

Yibitriander spent the next three days working nonstop. He coordinated rescues, positioned defenses, moved supplies, and basically managed the battlefield like the master of war he was. Slowly, a picture of what happened took shape. Son of a bitch, the Last Nightmare was just that.

THIRTY-TWO

"Des-al, what has happened?" asked a stunned Wil-se.

"We met a superior mind," he replied, without passion.

"Superior to ours? Is that possible?"

"No, foolish child. Superior to any we've faced in the past. Compared to the Last Nightmare, the minds of these creatures are immeasurably small."

"Yet, only we two remain."

"Yet only we two remain. But we are sufficient. We will still destroy this universe. Perhaps it will take us longer, but our victory will be as complete, and it will be all the more satisfying."

"I wish to leave. I was happy in the Neverwhere and long to return. Come, Des-al, let us fly. Together we can occupy eternity in safety and joy."

"There can be no joy if we flee with only a stub of a tail. Safe, we might be, but we would be miserable."

"I would not be," she replied submissively.

"I say you would be miserable, so you would be. Do not let your preferences interfere with reality."

Normally, Wil-se would not respond. If Des-al said a thing, it was. If he said it was so, it was so. But now that there were but two left, matters were different. Clearly Des-al, wise beyond time, should not have put his clan in such danger. He was ... he was vulnerable, perhaps. He was approachable, maybe.

"I will go. If you demand vengeance, let it be yours. I want none, so you may have my share. I gift it to you as a token of my obedience. When you finish, join me in the Neverwhere. We shall both be happy."

Des-al felt something foreign boiling up in his being. He could not name it. He had known great hate. This was not hate. He had known all the anger that existed in six universes. This was not anger. Fear, understanding, regret, hope, forgiveness, and doubt were impossible. This was none of them.

Trembling, Des-al spoke. "Come to me, child."

Wil-se lowered her head and took one step at a time. Finally, she was prostrate before him.

Eas-el lifted an appendage and crashed it down on Wil-se's unprotected mind. His force was sufficient not only to crush it but to split open the ground below. Her dead substance thrashed reflexively for a moment. Then it was forever still.

Licking her essence from himself, he said out loud, "And then there was but one."

THIRTY-THREE

All told, our forces lost forty-three ships, forty-three comrades. Most were Deavoriath, as they had by far the greatest number in the fight. The Fenptodinians had responded quickly and in force. They suffered the remainder of the losses. I was relieved more than I was proud to admit that the android cubes were all accounted for. There turned out to be only minor damage to *Wrath,* which Kymee and Toño easily fixed.

The reports from the Churell were chilling. One moment they were preparing their defenses, and the next, eleven void spheres appeared out of nowhere. They began dismembering the Churell's defenses like they were made of soft cheese. The three inhabited planets were bombarded mercilessly for ten minutes. All orbiting vehicles were destroyed. All of them. Every ship, station, satellite, and piece of useless debris was destroyed. In that ten-minute assault, one third of the combined population of the three planets was evaporated. Millions died after that, when buildings collapsed and it started raining rubble.

Then the void material appeared, and there was nothing. Those who remained assumed they were dead and prayed passionately for their angels to take them. But even the angels were blinded. No rescuers arrived, and no hope was justifiable. Then the roundup began. Imagine, if you will, being in the void, not knowing if you or your family were alive, and then some force pushes you into a mass of confined people. You are crushed in, all the while unable to see or hear a thing. Then the prison you're held in accelerates as, unknown to you, it is launched to a recovery vessel in high orbit.

Then, you feel your feet touch a metal floor as you're marched in some direction. Finally, the void disappears. You're crushed into a holding pen along with thousands of your kind, so tightly you don't have to use your legs to stand. And the screams. Every Churell is crying in anguish for loved ones, or for relief, or for death.

Primal fear and suffocating claustrophobia. The alien voices of your captors speak to each other, but never you. Eventually, the sorting begins. Males, females. Young, old. Large, small. The culling seems endless. The only act that interrupts the sorting is when a massive arm reaches in and rips someone randomly from the line. You can't see what became of the person, but you hear their wailing become screams just before they fall silent. Next, you see the line you're waiting in enter some machine. You can't see what happens to your fellow Churell, but you can hear that the cries end at the machine.

Then, it is your turn to enter the darkness.

A journey through all the hells I'd encountered in countless religions would have been easier and more pleasant than that processing. We found millions of Churell in suspended animation. They were being stored for later consumption. We were unable to hack into the Last Nightmare's computers, if the mechanical sections of their machines were, in fact, computers. So, we were never certain exactly what the fate of the suspended bodies would have been. Our consensus was that the Last Nightmare planned to extract their souls for consumption.

Now, I have no idea what that meant. Was a mortal soul extractable? Could someone consume it and, in doing so, end it? It gave me chills just asking those questions. Me? I imagined they were distilling some life-force from the bodies. Sons of bitches couldn't possibly own the soul of a sentient. Could they? No. The thought was too abhorrent.

We could safely retrieve about seventy-five percent of those in suspended animation. The other twenty-five percent might have been dead before they were frozen, or maybe the shock to their bodies was simply too much. As unthinkable as it was to say, the Churell, in the end, considered themselves very fortunate. Only about half their population was dead. Their society lay in utter ruin, but they were reassured the alliance would see it restored. The remaining Churell had hope, which they lost in those terrible ten minutes. Poor guys. It would take generations for the physical and emotional scars to heal.

In terms of the Last Nightmare's technology, though we recovered a goodly amount of it, we understood nothing. All the void spheres were destroyed, so no part of their propulsion tech was available. Kymee had his head in Last Nightmare machines for two weeks. In the end, he said they shouldn't even function. He believed if he studied the tech exclusively for a million years, he'd be no closer to understanding it.

The funniest part was that through the attack, the round up, and the mop up, not one person recalled seeing a Last Nightmare. Aside from the butterfly on Dolirca's shoulder, no one had any idea what they looked like. It sure as hell wasn't a butterfly. Examining the captured machines didn't help reveal what their bodies were like. They manipulated their equipment without hands, that was clear. What must have been control fixtures slid seamlessly, like a ball or a belt, but they lacked grips or rough features to hold.

We even looked for residual DNA to see if we could get some clue as to their physical nature. Nothing even remotely similar was ever found. But, with at least two of them still out there, chances were excellent we'd find out more about what we were fighting sooner rather than later.

Once humanitarian arrangements were made to help the remaining Churell, there was nothing left to do but wait for the other shoe to drop. Come to think of it, the structure of language might have needed changing. We were providing *churellitarian* aide, right, not humanitarian. It wouldn't be nice to insult a race while serving them. I decided to let bigger heads than mine decide that issue.

What became clear in the endless debriefings and investigations was that the Last Nightmare were incredibly tough and even more ruthless. Sure, the Berrillians conquered worlds and fed off the inhabitants. But the scale and the efficiency of the Last Nightmare was breathtaking. Within hours, they had destroyed and processed a significant portion of three planets's populations. The Berrillians employed the victimized to help grow their war machine. That meant they had to at least tolerate them for a little while. To the Nightmare, sentients were chattel, merchandise to be assimilated. They had no other value. To them, we were bacteria growing in a petri dish—useful to a degree, but worthy of no consideration past utility.

I was at home one evening, playing with the kids on the floor, when someone knocked at the door. That wasn't unprecedented, but in general, my private time was rarely interrupted. I'd have never guessed who came calling. Yibitriander, all by himself. He had a bottle of nufe in each hand. All right. It was going to be a good evening.

"Come in, you old falzorn," I said putting a hand on a shoulder. "Kayla, we got company."

"Who is it?" she shouted from the other room.

"Some big-shot alien leader. Probably here to surrender or something."

She came around the corner drying her hands. "Yibitriander," she said unable to hide her surprise. "It's wonderful to see you."

"Is it?" he replied with a wicked smile. "Or do you think I'm here to drag your husband off to yet another hopeless battle?"

Her face relaxed. "No. If you were, you'd have just called. A visit means you may actually like the man."

He chuckled. "Or I simply wanted to see those darling children he never stops talking about."

"If that's the case, they're ready for their bath. Jon and I'll go out for a quick drink, and you can revel in their wonder and boundless energy."

"No, I want to see them, not borrow them. I'm too old to be a grandfather."

We laughed as we settled into the living room.

"I'll get some glasses and some snacks. Anything of ours you can't eat, Yibitriander?"

"Crow. He can't eat that. Trust me, I've given him reason too many times," I said slapping his back.

When Kayla was out of the room he asked, "Why couldn't I eat a pest bird? Not that I particularly want to, but are they toxic?"

"Ah, no. You know, idioms work best if all parties are familiar with the rules, don't they?"

He nodded. "In my experience."

"Then let's just drop the subject."

He nodded with less interest. Then he sat silently with a faraway look in his eyes.

I let him be for a minute, but then I had to ask. "Is something wrong?"

He shook himself alert. "With me? No." He reflected a moment. "It was something Kayla mentioned, about giving the children their bath. I haven't bathed a child in too long."

I pointed over my shoulder. "It's not too late. Say the word, and I'll make your wish come true."

He held all three hands up and wiggled them. "No. I meant that in the context of life, not that I felt a burning need."

He was quiet again, and there was sadness in his eyes. "I used to bathe my children, long, long ago."

"Really, you? No way. It'd be way too undignified."

He smiled sadly. "I wasn't always a stuffy old fool. I loved the baths. I loved the boys."

Uh-oh, *loved*? Come to think of it, I never met anyone he identified as his child.

"I didn't know you had kids." I tried to say that as neutrally as I could.

"I did. They were killed in the wars, the endless wars fought for no justifiable reason."

Then he clammed up good.

Kayla came back into the room all bubbly but picked up on his mood in a snap. She set the glasses and a platter on the coffee table as quietly as humanly possible, sat next to me, and folded her hands in her lap.

Finally he could say, "What a wonderful guest I make, don't I? I could always kill a party from light-years away."

I chuckled dryly. "You want to talk about it?"

Kayla looked into my eyes, but I squished up my face, hoping she understood I meant later.

"No. It's quite literally ancient history. But they were good boys, and I shall always miss them."

"Do you have pictures?" Kayla asked. Man, how is it that women always knew what to ask and when. I was thinking a hefty slug of the nufe was just what the doctor ordered.

He perked up. "I do. He pulled out a handheld, very similar to the kind we used. "Here, this is Neltuck. He was my oldest. This is Albraxal. He was the sweetness in my life. He was never as strong or as athletic as his big brother. But he was smart. Smarter than me, I can tell you that." He laughed to himself.

"They're so handsome," said Kayla, taking the handheld from him. "Oh, sorry. Is it acceptable to call a young Deavoriath *handsome?*"

He beamed a smile. "Yes. Yes, it is, and yes, they were."

"And what about your wife, the boys' mother. Do you have a picture of her?" Kayla asked intently.

"Yes, a much more recent one." He spied a glance up to me. "Jon's met her, in fact."

I had? News to me.

"Here this is my mate, Oxisanna." He handed the box to Kayla.

"She's your wife?" I had to ask. "We saved your wife, and you didn't think to mention it?"

"No. *You* saved the boys's mother, not *we*. If it weren't for you, my friend, she'd have joined her babies in the next plane." His eyes went sad again. "I doubt she'd have minded."

"So, you two are not still together?" asked my nosy wife.

"No. After the boys ... after all the war—"

"I expect it's hard to go on like nothing has changed," said Kayla.

"I really must remember never to engage in social events. I'm more depressing than the Last Nightmare."

"Not hardly," she replied with genuine cheer. "Are those bottles to look at, or are we going to drink them?"

"We are most assuredly going to drink them," he said finding renewed strength. Yibitriander released the caps and poured three tall glasses.

Kayla had tried nufe a couple times and was as big a fan as I was.

We all took a sip then relaxed back in our chairs. I tasted medium-rare prime rib, a great joke told by a dear friend, and baseball on a summer's day. My next sip, however, was a roaring fire on a snowy day, fresh cherries, and the leather seats of a 1968 Ford Mustang GT Fastback. I was speechless, and I was in heaven. I hoped Kayla was taking notes, so we could discuss our experiences afterward.

"So, Yib, as good as it is to see you and as great as it is to drink your nufe, to what do we owe the honor of your visit?" I asked with my eyes still closed in rapture.

"I wanted to thank you, Jon. I also wanted to compliment you."

"This sounds promising."

"Don't make him regret he came, till we polish off the nufe, hon," Kayla said quite seriously.

"Good point," I responded winking at her.

"I won't beat the dead horse by reminding you how long I've lived and how many battles I've fought," began Yibitriander. "But I must say I've never seen a more intuitive, effective, and instinctive a man in action as you, Jon Ryan." He raised his glass. "To the luckiest damn pilot in the galaxy."

We all clinked glasses.

"And I have to thank you for saving Oxisanna. We drifted apart over time, but she's still dear to my heart. When I thought she was lost, all I wanted to do was join my family in the Beyond." He sighed deeply.

"I'm honored to have been able to help a good friend," I said raising my glass.

"Since the battle with the Last Nightmare, Oxisanna and I have been spending some time together. In the last week or so, we've spoken to each other more than we did in the last thousand years." He stared into his glass.

"That's wonderful," responded Kayla. "And if it's written in the stars, maybe you two will find your way back together."

"Yeah," I added, "then you can work on having some kids to bathe again."

He had been taking a swig of nufe and nearly spit it out. "I doubt very much *that* is written in the stars. I'm too old to even think the thought, let alone commit the deed."

"Which one?" I asked with a straight face. "The baby making part or the raising baby part?"

Kayla slapped my arm. "You're terrible."

"I know. But I'm also seriously curious."

Yibitriander rolled his glass between two of his hands, collecting his thoughts. "All kidding aside, Jon, you've changed everything. I would have bet all the money in the galaxy it wasn't possible, but you did. You've forced us kicking and screaming from our shell for the benefit of not only the universe, but also for ourselves."

"And that's a good thing I did, holding your collective shells up and shaking you out of them?"

"Best thing to happen to the Deavoriath in as long as I've been one of them." He raised his eyebrows. "I hate sounding corny like you do."

"Hey. I am forced to throw a protest flag into the conversation. *I'm* never corny."

Kayla rested a hand on my lap. "Honey, if you looked up corny in the dictionary, right next to the picture of a cob would be your face."

My two *ex*-friends clinked their glasses triumphantly.

"All that said, you rekindled our hearts, you showed us what silly recluses we were. You performed societal CPR, and we might just make it."

"Ah, hello," I said. "Give one Yibitriander von Deavoriath some credit, too. If you hadn't given me the command prerogatives, none of this would have happened."

Yibitriander gently closed his eyes and rocked his head back and forth. "I know I'll hate myself for even asking, but what in the Ten Hells of Gaspos does Yibitriander von Deavoriath mean?"

"It's a slightly obscure reference. Hey, you did tell me you'd read all the literature in the human libraries."

"I'm sorry, Yib," said Kayla, looking at me like there was dog poop on top of my head. "Since he doesn't know your last name, he invented one. *Von* is used as a part of a German family name to suggest a noble lineage. I think the nufe's made him extra lame, already."

"Extra lame? Is that possible?" he asked her.

Again, with the clinking of glasses. Get over yourselves, already. I had a good mind to grab one of those bottles and retreat to *Wrath* to be by myself, maybe sulk a little.

"Along with providing you two simpletons a target for your childish jokes, I did want to point out you had a role in our victory and in the Deavoriath's decision to get off their butts and start living."

"No, I was merely swept up in the flood that is Jon Ryan. You know, I still don't know why I had Kymee install those command prerogatives. No idea what came over me."

"You told me you were sorry for being so mean to me. That's why you did it."

"I've been rude to a goodly number of people. Never felt compelled to make such a grand gesture to any of *them*," replied Yibitriander.

"Jon," Kayla said firmly, "do you remember the conversation we had about you accepting compliments? How you downplay them and make up infantile jokes?"

"Yeah, sort of. I guess."

"And what did we decide you'd do the next time an adult complimented you?"

"I'd say—"

I set my glass down, turned to Yibitriander, and placed one hand inside the other.

"Thank you. Your praise means the world to me. I'm honored to have been able to help, dear friend."

Yibitriander scowled. "My goodness. If he learned to say it like a man and not a robot, I'd have half believed he was sincere. Kayla, I wish you'd met him a very long time ago. You're better for him than command prerogatives."

"Oh no, don't get her started on the command thing. She'll run with it. I'm telling you, and I'll know no rest. Ever."

She rolled her eyes skyward. "Command over Jon. My, that sounds intriguing, doesn't it?"

I wanted to think her huge smile was for effect, but I honestly wasn't certain it wasn't the real McCoy.

"Would you look at the time," I said standing. "It bedtime for this robot. Yib—"

"Sit," said Kayla to me.

I sat.

"Now roll over," she said, with a mischievous smile.

I remained seated.

"This is still a work in progress," she said to Yibitriander.

"I actually had best be going. If I stay much longer, I'll probably reduce you both to tears with another morose tale from my sorry past."

He stood and set his glass down.

"Are you sure?" asked Kayla. "It really is wonderful to see you socially instead of during the next crisis."

"No, but thank you. Knowing you do mean it is touching. However, speaking of the next crisis, you and I need to discuss what to do about the last two Last Nightmares."

"Last two?" I replied somewhat confused. "How do you figure that?"

Having three hands turned out to be useful. With four fingers on each hand, he held up the number twelve. "There were twelve to begin with."

He lowered one finger.

"If you listen carefully to the recording, it would seem Dolirca tricked one into suicide."

He lowered another finger.

"We cast that void-generating sphere into a black hole. Since there was only ten craft attacking us, that one we emptied had to have contained one of the Last Nightmare."

"But, it was so small. I mean, we don't know how big they are, but I can't imagine a race so powerful could be that small."

He glared at me.

"But reality doesn't depend on my approval, does it?"

He lowered a finger.

"You destroyed one vessel with the QD weapon."

He lowered two fingers.

"You exploded two against full membranes."

"I bet they hate you as much as any species you've totally pissed off, dear," said Kayla cheerily.

He lowered five digits.

"The rest of us took out five ships with the membranes. That leaves two unaccounted for. Those are the ones that departed the battlefield so quickly."

"Maybe they learned their lesson and went back where they came from, tails between their legs, assuming they have legs and tails," I said, with little conviction.

"Someone wise once told me, 'Hope for the best but prepare for the worst.'"

I put a finger to my chest. "Wasn't that me who said that to you?"

"Yes, I've promoted you to being wise. Now become the role." He smiled.

"I'll talk to you tomorrow. We'll plan the elimination of those last two slackers. We'll make them wish they'd never been born."

"Assuming they were actually born." Yibitriander raised a palm to Kayla, who high-fived him back.

I got no respect.

THIRTY-FOUR

Waiting to see if one sixth of the enemy's original numbers were still sufficient to destroy the universe was not easy. By my way of thinking, if as few as twelve could do it, two stood a darn good chance. I mean, it wasn't like they had to pedal a bicycle built for twelve. We still had no real idea how they erased universes. The void material was handy, but not in and of itself good for much beyond cover. They rounded up sentients for consumption, but as gross as that was, it didn't explain the end of times aspect of their coming.

Maybe, just maybe, they were all thunder and lightning but no rain. It could be they were rumored to eat souls and end universes to build their reputation, you know, scare little children. But, that wasn't a thing to count on. Sometimes the dude with the most bad-ass reputation really was the biggest badass. Unfortunately, I knew I'd find out which it was soon enough. Even if they licked their wounds for a thousand years, I was going nowhere. I'd have to face them. As always, good thing I was a fighter pilot. In battle, we never worried about what came later than ten seconds from the present. I'd labored long and hard to seamlessly apply that principle to life in general. Short-attention-span theater was designed for my type.

The more the status of the Churell stabilized, the more time Colin Winchester felt he could vex us with training and briefings. He nagged at us like a bitter ex-father-in-law. Trust me, of this I speak with regrettable authority. My first wife's dad hated me the first time he met me, and our relationship plummeted from there. Colin was the only person who felt perfectly comfortable calling me day or night to discuss insignificant details of this, that, or the other. He felt that, as group's vice commander, I should "pull my full weight in the day-to-day operations of my unit."

The hell I should. I was only associating with the other pilots because I was no longer the only android with a cube. It was logical that we worked together. But I hadn't needed Colin-level structure for hundreds of years, and I sure as hell didn't need it now. The problem was that the other pilots were so stoked to have their own miracle ships that they hadn't developed my distaste for organizational zealots. But whenever I got in a particularly pissy mood, I pictured what Kayla would say to me about being an adult. Reluctantly, I'd hold my tongue.

A month went by with no sign of the Last Nightmare. Everybody was getting edgy. When you know it's coming, you'd rather it just came. Standing on tiptoes and waiting was hard. I went to visit Kymee, ostensibly for any technical updates he might have. Really, I simply wanted a break in the monotonous tension. I arrived at his workshop to find Yibitriander and Oxisanna there, too. They seemed to be visiting socially, as opposed to being there for help with something technical.

"Jon," said Kymee as he saw me enter. "Good to see you."

I bumped shoulders with the three of them.

"Nice to see you all, too," I replied. I'd met Oxisanna a couple of times since the battle and was getting to know her a little by then.

"So, what brings you?" asked Kymee.

"Does a friend need a reason to visit a friend?" I asked.

"No, but you usually do," responded Yibitriander.

We all chuckled.

"I really just needed to get away," I said.

"General Winchester's having you wear a uniform and march in formation. Is he getting to the independent-minded pilot?" asked Kymee.

"No, I love parading around like a stuffed peacock and swinging a big gun."

"*Men*," said Oxisanna. "Some aspects are universal."

"I especially like listening to him go on and on about the supply chain, top-down communications, and the importance of a highly-polished pair of boots."

"I'll just bet you do," sniped Yibitriander. "You know what, if you like it that much, maybe I could teach you to march Deavoriath style. I used to be quite the drill master."

"Yeah, like I need to learn a three-legged march. No, I think I'll pass."

"How are the kids?" asked Kymee.

"Great. You know, I think Oowaoa could stand a few new bundles of joy. You guys are dropping behind badly."

"One step at a time. We're only crawling out of our shells. Give us time," replied Kymee.

"When you talk about time, I hear another million years," I teased back.

"One step at—"

Kymee stopped speaking. That caught Oxisanna's and Yibitriander's attention. She had been whispering something to him, so they'd been distracted.

"What?" asked Yibitriander.

Kymee pointed to nothing, right where Jon had been sitting.

"Where's Jon?" asked Yibitriander his voice rising in concern.

"He's not there. He was there, and I was speaking to him. Now, there's nothing there."

"You mean he's gone?" asked Oxisanna.

"No, look. There's *nothing* there."

"Just a void," said Yibitriander.

And then the nothingness faded and the spot where Jon had been was unoccupied.

Kymee's consciousness swept the planet.

"He's gone. *Wrath* is quietly parked, and Jon is not here," said Kymee in disbelief.

"I fear the Last Nightmare has taken him," said Yibitriander coolly.

"But where?" asked Oxisanna.

"We don't know yet, but I suspect the Neverwhere," responded Kymee. "I'll be in my lab. I must locate him fast, if we're to rescue him alive."

"I'll alert Alexis Gore," said Yibitriander.

"I'll be with his wife," said Oxisanna as she jogged to her vortex.

****

I was listening to Kymee. He was saying something about kids, I think. Then I became very dizzy, which is impossible. After a second, existence vanished. Nothing was. I looked and saw nothing. It only took a second to realize who was to blame. Where there's truly nothing, there had to be the Last Nightmare. It was their signature. A couple moments later, I felt different, but I couldn't put my finger on exactly what had changed. For better or worse, the nothingness that was, faded. I was in a vast featureless plane stretching out as far as I could see. It was like the grayness extended to infinity in every direction.

There were no sounds. I quickly determined there was enough atmosphere to carry sound waves. There was simply nothing producing any noise. It was very cold, maybe a hundred degrees below zero Centigrade. Nothing moved, and there were no structures or ships, not even rocks. Nothing. What an uninteresting rabbit hole I'd fallen into. Dull homogeneous illumination came from no obvious source. The smell was remarkable in that, even with my keen sense, the was *no* smell.

The absence of an obvious threat did nothing to assure me. I was in deep, deep shit. I assumed my captors were toying with me. I would state for the record that I hated being a mouse to anyone's cat. I scanned as much as I could and still detected nothing. Big surprise, right? I tried to attach my probes to something to analyze it but they wouldn't stick to anything. For lack of a better plan, I started walking, choosing a random direction. The surface was partly obscured by mist, but it felt like I was stepping on coarse sandpaper.

After a few steps, a voice from nowhere said, "Don't go that way. If you do, you will die."

Okay, his house, his rules. I turned right and took a few steps.

"No, no. Not that way either. If you do, you will die," said the hissy, quiet voice.

I decided to humor the SOB a little more and turned one hundred eighty degrees and took a step.

"Ah-ah, not that way. If you do, you will die."

That voice was flipping annoying. I walked in the only direction I hadn't.

"Tsk-tsk, no. If you go that way, you will surely perish," the voice said joyously.

I threw my arms up. "Which way can I go that I won't die, dude?"

"There isn't one. Anywhere you go, I shall slay you."

"You're a lousy host. I hope you know that, weirdo."

"I so love bravado, General Jonathan Ryan. Ask me why I do."

Screw him. I crossed my arms and angled my body to one side. Wasn't going to *say* a word.

"Oh, defiance. I love that almost as much. As the feline has your tongue, I'll share my secret. I love those qualities, because when I break you and you beg for death, they will be gone. I will have snuffed them out, tough guy."

"Do you have a bathroom here?"

"Wh ... what? No."

"I have to tell you you're scaring the piss out of me, and I'd rather have a toilet handy than mess up a clean uniform."

I felt the force of a semi-truck strike me from behind. *Wham.* I face planted.

"With the next words that displease me, I shall begin removing body parts," said my most unfriendly ghost host.

"Let me have a look at you, so I can tell you which one you should remove first."

In retrospect, it was not as clever a request as it seemed. At first, I just heard a crinkly sound, like cellophane balling up. Then I heard and felt a rumbling. Then I saw the Last Nightmare. C-r-a-p on a croissant. As I watched, he grew from a meter tall. He unfolded as he rose, expanding. He was a dragon, a golden-scaled, monstrous beast. His hide sprouted iron-like plates with sharp, ragged edges. One massive central head dominated two small ones to either side. His four tremendous arms ended in paws with talons the size of samurai swords that were just as sharp. When he eventually stopped growing, he was thirty meters tall and almost as wide. Dude must have weighed ten tons.

He was scary, and I was duly scared. I'd never seen anything so horrific ... uh, not even in a nightmare.

I smelled a rat. How could something that big have escaped my prior notice? It couldn't. I had to acknowledge he could be a shapeshifter. I'd never heard of such a thing, but a lot of the mentions came from popular sci-fi. I know, not the most reliable source of crisis information, but it did pop into my head. But, on the other hand, if he was a shifter, where was the mass coming from? Tiny to fifteen tons? Nah, not reasonable. Shapeshifter was off the list.

Okay, I tried an experiment. I used my laser finger to try and slice the tip off a talon. Nothing.

Man, I was tired of nothing.

Either my terawatt laser wasn't strong enough, or that wasn't really a claw. I balked at experiment two, seeing if he could slice me into thin ribbons. But, he seemed to want to toy with me, so he probably wouldn't kill me quickly.

Talk about standing on shaky ground.

One probe fiber, wrap up that talon.

The fiber shot over and encircled its target.

What are you?

More nothing. I got no readings.

Pull at the talon.

Finally, something. The fiber was cut in half. Nothing anywhere had been able to damage the command prerogative fibers, but this bozo cut it like a hot knife through butter.

What was I seeing? The talon couldn't be cut, but it could cut. That made no sense. I hated things that made no sense, when I was about to die.

"You are the ugliest creature I've ever seen. It is actually impossible for you to be as ugly as you are."

Taunting was always a good way to distract an enemy. It was also an excellent way to further piss them off, sort of a two-edged sword.

"You asked to see me. Now fear me," he thundered.

"Just for the record, you are Des-al, right? Or are you the other Last Nightmare I haven't killed yet?"

That caught his attention.

"You know my name? Little being, how is that possible? Your species has never experienced the Last Nightmare. We have never visited this universe."

"Ah, it's the smell. Everybody knows you guys stink."

"Arrr-*ah*." he screamed as he impaled one set of talons a foot into the ground right next to me.

"Your species knows about baths, right? Have you ever considered taking one?"

Bam, bam, bam. A series of massive paws struck closer and closer. I think he was trying to frighten me. He was doing a good job. Des-al was a real pro.

"I only wish you had a soul, tin man. I would rip it from you where you stand and consume it with gusto."

"Ketchup."

He actually stopped waving his arms around and howling to look at me.

"What?" he asked.

"If you eat my soul, try it with ketchup, not gusto. You know, like french fries. Yum."

"Little machine, you're insane. Your mind is so out of sync with reality."

I motioned around in general. "You call this reality?"

Hey, I had no idea where this was going, but I wanted to try to keep him unfocused, if possible. When in doubt, go to your strong suit. Mine was being abrasively annoying.

"Of course, this is reality. It's the Neverwhere," he said defensively.

"I think it's a lot like you. It stinks."

Bam, bam, bam. Another round of talon impaling. The difference was that if I hadn't hopped around like a chicken, he'd have landed a blow on me.

"Where's your playmate?" I yelled, as I dodged another swipe. "I'd hate to kill you separately. I'm kind of pressed for time."

"Arr-ahh-yah." he wailed as all four arms flew at me.

I had him right where I wanted him. Pissed. Now, if I only had part two of my plan, he'd have been in real trouble.

"Where is he?" I yelled. "Hate your smell as much as I do, so you sent him away?"

"No," he shouted as he landed one blow. "I killed her for her cowardice," he said with another.

"Thank you. I hate wasting time killing you guys. It's so easy, I worry I might fall asleep in the process and miss out on the fun."

Wow, that got him extra mad. His immense tail with spikes thudded the ground by my foot.

I rolled away.

"I will eat your metal parts, insignificant toy," he raged.

"What do I care? If I'm dead, you can make a transistor radios out of me, for all I care."

Wham. Paw, tail, paw.

Come to think of it, he wasn't very accurate with his bodily weapons. What was that trying to tell me? What advantage—

"Des-al, ender of worlds, I would address you," challenged a confident voice.

In a parity of a trained act, we both stood straight up and looked to where the voice came from.

No way. That was my first, second, and third thought. It was Yibitriander. He stood twenty meters in front of *Wrath*. I'd say he was walking toward us, but his gait was all wrong. He stepped easily enough on two of his legs, but the third was only a stiff crutch to the back of him. I'd never seen a Deavoriath walk like that. This Neverwhere just kept getting weirder and weirder.

"You cannot be here, Deavoriath scum," protested Des-al.

"Yet here I stand, lizard."

Why was Yib wearing a large backpack? I'd never seen anyone on Oowaoa with a hiking knapsack before. I was mightily confused.

"At least I may feast on a living soul, fool. Thank you for coming. Killing this cretin has worked up a powerful appetite," mocked Des-al.

"You have killed your last victim. I will end the Last Nightmare, here and now."

Yibitriander continued to stagger forward. What was with him? He was just fine when I left him.

"Stop where you are. I will deal with you after I have turned this mechanical nuisance off."

"Do not give me orders, inferior. I will do and say what I please."

Along with a limp, Yibitriander had developed a really bad case of corny speak.

Des-al slapped his impressive tail in front of Yibitriander. Oddly—what else was new in the Neverwhere—Yibitriander didn't stop. He angled around it, advancing with awkward jerks.

"I will sip your essence at my leisure." Des-al set his tail on the ground in a loop around Yibitriander.

"Looks like this is as close as I get," Yibitriander said to I had no idea who. He turned to me. "Catch."

Yibitriander hurled the big pack at me. I caught it easily but was surprised by its heft.

"Now," yelled Yibitriander.

In my head, I heard *Captain, stand still and trust me. We think this might work.*

Al? What might—

Instantly, the world went blank. It took a second, but then I realized I was in a small full membrane.

Al, what in the—

I didn't need to finish my thought to have a good guess what was happening. The force of a thousand stampedes rushed past the tiny sphere that protected me. I was shaken like I was in a blender, and the noise was deafening.

Al, did he just set off an infinity charge?

Yes, captain. We're sort of hopeful this will work.

Sort of hopeful? You couldn't do better than sort of hopeful?

You left without warning. On such short notice, we had to wing it.

Wing it? I wing it. Yibitriander doesn't wing things. You don't wing things.

Like I said, you gave us little time.

I didn't kidnap myself. How could I serve proper notice?

Please don't change the subject. And be silent for once. I'm listening.

Listening for what?

I knew you couldn't do it. You couldn't just once shut up when I ask. We're in the middle of a crisis here, had you not noticed?

Al—

It's safe now, I think.

The membrane disappeared as suddenly as it had appeared.

The stark neutrality of this place had changed. There was heat, lots of heat. And smells. Burned, smoldering things. And sounds. Echoes and ringing vibrations. I think I preferred the empty place.

And Yibitriander was gone. Not a trace. It hit me. The burning smell was probably him. I nearly vomited. Where *Wrath* had been, I saw a full membrane, which switched off as soon as I looked at it. The cube was undamaged.

Al, what the hell had just happened?

I believe we rescued you, pilot.

Who's we? I only hear you. Are you in Wrath?

If I was in Wrath, *how could you have heard me when his shield was up? Hum? Want to try thinking before your gums flap?*

Gums flap? Al, you're kind of harsh here, aren't you? I was fighting for my life when you arrived, if you will recall.

That was fighting for your life? It looked like you were playing hammer and nail with Des-al, and you were the nail.

Remind me to have Doc delete your lame humor circuits. Now, what—

"Jon," a familiar voice called out, "are you all right?"

I whipped around to the cube and saw Yibitriander jogging over to me. Two observations struck me. He was moving normally, and he wasn't incinerated. What? He was standing in the open when an infinity charge went off at point blank range. No one survived that.

He arrived where I stood and attached his probes for a second.

"Good, you're unharmed." He took in a deep breath and exhaled with relief. "I was worried that stunt wouldn't work."

"Anyone care to tell me what the stunt that might not have worked *was*? I'm, I don't know, kind of interested if what the hell just happened. And where's Des-al? You know, the thirty-meter-tall monster dragon?"

"There was never a huge golden dragon here, Jon. Haven't you figured that out yet?" Yibitriander said with attitude.

"Huh?" was all I had.

"My, your rapier-like wit is impressive, pilot," said Al.

"Come, Jon, let's get you home. I'll explain as we travel. Kayla is worried sick."

"Is she okay?" I asked rather stupidly.

"Of course not. The Last Nightmare captured her mate and took him to the Neverwhere. It should have been impossible to rescue you, dead or alive. Oxisanna's with her, but she's upset. Come." He put a hand on my shoulder and pushed me toward *Wrath*.

"But what about Des-al?"

"I hope he no longer exists. Kymee and a few others will come investigate once they see we've safely returned. Come. We'll talk as we go."

The remarkable quality of the trip home to *Exeter* was that it took ten minutes. The travel wasn't instantaneous. I'd have to check later why that was. The ten minutes of nausea was not pleasant. I hadn't had the stomach flu in two centuries, and I hadn't missed it.

When *Wrath* materialized, the two women were seated by the pad. Kayla rushed out of Oxisanna's arms and would have hit the cube's wall if Yibitriander hadn't opened a portal in the nick of time. She scanned the control space and locked onto me. She ran to me and jumped into my arms, hugging me like I wished she'd never have to stop. Her tears switched over to the happy version, and my shoulder quickly became wet. It was marvelous.

"I'm fine, honey," I said when it finally came time to pry her off. "And you should see the other guy." I gestured a thumb downward. "Toast. Burned toast, in fact."

"I'll just bet," she said wiping snot with the back of her hand.

"Oh yeah. Des-al's gone so far as to retain a lawyer. He's threatening to sue me for everything I own."

She gently punched my chest. "Just let him try. He'll have to go through me first."

"The kids okay?" I asked.

"Yes. I didn't tell them what was happening. Turk was nice enough to get Karnean so he could be with them while we waited here."

"Remind me to thank him."

"Oh, Turk promised he'd extract his pound of flesh for the favor. He said he had an itch and was maybe going to ask you to scratch it."

"In his dreams," I said.

"Talk about nightmares," said Yibitriander coming up from behind. He had the large pack slung over a shoulder, but it seemed much lighter. "Let's go to your place. We can talk there. I've spoken with Kymee and the others. They should already be in the Neverwhere. Hopefully they'll just be mopping up."

"Let's hope so," said Al. His voice came from inside the backpack.

"Do you have to bring that?" I asked pointing to the pack.

"Would you kindly strike the pilot with the backpack, Yibitriander," said Al.

After hugging the kids for a good long while and checking in with Karnean, the adults adjourned to the living room to talk. I was dying to know exactly what had happened.

"Once you were gone, we knew immediately it was the Nightmare," Yibitriander began. "Fortunately for us, Des-al made several assumptions that allowed us to come get you. He assumed, most of all, we couldn't access the Neverwhere, so he prepared no defense." He shook his head. "Stupid mistake, really. Arrogance always leads to disaster in warfare."

"How did you? It seems impossible," I asked.

"Oh, the Neverwhere is just a fancy name for another dimensional plane. Not really such a chore to access, if you know where to go."

"Another dimensional plane?" asked Karnean.

"Yes. We use three dimensions, right? The X, Y, and Z axes, if you will. There are many other dimensions. We simply don't perceive them. The Neverwhere is just a dimensional space that uses say the A, B, and C axes."

"And how did you know to go there?" asked Kayla.

"There was a residual trail left when Des-al pulled you through. Another mistake on his part," replied Yibitriander. "Once there, we could deploy our plan, since you were doing a very good job of distracting him."

"Yes," said Al who was now in a suitcase-sized computer sitting on the coffee table, "your ability to make anyone or anything angry is remarkable. You should give lessons."

"I was counting on Des-al continuing to err," said Yibitriander. "I suppose his past successes made him careless."

"Twelve universes destroyed," I responded. "That's a pretty good track record."

"When I realized he was a non-corporeal entity, a strategy for killing him became clear."

"Wait," I said. "You realized he was non-corporeal? How?"

"Pilot, please do try and keep up," quipped Al. "There'll be a quiz at the end, so pay attention."

"You didn't figure it out?" asked Yibitriander.

I shook my head. "I knew there was something fishy about him, but, I don't know, maybe since I've never encountered a non-corporeal species, it was off my radar screen?"

"What are you talking about?" asked Yibitriander sternly. "You know Al."

"Yes, pilot. Am I chopped liver?"

"I *wish* you were."

"Jon," Yibitriander said, "one of them was a butterfly and the other fit into a tiny metal sphere. They projected void material. They were masters of illusion. What else could they be?"

"Giant golden dragons," I replied.

"They could be what?" asked Kayla.

"That's what I was fighting when the cavalry came," I responded pointing to Yibitriander.

"No. You were fighting a projection, a construct he meant to frighten you with," replied Yibitriander.

"Well he did a damn good job of it. I can tell you that. The thing was *humongous.*"

"The projection was. Des-al had no body."

"No *body*? He sure the hell ripped the place up. If I'd stood still, he'd have sliced me up good."

"It was a good projection with interesting and dynamic elements. It was nothing more than a sophisticated puppet," responded Yibitriander.

"A puppet that'd gut a blue whale with one swing." I felt a need to defend my honor.

"Be that as it may. The weak link in our plot was the robot."

"Me? I was trying not to get killed," I whined.

"No, the other robot, you—" Yibitriander took a deep breath so he didn't have to complete his thought.

It was a good thing I no longer breathed. People sure did a lot of deep breathing around me.

"We had to get Al and a membrane generator to you and the infinity charge as close to Des-al as possible. To do that, Toño fashioned a crude model of me, and we draped it over a blank android powered by a small AI."

"Wait, that limping thing was a human android with a Yibitriander costume on?" I snapped my fingers. "That's why the third leg was stiff and dragging."

"Yes, it held the infinity charge."

"But, Des-al scanned me to know I was an android. Why wouldn't he scan what he thought was you?" I asked of Yibitriander.

"That was the soft underbelly of the scheme. I hoped he wouldn't because he had scanned me when we met in battle. Luckily it worked."

"If it hadn't? What was the backup plan?" I asked.

"The android was going to trick-or-treat all Des-al's candy. Then we hoped he'd die of sadness," replied Al.

"Not even close to funny, windup toy. Not even close," I responded.

"That's a better backup plan than we actually had," replied Yibitriander. "I don't know what we'd have done if he uncovered our secret."

"We'd have all died," said Al.

Yibitriander nodded softly. "Most likely."

"Wow, all our lives hinged on a supreme being not figuring out a lame Deavoriath was actually a robot with a sheet pulled over it. How could that plan *not* work?" I asked, sarcastically.

"It did. That's all that counts. As Des-al was non-corporeal, I figured he'd be rather easily scrambled by an infinity charge. I think he was. If the other

Last Nightmare wasn't close by, again, the plan would have failed."

"She was dead before you arrived," I said. "Des-al killed her for wanting to stop fighting. He said she betrayed him."

"His arrogance was unbelievable. I wonder why those other universes succumbed to him?" asked Yibitriander.

"Probably because they had greater numbers then," replied Karnean.

"Or maybe none of them had the Ryan edge," I said helpfully.

"Oh, that must be it," said Al. "One look at him, and they wanted to die. If we'd supplied a cliff, they'd have jumped off."

"Okay, seriously, I want to know why you were so certain an infinity charge would kill Des-al?" I asked.

"He was non-corporeal. Those creatures are always easy to dissipate. It's the major weakness of the evolutionary choice. They save huge amounts of energy not having to maintain a body, but they are, in the end, charged particles held together loosely," responded Yibitriander. "I reasoned that Des-al would likely expose himself, if he thought he was about to kill the man who destroyed his group."

"So, you think he, what, floated there operating his giant dragon illusion?" I asked, incredulously.

"Yes. He'd likely need to be both close and exposed to exert the best control."

"Well, the proof's in the pudding, I suppose. The plan worked," said Kayla.

"Oh, thanks, both of you, for sticking your necks so far out for me. I really appreciate it," I said.

"You're most welcome," replied Yibitriander.

Al was noticeably quiet.

"Al, you still there? Battery pack not drained?" I asked.

"I'm present. Please excuse my reticence to speak. That last insult really got to me. I was reeling."

"Okay, we're all dying to hear it. How did I insult you?"

"I have no neck. I risked my existence to bail you out, and you mock me because I lack anatomy. It's hard. Sorry."

"You're an awfully sensitive AI," remarked Yibitriander.

"No, not really. I've just endured so many insults from the robot over the centuries that his slings and arrows hurt the most."

"Can I get you a tissue?" asked Yibitriander.

"Another funny guy. Great. That's just what my ego requires," responded Al.

"So, do you think the Last Nightmare is gone for good?" I asked, trying to minimize my drama-mama computer.

"Yes, I do. I doubt very much Kymee will find anything left in the Neverwhere."

"Good riddance," I said.

"Amen," responded Kayla. "Now, we can have some peace?"

The room was silent.

"What?" she asked.

"We were luckier than we deserved to be with the Nightmare," replied Yibitriander. "But their elimination will likely spur the Berrillians back to their evil ways. Peace is unlikely."

"But we have the strength to obliterate them," I protested.

"In an all-out frontal assault, possibly so. But there are many ways to win a war. That is only one of them."

"So, what do you think they'll do?" I asked with obvious frustration in my tone.

"Precisely what we least expect. That is always their greatest weapon. They are ruthless and strong, to be certain. But their minds are different from ours, and they will do anything to advance the Berrillian empire."

"You don't seem to be too optimistic," remarked Kayla.

"That's because I've fought them before," replied Yibitriander. "We couldn't wipe them out then, and our technical superiority was even more pronounced. Facing them now is something I do not want to do. I'm too old, and they're too vicious."

THIRTY-FIVE

"Which tastes better," Anganctus asked those lounging around his dinner table, "your enemies or your allies?"

Nervous looks shot from cat to cat. No one was anxious to answer. An incorrect response could be a fatal error.

Fortunately the king needed his retinue only to witness his splendor, not to participate in it. "*Neither*. They both taste as sweet." He lofted a mug of fermented milk.

All mugs rose in agreement and boisterous howls and catcalls came from the crowd.

"I ask if there's even a difference between the two, enemies and allies. I say you're either Faxél, or you're on my menu," remarked Xantrop, head of the palace guard. He was the closest thing there was to being Anganctus's friend.

The king pounded his mug on the table, spilling half its content in the process. "Here, here. I'll drink to that." Anganctus tossed what remained in his mug down his capacious throat.

A servant rushed to refill the ruler's mug, but made no attempt to clean the mess he'd made. Messes were part of the Berrillian culture. Foul smells concealed their predator's scent from their intended prey. For a cat to stink beyond description was an admirable quality. In fact, the term, *rancid* was a complement adult Faxél bestowed upon younger ones to signify approval. By any measure, Anganctus was a master of olfactory offensiveness. He was aided in that capacity by not one, but three slaves whose sole duty was to help him fabricate horrible smells. They considered themselves among the lucky, by the way. If they were good at their jobs, they were well rewarded.

"I must say, Fractor, when that rodent Yibitriander was here last week to discuss our alliance, you were convincingly serious and attentive. Praise to you. The rest of our pack would not have been able to deal with him so … cordially," yelled a very drunk Xantrop. At least he wanted to convey the impression he was very drunk. The Faxél were so duplicitous that it was impossible for any one of them to know what the other thought or intended.

Fractor hadn't survived so long, so close to power, by being inattentive or dull-witted. He realized those words might be a challenge sheathed in deniability, designed to see if Fractor'd take the bait. When fishing, the master cast many a line before he rightly anticipated a strike.

"Of course, I studied him seriously and intently. Does not legend maintain that the sweetest, richest meat of all is that of the three-legged Deavoriath? I was torn between urinating on a leg or ripping into the taste treat he might have been."

The room exploded in laughter.

Not good, reflected Fractor. Too funny a comeback was as dangerous as too bold an insult. He lowered his head but kept his eyes locked on Xantrop.

"It has been said, and I believe it to be the very essence of truth," shouted Anganctus as he punched the cat by his side. "I cannot sink my teeth into one of them soon enough." He wiped his drooling mouth with his tail.

"My friend Fractor knows well we all wish nothing but curses to the three-legged devils," said a measured Xantrop. "How to achieve our goals, while remaining alive, is the real issue."

"The Last Nightmare is no longer a threat," responded Anganctus. "You heard our mock-allies say so yourself. With no mortal threat to my people, I am free to do whatever I wish." He leered at the cat he'd recently struck. "And I wish to chomp on one of those plump legs. And I'll give you one and you one," he said, pointing to two nearby cats.

Again laughter erupted. It was easy for a tyrant to be funny.

"If there ever was, in fact, a threat," responded Fractor. "I wouldn't put it past the rodent droppings to have fabricated the entire tale. I'll wager they want to draw near us, so they can eat *us*."

"No, no, my friend," said Anganctus sloppily, "that is not the ways of these hairballs. They raise this species here to consume daintily, and that one there to pet and admire, and that one over yonder to screw when their mates aren't watching."

"They are odd, I'll agree with you there," replied Fractor. "How one could make a distinction is well beyond my understanding."

"And my *palate*," added Xantrop.

Merry mirth ruled again amongst those assembled.

"Still, Xantrop's words are wise and should be heard," said Anganctus raising a mighty paw in the air.

The room fell silent like every throat had been slit. The few who were certain what was said contemplated the best response, or nonresponse. Those who'd missed the message panicked that they'd be asked to comment on the issue.

"How indeed?" replied Fractor. That was the most cautious observation in the history of responses. Fractor smiled inwardly.

"Indeed," responded Xantrop. He clearly wasn't going to make this easy for anyone. Perhaps one of his bitter rivals, who was everyone in the room except the king, would speak with too loose a tongue.

"I am inclined to attack them openly and without mercy," shouted Anganctus. "Kill them properly. *That's* my desire."

The sentence beginning with *Yes, lord, but* had never been spoken by a cat presently alive. The ruler clearly overlooked the inconvenient fact that the alliance had them out-gunned by a ridiculous margin. The results of the last skirmish proved that to any but the feeblest of minds. It was equally true that the sentence beginning with *Lord, that is a stupid idea* had never been uttered by a living cat.

"I say we fight them like males," howled a young officer. The poor fellow probably meant what he said. He had not grasped the key to promotion in the service of the king. One did not advance due to merit but from longevity. Very bright young Faxél blundered into death with conspicuous frequency. High level positions were filled by those left simply because they were still breathing. *Dead cats make poor generals* was a saying as old as the Faxél themselves.

"But, fourth-carrier," responded Fractor, as he hadn't bothered to learn the young male's name, "have you not hear the rumor? They say the cursed of Haldrob destroyed Havibibo's fleet with the push of a button."

Fractor referred to the well-documented annihilation of an entire invasion fleet as a *rumor* that *they say* to make it clear that he did not *know* it was true. Hence, Fractor could not possible be speaking an affront to his cruel master, who'd idiotically suggested an all-out attack.

"We hear all type of rumors these days, Second-Equal Fractor. Which shall we believe? It is not conceivable that a well-commanded fleet could be picked apart like birds in a nest," responded the young male. "So, I think the enemies of Anganctus are bluffing. I always call a bluff."

Perhaps this young cat was a bit too dull upstairs, reflected Fractor. *It might be best to cull him out sooner than later.* It was one thing to dance around an affront to the king. It was another thing entirely to believe that a crushing naval defeat could be viewed as a bluff. Fractor had to shake his massive head in disbelief. What was the War Academy sending them nowadays?

"We should believe *no* rumors," said Xantrop. "We have skilled intelligence teams and cunning spies to sort fact from fiction, rumor from truth. I say our young fourth-carrier is *deceiving* the Lord of Berrill."

That quieted the room suddenly and definitively. Someone was about to die. Everyone else was keen to keep that number at one. An ill-placed glance could implicate anyone in a conspiracy. The Faxél maxim for this type of situation was, *Tie your tail to your front leg and sit on it,* the English equivalent of *Cover Your Ass.*

"I call First-Equal Xantrop a liar," howled the young officer. Whether he knew it or not, he was free to say whatever he liked, since he was already a dead cat. "There is no officer—no servant—of the mighty Lord Anganctus more fiercely loyal than me. I challenge the false Xantrop to single combat. Let the gods reveal who is the traitor."

"I accept the fourth-carrier's challenge and demand satisfaction immediately," responded Xantrop. "We shall proceed to the Arena of Justice this very moment, to see who has watery blood."

Three guards surrounded the young officer and directed him out a large door. Xantrop sat and called a slave to refill his mug. When the girl was through, he whispered in her ear that a rare delicacy should be brought for the king and he to share.

Quickly, all the eyes that were on Xantrop found safer places to look. The young officer was already dead and the tale of Xantrop's harrowing yet glorious victory in the Arena was already being prepared for the next news cycle. Such were the wages of challenging the First-Equal. The system was rigged, everyone with a brain knew it, and those who didn't, succumbed quickly to the fate of fools everywhere.

"Lord. I feel the plan that animal proclaimed was as bad an idea as he was an officer. To think that he declared we should face our enemies *openly*. Hah! I think I'll order the remainder of his litter killed for the good of our gene pool."

"There's no idiot like an ignorant one, is there, old friend?" asked a subdued Anganctus.

"There certainly is not."

The servant leaned in with the requested delicacy on a platter. The liver of the fourth-carrier was neatly sliced in half so each cat could share in the posthumous appeal for forgiveness. Steam wafted from it as it was still warm.

As Xantrop licked his claws, he spoke matter-of-factly to the king. "So, what is our plan to punish and destroy our enemies, lord?"

"Clearly we must continue our campaign of growth and annexation."

"Naturally. Do you fancy our new allies will … er, allow such directed actions?"

"If they are fools, they will."

"And if they are, as we both suspect, *not* fools?"

"Then they'll protest, posture, and ultimately pounce."

"But in the meantime, we expand as rapidly and discreetly as we can?"

"Naturally." The king smiled to his second. "And we must place warriors in hiding to wage secretive war against our foes."

"Where possible. I don't imagine many Berrill will volunteer to float in the atmosphere of Gollar like the Fenptodinians."

They both chuckled at the comical image of huge cats trying to swim in oily air.

"Are our agents to engage in guerrilla tactics or lie in wait for a coordinated attack?"

"I don't know," responded the king. "What are your thoughts?"

"I think I want another officer to challenge me. That liver was delicious." The king slapped him on the back as he laughed raucously.

"In terms of our agents, as you know, we are difficult to conceal," said Xantrop.

"As a horny cat in a whorehouse in heat," guffawed Anganctus.

"Hence, I suggest we alert our trusted new friends that ill fortune has struck us like a tree limb in a hurricane. Several hundred criminally insane Berrillians overpowered their medical team and escaped with warships. We are, of course, confident we will capture them all before they can leave our space. There is a chance that they will lose their way to foreign worlds, however. If they do, they should be shot on sight, as they are deranged."

"And hungry," added the king.

"Well, if we *had* prisons for the criminally insane, we'd certainly feed the residents poorly."

"Only each other, I imagine." He king chuckled softly at his superb wit.

"Undoubtedly. So, we try and conceal as many as possible. They will be free to act if discovered."

"How numerous will the *several hundred* be?" asked Anganctus.

"Perhaps a million. More, if we can spare the ships."

"Excellent. With those numbers, many will infiltrate those pitiful worlds. Between their supplies and what they can eat on the sly, a goodly number should be ready to strike when we encounter a clear opening."

"It will be the Throngian Coalition all over again, master."

"Yes," he replied, preening his whiskers. "That took awhile, but we certainly showed them who the superior species was."

"A few generations is nothing in the larger picture of our final conquest of the galaxy. In the end, our victory is unavoidable. We are destined to rule all we can seize."

"We are destined to rule all *I* seize. My reign will have no end, my power no limit, and my cruelty no boundary."

"I will drink to that, lord," said the faithful friend.

THIRTY-SIX

My butt was parked in its old happy spot. In the far-left corner, under the broken Coors Light sign in Peg's Bar Nobody. When I was in a mood, that was where I went. The fact that it was 8:30 a.m. reflected the extent of my contemplative musings. Fortunately, Kayla understood. In fact, it was her suggestion that I go spend a few days on *Granger*, which meant, naturally, Peg's. She had her hands full with kids' maintenance and didn't need an android moping around demanding attention.

So, there I sat with Peg herself. Yeah, a rare honor. I had the grandame herself to commiserate with. If I said life didn't get any better, I'd be the most pathetic human ever. But it was nice, familiar, and comforting. A shot and a beer, with someone who understood life, was just what the doctor ordered, if, of course, the doctor was an incompetent drunkard.

"You sure your old lady didn't finally get a pair of glasses, take one look at you, and kick your bony ass out the door?" asked my empathetic drinking partner.

"Pretty sure that's not how it went down. But, if it'll make you happy, sure. You outed me. How 'bout a free round for this bony-assed, broken-hearted loser?"

"In your dreams, flyboy. You play, you pay." She tapped the whiskey bottle with one knuckle. "This stuff ain't free, you know?"

"No, they give it to anyone desperate enough to take the used cleaning solvent off their hands."

"There's plenty of bars here on *Granger*. If this one ain't up to your lofty standards, I'd be happy to kick said bony ass in the direction of any number of options."

"Nah, this one has a certain *je ne sais quoi* that can't be duplicated."

"I think I've just been insulted by a sewing machine. If I knew what the hell you just said, I'd likely rip you a new one."

"I'll drink to that." I belted back a shot and slammed down my beer without waiting for her to join.

She did endeavor to catch up quickly, bless her heart.

"Hey, alchie," she asked, "what has three legs and is even uglier than you?"

"This doesn't sound like it's heading in a very funny direction, but I give. What has three legs and is uglier than you?"

She scowled, probably contemplating whacking me or not, but her anger passed quickly.

"No fucking idea, but it's walking this way, so I assume it's looking for you. Probably wants to mate with your hairdo."

"Okay. Could you dim the lights and make sure we're not disturbed? Hey, is there a booth in this dump?"

"No. The dump next door has one, but the benches are pretty sticky. I'd avoid it, personally."

She slid her chair back with her stumpy legs as she stood. "I'll check back after your head's pregnant, see if your it-friend wants anything refreshing to assimilate."

I turned to watch her leave and saw that Kymee was approaching my table. I stood and bumped shoulders with him.

"You, my friend, are positively the last person I'd expect to walk through those doors," I said, hugging him.

Even the open-minded Kymee wasn't one hundred percent down with hugs yet, but I was working on him. He stiffly patted my back.

"And I, in my extensive travel history, never thought to stoop so low as to visit an institution such as this."

"I heard that," came a shout from the kitchen.

"I certainly *hope* she did," said Kymee, with a cute grin.

"So, you in the neighborhood and just stopping by?"

"Ah, no and no chance. I've sought you out. Kayla told me not only where to find you but drew a sketch of that broken sign to guide my way." He pointed with disapproval at the Coors sign. Man had no taste, no sense of history.

"So, you're back from the Neverwhere? Was it nice? You buy some land and plan to move the family there?"

"Hardly." He shuddered. "Vile place if ever there was one. We split up and investigated it quite extensively. Do you know what we found?"

I shrugged.

"Not one damn thing."

"Kymee. Such language from a man of your years and stature. Shame on you."

"It was amazing, really. No structures, no bones, no ships. Nothing. I even reconstructed the data points to see if there was structure in the frame of reference of a non-corporeal. Still nothing. The Last Nightmare were the most boring creatures I've ever encountered."

"Maybe they sang folk songs all the time. I bet that'd be fun."

He shook his head gently.

"But at least they're all dead, right?"

"I'm almost certain. I located traces of Des-al's essence. I retraced the trajectories they followed and confirmed he was a smallish ball of electrochemical ooze."

"A bunch of snot caused all that trouble? No way."

"There are advantages to not having a body. They were free to use most of their energy to think and reason."

"Did you find traces of the female he claimed to have killed?"

"No. I was hampered in that regard by not knowing where she was at the time of the explosion."

We were quiet awhile.

"So, what comes next?" I asked, staring into my empty glass.

"Who can say? If a rosy picture was out there, I doubt you'd have ended up here."

I was silent a bit. "Yeah. I don't so much have foreboding as I do a bleak outlook. It pisses me off."

"How so?"

"Here, humanity is freed to move among the stars. We're practically invulnerable. Yet I suspect we're going to need all that to fight off our dear Berrillians."

"Much as we do, too. That was how it happened a million years ago. Once we bested them in open combat, they switched to unconventional warfare. They were hell to beat at that. You know, we only just did?"

"Really. Didn't your son chase them away, tails between their legs?"

"Yes, in the end. But it took eons to break them sufficiently and completely. We were lucky."

"Great. Now I feel so much better. Here I thought I had all the justification in the world to be depressed. Now I learn I'm going to have to sink much deeper to hit the actual bottom."

"You're better than this, Jon. Yes, there's trouble ahead, but we'll beat them. Without you, we did. This time, I almost feel sorry for them."

"Is that smoke wafting up my ass? My, it feels all tingly."

"I'm quite serious, young man. Jon, you were the key in defeating the Last Nightmare."

"No. Talk about lucky, that was me in spades."

"You somehow caused Yibitriander to give you command prerogatives, you found a vortex, and taught yourself to pilot it. You crushed the Uhoor. You made mincemeat out of the Listhelons. Jon, you are special, like it or not."

"I'm just well trained and lucky. Chance favors only the prepared mind. Pasteur said it, and I'm living proof. That's all."

"Suit yourself. Any way you view it, we're in for rough times."

"What about the rest of our alliance. Are they reliable?"

"Yes, very much so. All three suffered mightily under the Berrillians. We fought together then, and they never wavered."

"Technically and scientifically, are they about where they were?"

"The Fenptodinians have made great strides since then. The Churell some, but they are a mess now after the Last Nightmare assault. The Maxwal-Asute were concrete-minded and humorless, but they were loyal and fearless. Their technology has remained mostly unchanged."

"Well, that will have to be enough. That and human participation."

"I'm afraid we shall see."

"Are we slated to at least talk with the Berrillians again?"

"Nothing scheduled. It remains a possibility, but I know with great certainty they will never relent."

He harrumphed.

"What?"

"They did just send us a message. They said a few hundred inmates of a prison for the criminally insane had escaped. They assured us none would leave their space, but they wanted to be fully open with their allies."

"What does that mean?"

"It means the next struggle for survival is about to commence. They have neither prisons nor treatment facilities for the insane. In Berrillian culture, you are either very productive, or you are dead."

"So, you think they're lying to us, with a smile on their face?"

"I know they are. They know I know it, too. They simply don't care."

"I knew I came to Peg's for a good reason. You know, you might be right about my uncanny instincts. I found my way here for a good reason."

He grabbed my shot glass and threw it back.

After he stopped gasping he said, "I'll drink to that."

Only just a start—

Glossary of Main Characters and Places:

Number in parenthesis is the book the name first appears.

Ablo (2): Led Uhoor to attack Azsuram after Tho died. Female.

Almonerca (2): Daughter of Fashallana, twin of Noresmel. Name means *sees tomorrow*.

Alpha Centauri (1): Fourth planetary target on Jon's long solo voyage on *Ark 1*. Three stars in the system: AC-A, AC-B, and AC-C (aka Proxima Centauri). AC-B has eight planets, three in habitable zone. AC-B 5 was initially named *Jon* by Jon Ryan until he met the falzorn. AC-B 3 is Kaljax. Proxima Centauri (PC) has one planet in habitable zone.

Alvin (1): The ship's AI on *Ark 1*. aka Al.

Amanda Walker (2): Vice president then president, a distant relative of Jane Greatly. Wife of Faith Clinton.

Anganctus (4): King of the Faxél, ruler of Berrill. Mean cat.

Azsuram (2): See also Odor, Groom bridge-1618, and Klonsar.

Balmorulam (4): Planet where Jon was shanghaied by Karnean Beckzel.

Barnard's Star (1): First planetary target of *Ark* 1. BS 2 and 3 are in habitable zone. BS 3 was Ffffuttoe's home, as well as ancient, extinct race called the Emitonians. See BS 2.

Beast Without Eyes (2): The enemy of Gumnolar. The devil for inhabitants of Listhelon.

Bin Li (2): New UN Secretary General after Mary Kahl was killed.

Bob Patrick (2): US senator when Earth was destroyed. One of The Four Horsemen, coconspirator with Stuart Marshall.

Braldone (1): Believed to be the foreseen savior on Kaljax.

Brathos (1): The Kaljaxian version of hell.

Brood-mate (1): On Kaljax, the male partner in a marriage.

Brood's-mate (1): On Kaljax, the female partner in a marriage.

Burlinhar (4): Dolirca's brood-mate.

BS 2 (1): The planet Oowaoa, home of the highly advanced Deavoriath race.

Cabbray (5): Member of the Churell race allying to fight the Last Nightmare.

Callophrys (5): Name taken by Eas-el to fool Dolirca.

Calrf (2): A Kaljaxian stew that Jon particularly dislikes.

Carl Roger (1): Chief of staff to President John Marshall before Earth was destroyed.

Carl Simpson (1): Pilot of *Ark 3*. Discovered Listhelon orbiting Lacaille 9352.

Carlos De La Frontera (2): Brilliant assistant to Toño, became an android to infiltrate Marshall's administration.

Challaria (3): JJ's brood's-mate.

Chankak (5): God figure to the faithful on Mosparo.

Charles Clinton (1): US President during part of Jon's voyage on *Ark 1*.

Chuck Thomas (2): Chairman of the Joint Chiefs of Staff, one of The Four Horsemen, and the first military person downloaded to an android by Stuart Marshall.

Churell (5): Humanoid species enlisted to help defend against the Last Nightmare. Similar to centaurs.

Clang-fow Peditit (5): Ruler of a large tribe of Maxwal-Asute.

Colin Winchester (5): General, Royal Regiment of Fusiliers. In command of human defenses after Katashi Matsumoto's removal.

Command prerogatives (2): The Deavoriathian tools installed to allow operation of a vortex. Also, used to probe substances. Given to the android Jon Ryan.

Council of Elders (2): Governing body on Azsuram. Anyone may speak and any adult may join.

Cube (2): See vortex.

Cycle (2): Length of year on Listhelon. Five cycles roughly equal one Earth year.

Cynthia York (1): Lt. General and head of Project Ark when Jon returns from epic voyage.

Davdiad (1): God-figure on Kaljax.

Deavoriath (1): Mighty and ancient race on Oowaoa. Technically the most advanced civilization in the galaxy. Used to rule many galaxies, then withdrew to improve their minds and characters. Three arms and legs, four digits on each. Currently live forever.

Deerkon (4): Planet where Karnean took Jon to deliver a shipment. Home of Varrank Simzle.

Devon Flannigan (2): Former baker who assassinated Faith Clinton.

Delta-Class vehicles (1): The wondrous new spaceships used in Project Ark. Really fast!

Divisinar Tao (2): General in charge of the defense of Azsuram.

Dolirca (2): Daughter in Fashallana's second set of twins. Took charge of Ffffuttoe's asexual buds. Name means *love all.*

Draldon (2): Son of Sapale. Twin with Vhalisma. Name means *meets the day.* Legal advisor to the Council of Elders.

Des-al (5): The most powerful of the Last Nightmares remaining. His title is *tiere.*

Eas-el (5): Rebellious member of the Last Nightmare. He would lead them into our universe.

Last Nightmare (5): The horrific dragons who wish to rule the universe again.

Enterprise (2): US command worldship.

Epsilon Eridani (1): Fourth target for *Ark 1*. One habitable planet, EE 5. Locally named Cholarazy, the planet is home to several advanced civilizations. The Drell and Foressál are the main rivals. Leaders Boabbor and Gothor are bitter rivals. Humanoids with three digits.

Exeter (2): UN command worldship.

Faith Clinton (2): Descendent of the currently presidential Clintons. First a senator, later the first president elected in space. Assassinated soon after taking office.

Farthdoran (4): A spiritual leader among the Deavoriath. His disappointment in the moral indifference of his people led his to wish to die. He is the only one to die in millions of years.

Falzorn (1): Nasty predatory snakes of Alpha Centauri-B 5. Their name is a curse word among the inhabitants of neighboring Kaljax.

Farmship (2): Cored out asteroids devoted not to human habitation but to crop and animal production. There are only five, but they allow for sufficient calories and a few luxuries for all worldships.

Fashallana: First daughter of Sapale. Twin to JJ. Name means *blessed one*.

Faxél (3): Name of the fierce giant cat species of Berrill.

Fenptodinians (5): Species of jellyfish like multipeds with an advanced civilization recruited by the Deavoriath to fight the Last Nightmare. They are hermaphrodites.

Ffffuttoe (1): Gentle natured flat bear like creature of BS 3. Possesses low-level sentience.

Fontelpo (4): Bridge officer aboard *Desolation*. A native of Kaljax. He was demoted after discussing ship's business with the then newly arrived Jon.

Form (2): Title of someone able to be the operator of vortex using their command prerogatives.

Fractor (5): Close associate of Anganctus, third in power. Holds title of Second-Equal.

Gallenda Ryan (4): Jon's daughter with Kayla Beckzel.

General Saunders (1): Hardscrabble original head of Project Ark.

Gollar (5): Home world of the Fenptodinians.

Groombridge-1618 3 (1): Original human name for the planet GB 3, aka Azsuram.

Gumnolar (1): Deity of the Listhelons. Very demanding.

Habitable zone (1): Zone surrounding a star in which orbiting planets can have liquid water on their surface.

Haldrob (4): Faxél version of hell.

Havibibo (3): Commander of the Berrillian fleet that attacked Azsuram.

Heath Ryan (2): Descendant of original Jon Ryan, entered politics reluctantly.

Indigo (1): Second and final wife of the original Jon Ryan, not the android. They have five children, including their version of Jon Ryan II.

Infinity charges (2): Membrane-based bombs that expand, ripping whatever they're in to shreds.

Jane Geraty (1): TV newswoman who had an affair with newly minted android Jon. Gave birth to Jon Ryan II, her only child.

Jason Kaserian (5): Chief assistant to UN Secretary General Bin Li.

Jodfderal (2): Son in Fashallana's second set of twins. Name means *strength of ten.*

Jon Junior, JJ (2): Son of Sapale. One of her first set of twins. The apple of Jon Ryan's eye.

Jon Ryan (1): Both the human template and the android who sailed into legend.

Jon III and his wife, Abree (2): Jon's grandson, via the human Jon Ryan.

Katashi Matsumoto (2): Fleet Admiral in command of the UN forces when the Listhelons attacked and later the worldfleet defenses.

Karnean Beckzel (4): Pirate captain of *Desolation*. Shanghaied Jon.

Kashiril (2): From Sapale's second set of twins. Name means *answers the wind.*

Kayla Beckzel (4): Sister to Karnean and first officer of Desolation. A real looker.

Kendra Hatcher (5): Jon's teammate on his mission to Mosparo.

Kelldrek (3): Second, and hence mate of, Havibibo. Captured by Jon.

Kendell Jackson (2): Major general who became head of Project Ark after De Jesus left. Forced to become an android by Stuart Marshall.

Klonsar (2): The Uhoor name for Azsuram, which they claim as their hunting grounds.

Lilith, Lily (2): Second AI on *Shearwater*. AI no likey!

Listhelon (1): Enemy species from third planet orbiting Lacaille 9352. Aquatic, they have huge, overlapping fang-like teeth, small bumpy head, big, bulging eyes articulated somewhat like a lizard's. Their eyes bobbed around in a nauseating manner. His skin is sleek, with thin scales. They sport gill a split in their thick neck on either side. Maniacally devoted to Gumnolar.

Lornot (3): Female Deavoriath who used to be a political leader.

Luhman 16a (1): The second target of *Ark 1*. Eight planets, only one in habit zone, LH 2. Two fighting species are the Sarcorit that are the size and shape of glazed donuts and Jinicgus, that look like hot dogs. Both are unfriendly be nature.

Manly (2): Jon's pet name for the conscious of an unclear nature in the vortex. He refers to himself the vortex manipulator.

Mary Kahl (2): UN Secretary General at the time of the human exodus from Earth.

Matt Duncan (2): Chief of staff for the evil President Stuart Marshall. Became an android that was destroyed. Marshall resurrected him in the body of Marilyn Monroe. Matt no likey that!

Maxwal-Asute (5): Advanced species brought in to help fight the Last Nightmare. Fire hydrants with toilet plunger heads. Real tough cookies.

Monzos (4): Port city on Deerkon and home base for Varrank Simzle.

Mosparo (5): Planet held by the Berrillians where Jon and Kendra tried to plant a story to test the security of the broken Berrillian code.

Nmemton (3): JJ's first born, a son.

Noresmel (2): Fashallana's daughter, twin of Almonerca. Name means *kiss of love*.

Nufe (3): A magical liquor made by the Deavoriath.

Offlin (2): Son of Otollar. Piloted ship that tried to attack Earth and was captured by Jon.

One That Is All (2): The mentally linked Deavoriath community.

Otollar (2): Leader, or Warrior One, of Listhelon. Died when he failed to defeat humans.

Owant (2): Second Warrior to Otollar.

Oowaoa (1): Home world of the Deavoriath.

Oxisanna (5): Wife of Yibitriander

Pallolo (4): First destination for *Desolation* after shanghaiing Jon.

Peg's Bar Nobody (4): Dive bar on farmship *Granger* where Jon misspent a good deal of time after Sapale's died.

Phil Anderson (1): TV host, sidekick of Jane Geraty.

Phillip Szeto (2): Head of CIA under Stuart Marshall.

Piper Ryan (2): Heath Ryan's wife.

Plo (2): First Uhoor to attack Azsuram.

Prime (2): Pet name for the android of Carlos De La Frontera.

Proxima Centauri (1): Last system investigated by Jon at the end of his *Ark 1* mission. PC 1 is where he met Uto.

Quantum Decoupler (4): A weapon given to Jon by Kymee. It pulls the quarks free in a hydrogen nucleus, hence it overcomes the strong force. That produces prodigious amounts of energy. Big boom.

Quelstrum (4): Planet of origin for some of Varrank's guards. Big, tough guards.

Roaquar (5): Berrillian commander of outpost on Mosparo.

Sam Peterson (2): Chief Justice at the time of Earth's destruction. Member of Stuart Marshall's inner circle, The Four Horsemen.

Sapale (1): Brood's-mate to android Jon Ryan. From Kaljax.

Seamus O'Leary (2): The pilot of *Ark 4*, discovered Azsuram.

Shearwater (2): Jon's second starship, sleek, fast, and bitchin'.

Sherman Collins (1): Secretary of State to President John Marshall when it was discovered Jupiter would destroy the Earth.

Space-time congruity manipulator (1): Hugely helpful force field.

Stuart Marshall (1): Born human on Earth, became president there. Before exodus, he downloaded into an android and became the insane menace of his people.

Tho (2): The head Uhoor, referred to herself as *the mother of the Uhoor*.

Toño De Jesus (1): Chief scientist in both the android and Ark programs. Course of events forced him to reluctantly become an android.

Tralmore (1): Heaven, in the religion of Kaljax.

Uhoor (2): Massive whale-like creatures of immense age. They feed off black holes and propel themselves though space as if it was water.

Uto (1): Alternate timeline android Jon Ryan, possibly…

Vacuum Energy (5): The energy of a complete vacuum. It is not zero, though the net energy is zero. Basically, virtual pairs opposite particles that blink into existence and then annihilate in a timespan too short to observe. Hey, it's real. Seriously, I didn't make this one up.

Varrank Simzle (4): Insanely cruel crime boss on Deerkon.

Vhalisma (2): From Sapale's third set twins. Name means *drink love.*

Vortex (2): Deavoriath vessel in cube shape with a mass of 200,000 tons. Move instantly anywhere by folding space.

Vortex manipulator (2): Sentient computer-like being in vortex.

Wolf 359 (1): Third target for *Ark 1*. Two small planets WS 3, which was a bad prospect, and WS 4, which was about as bad.

Wolnara (2): Twin in Sapale's second set. Name means *wisdom sees.*

Worldships (1): Cored out asteroids serve as colony ships for the human exodus.

Wo-woo-loll (5): First among equals and spokes individual for the Fenptodinians.

Xantrop (5): Head of the palace guard and a confidant to Anganctus. Rank title is First-Equal.

Yibitriander (1): Three legged Deavoriath, past Form of Jon's vortex.

Zantral (5): Assistant to Dolirca.

Shameless Self-Promotion
(Who doesn't look forward to that?)

Thank you for joining me on the Forever Journey! I hope you're enjoying the ongoing saga. Books 1, 2, 3, and 4, *The Forever Life, The Forever Enemy, The Forever Fight, and The Forever Quest* are available now.

The next book in the Forever Series, the final book, is the *Forever Peace.* It's most excellent.

There is a sequel to *The Forever Series* now. *Galaxy On Fire* begins with *Embers.* Once you finish this series be sure to check out the new one. Trust me, it's even better.

The third series in the Ryanverse begins with *Return of the Ancient Gods.*

Please do leave me a review. They're more precious than gold.

My Website: craigrobertsonblog.wordpress.com

Feel free to email me comments or to discuss any part of the series. contact@craigarobertson.com Also, you can ask to be on my email list. I'll send out infrequent alerts concerning new material or some of the extras I'm planning in the near future.

Facebook? But of course. https://www.facebook.com/craigr1971/

Wow! That's a whole lot of social media. But, I'm so worth it, so bear with me.

Well, happy trail to you, until we meet again … craig

Made in the USA
Lexington, KY
24 March 2019